M000313010

Also by

DAVID ABIS

THOUGH I WALK THROUGH THE VALLEY

PURE CANE

VILLAGE IDIOTS

CALAMITY IN SWEETSPOT:

A POLITICALLY UNCORRECT
WHIRLWIND REDNECK ROMANCE

by

DAVID ABIS

Sweet Spot Publishing

Calamity In Sweet Spot:
A Politically Uncorrect Whirlwind Redneck Romance

Sweet Spot Publishing

Paperback Edition

Copyright 2015 David Abis

All rights reserved.

Images courtesy of mikesch112, Fotolia, imagedepotpro, & istockphoto.
Cover by Joleene Naylor.

ISBN 978-0-9907739-7-9
eBook ISBN 978-0-9907739-6-2

Chapter 1

The town of Sweet Spot was anything but. Like the land that time forgot, Sweet Spot, Mississippi was as backward as a coonhound fell upon an ornery skunk's den. Outsiders presumed it was the government to blame for the town's plight, just another pathetic little victim of government neglect. But it weren't nothin' of the kind. In fact, t'were just the opposite. See, the proud folks of Sweet Spot never took no courses in victimology, and they had no intention of winding up beholden to no nosey government do-gooders bearing handouts. No, there was a reason Sweet Spot was so backward. 'Cause that's how the Spotters liked it. Anything an inch above their station in life just weren't worth the effort. It was sloth, pure and simple, just like in the Bible. And that's all there was to it.

But Buck Jones was a man of vision. The 38-year-old mayor of Sweet Spot felt obliged to lead his subjects from the valley of naught into the promised land, even if they had no aspirations to do so themselves. That's the very reason Buck sent his man Pedro up on the roof of his trailer home with that can of barn-red paint.

"Damn it, Pedro. I ain't askin' ya to paint an actual eye. You don't need to be no Picasso to paint a bull's-eye. It's just a target. You know, red rings, like for shootin' practice," he called up to the Mexican standing on top of his trailer.

Buck wasn't too sure about Pedro. There were a lot of things Buck didn't know about his illegal alien, or "undocumented worker" as they were callin' 'em nowadays. For one, Buck didn't actually know if the man was even Mexican. Didn't care. The fact that he had a great tan and a Spanish accent was good enough for Buck. Buck also didn't know the man's real name. But Pedro seemed a fittin' enough name for a wetback paintin' a bull's-eye on your roof. That's what everyone called him, and he never complained. But Buck knew that he understood English. So why the concept of a bull's-eye seemed to confound the man so, seemed a conundrum.

"Well, why for you want a big bull's-eye on your roof anyway, Meester Buck?" came Pedro's reply, thick with south-of-the-border flavor.

"Just tryin' to make history, Pedro," Buck answered with a grin. "That's all. Gonna catch us a tornado." Buck Jones knew it was only a matter of time. You see, there was a reason the town was called Sweet Spot. Despite representing the very buckle of the tornado belt, Sweet Spot was the only town for miles around never been hit by a twister. Never. And the mayor was of a mind that that was just what was wrong with the place, the cause of its economic downfall.

Smack dab in the middle of Tornado Alley, the town was just a dilapidated collection of flimsy tin-roofed shacks already suffering from the effects of gravity such that the simple blowing out of birthday candles represented a bonafide risk to the town's very existence. The mayor's trailer home wasn't just the icing on the cake, it was the cherry on top. If that didn't just call for a twister, nothin' did. Well now they had a goddamned bull's-eye to boot. Just what else could a twister ask for?

Pedro leaned out over the edge of the roof to look down at the mayor with one eyebrow raised, a finger twisting in his ear to clear out any wax buildup. Maybe he hadn't heard right.

"You say you're looking for a tornado to hit your house, Meester Buck?" asked Pedro.

Buck smiled. "You're thinkin' small, Pedro. That's the problem with this whole town. They think too small. No vision. That bull's-eye's not just for my house. It represents all of Sweet Spot."

Pedro just stared for a moment, but he knew better than to give it much thought. Thinking was never one of Pedro's strong points.

"Sounds kind of loco to me, Meester Buck," as he went back to the task at hand.

Buck just laughed. "That's what they said about all the great ones. Galileo. Columbus. Jack Daniels. History will vindicate me. A visionary. That's what they'll inscribe on my statue."

As Pedro disappeared from view up on the roof, Buck turned to the east in anticipation, and sure enough thought he could make out a dust cloud off in the distance. No, it wasn't a tornado. That woulda' been too much to ask for. But it was the next best thing. It was just another part of Buck's master plan.

Everyone in town could recognize that little cloud of dust whenever they saw it coming. It was a sign, just like Indian smoke signals. And this smoke signal announced the arrival of one particular Native American named Chief Firewater.

At least that's what everyone called him. The reason for his name explained the cloud of dust that always preceded him. You see, it was the chief's propensity for whiskey that resulted in the permanent loss of his driver's license. So the chief resorted to getting around on a tiny John Deere riding mower. And that little sucker managed to kick up quite a trail of dust when the chief threw her into high gear.

Just a matter of time now, thought Buck. Pedro's bull's-eye wouldn't take long. Just in time for the chief to begin his rain dance. Only this time, Buck convinced the chief to put a little razzle-dazzle in his step in exchange for a full jar of Jeb Clancey's famous moonshine. Chief Firewater assured the mayor it was only a matter of a little razzle-dazzle to upgrade from downpour to twister. And the incremental cost in moonshine was a bargain. Buck couldn't help rubbing his hands together in anticipation. That twister was practically in the bank. He'd seen the chief at work before. Rain, even snow. Shoot, he'd seen the chief produce hail stones the size of Rocky Mountain oysters. Yep, it was just a matter of time now, a sure thing. Sure as sweet young Becky Pike the day before the rent was due.

As the chief's cloud grew larger in its approach, Buck recalled that fine day his master plan took shape. He and his friend Jefferson were in Pottsville, the next town over, sittin' in their foldin' chairs on the sidewalk outside the Sears and Roebuck watchin' the Ole Miss football game on one of them flat-screens for sale in the display window out front. They had to run over to Pottsville since the day all broadcasting went digital. Buck's little old black and white, the last workin' set in Sweet Spot, didn't speak no digital.

During halftime they cut to a news story about them floods in Nashville and about how, with little media coverage, federal assistance had been slow in coming. Meanwhile, the reporter pointed to the billions of dollars ultimately given to victims of Katrina in New Orleans and all them hurricanes over in Florida, not to mention that earthquake in Haiti.

One of the local Pottsville boys couldn't help clickin' his tongue and shakin' his head.

"I sure could use some o' that ol' FEMA money myself. Why can't we have no damn disaster blow some money our way?"

"Shoot, you wouldn't get none of it anyhow," answered Jefferson. "Didn't you hear the man? Nashville had to fight for every penny they got. Even with Katrina, the Mississippi gulf got hit damn hard as New Orleans but hardly anyone even heard a peep 'bout them poor souls."

"That's cause they didn't play their cards right is all."

"Yeah, well, that's cause they didn't have the right card," Jefferson replied.

"And what card is it you're talkin' 'bout exactly?"

"I'm talkin' 'bout the race card."

The boys all stared at Jefferson Washington, the only black man among them. "What's that supposed to mean?"

Jefferson rolled his eyes. "Do I have to spell it out for you yahoos? You know, cultural diversity, minorities. Them folks in Nashville and Biloxi didn't have enough of what the liberal media and them D.C. politicians consider victims. Shoot, bunch o' white crackers like y'all ain't never gonna see no FEMA dough. You ain't earned your degree in victimology."

"Jefferson, if you wasn't black and all, I'd say you was soundin' just a tad racist there."

"Hey, don't shoot the messenger. I may be politically uncorrect, but it's Uncle Sam all hung up on race, not me. All I'm sayin' is it seems pretty obvious to me you gotta check the right box on that census form 'fore you be receivin' no FEMA dough. I ain't sayin' it's right. But it is what it is."

The rest of the boys pondered Jefferson's words in silence. As cynical as it appeared, they began to think maybe Jefferson was onto something, that his theory might just hold some water. And snow-white Pottsville didn't have no minorities, unless you counted that Catholic couple with all them kids recently come to town. So Pottsville's fleeting dreams of disaster and its subsequent pecuniary windfall faded from consciousness.

But not so for Buck. Buck Jones was a visionary. The wheels started turning that day and hadn't stopped since. Buck didn't wanna believe what Jefferson was sayin', that you needed a certain ethnic mix to receive government aid. He thought maybe the man had been listenin' to a little too much talk radio.

But even if Jefferson was right, Buck had that contingency covered. After all, Sweet Spot was a veritable rainbow of cultural diversity. Pedro was brown. The chief was red. And yes, they even had black folk, well one anyways. Jefferson Washington himself.

There was only one problem. Jefferson was a Republican. Buck wondered if a Republican could ever really be considered a victim, but the concern didn't last as he felt fairly confident that race trumped party affiliation in the game of victimhood.

So that settled it. All Sweet Spot needed now was a disaster and they'd all be livin' on easy street. A rickety collection of shacks with a trailer home for the mayor's mansion right in the middle of Tornado Alley, and now ol' Chief Firewater here to work his magic. Yes sir. Prosperity danced right around the corner.

In fact, maybe it was just his imagination, but as Buck watched the Chief's John Deere approaching in slow motion, he thought maybe he already felt a breeze kickin' up. He looked up at the sky and could have sworn them clouds came out of nowhere.

"Hey Pedro," he called up to the unseen worker on his roof. "Better git 'er done. Looks like we may be in for some weather." Buck Jones could hardly contain his glee.

Chapter 2

The last thing Jennifer Steele remembered was flying through the air and hitting the back of her head on a straw-covered floor.

Just open your eyes and maybe you'll know where you are, she thought. She didn't recall how she'd ended up flat on her back, unconscious. But as the stars swirling behind her eyelids began to dissipate, she wondered if it had anything to do with the pain at the back of her head and the pounding of loud country music. When she finally dared open her eyes, the room began to spin out of control and she wasn't sure if it was from the bump on her head or the tequila in her belly. But she really knew something was amiss when she dared peek through one eye again and observed a crowd of concerned folks in cowboy hats looking down at her.

She remembered her name, so she wasn't completely brain-damaged. Jennifer Steele, graduate of the Columbia School of Journalism, as yet a low-level writer for CNN, based in New York City. All she had to do now was figure out how she wound up drunk and unconscious after a blow to the head, surrounded by a bunch of cowboys. Then it got worse, if such a thing was even possible.

A sickeningly gorgeous blonde face framed in big hair and cleavage broke through the circle of cowboys snorting in uncontrollable laughter, exposing a perfect set of pearly whites. Her thick Southern drawl reminded Jennifer of Gone With The Wind with a Dukes of Hazard makeover, almost too cute to be real.

"Shoot, girl. I do declare that was the funniest thing I ever seen. That dang bull must have thrown you ten feet in the air." Turning to the circle of cowboys, "Y'all ever seen anything like it in all your days?"

As Jennifer watched the previously concerned boys start to laugh along with the beauty queen, she tried to gather her senses. She recalled going out for drinks with the gang down at the news station. So how did going out for drinks in Manhattan lead to cowboys and bull riding? She just knew the blonde had had a hand in this somehow. That's when it all started coming back to her. Scarlet Witherspoon, that Southern-bred, charm school graduating, beauty pageant winning white trash weather-bitch from down at the station. This was all her idea. Drinks at the only country western bar in New York City, where a bunch of losers from Brooklyn wearing cowboy costumes could remind her of back home.

Scarlet Witherspoon was Jennifer Steele's nemesis. While pale Plain Jane Jennifer worked her ass off earning a master's degree in journalism, blondie here, the tanned goddess, won a beauty pageant in Atlanta and landed her generous tits in front of the camera as a weather girl, earning five times Jennifer's pitiful paycheck writing the words that came out of all the pretty faces on the news. It took beaucoup shots of tequila to help assure Jennifer that looks, money, and popularity weren't as important as brains. That same tequila might also explain what made her try to ride that ridiculous mechanical bull.

"If you're all done laughing, I'd like to get up," she growled, struggling to her knees. One of the boys picked her up and placed her on her feet like a fallen toddler, all five-foot nothing 98 pounds of her. Jennifer pushed them all out of her way with a scowl on her face. She might be small, but she was wiry. Jennifer Steele was a short-fused little powder keg, always ready to go off at the slightest spark of confrontation. Standing next to the nearly six-foot Witherspoon, Jennifer wanted to kick the mannequin in the shins. But her balance was still questionable.

"Whatever gave you a mind to ride that thing, Jennifer?" asked Scarlet.

Jennifer could have answered in words small enough even Scarlet might have understood, but Jennifer couldn't even admit it to herself, let alone give Scarlet the satisfaction of knowing the truth. She'd never say how much she hated everything about her life. Despite all her hard work and academic achievements, it just didn't seem fair. Short, plain, underpaid, and alone. That about summed it up. While all the statuesque beauty hovering over her had to do was read the words Jennifer spoon-fed her from the teleprompter, collect her gargantuan check, and pick her next boyfriend out of the crowd.

Jennifer'd even given up claiming she was 29 years old and started admitting to all thirty-two of her years. So she went out with the gang from the station. It was that or go home to another frozen dinner alone. But that didn't mean she had to suffer it sober. So she sat at the bar, always on the outside looking in, throwing back tequila shots, drowning out the pain. That's when that damn mechanical bull started calling to her.

First it was that obnoxious braying sound it made whenever someone got thrown. Then Jennifer was convinced it was making eye contact with her, challenging her, daring her to give it a go. Jennifer Steele may have been insecure about a lot of things, but, not the most introspective of the bunch, she didn't know it. On the contrary, her response to any challenge was to take it head on and never back down. And that bull was beginning to piss her off. Her fuse was lit.

But there was nothing like a concussion to get something out of your system. So she let Scarlet lead her back to a seat at the bar to lick her wounds.

"Would you just look at that tacky outfit?" remarked Scarlet, looking up behind the bar. "Good Lord, who dressed the poor girl?"

Jennifer looked up to see what fashion show had so intrigued her skin-deep colleague only to see a weather bulletin on the television behind the bar. While Scarlet concentrated on the weather girl's outfit, Jennifer read the closed-captioned headlines scrolling under the picture. Something about a series of tornadoes flattening a bunch of trailer parks in rural Mississippi. They call that news?

Just as she and Scarlet were staring at the television, their cell phones went off simultaneously. Too noisy in the bar to make out the details, they understood they were receiving a special assignment, something about a natural disaster, going on location, and getting their asses to the airport.

Scarlet seemed all atwitter with excitement. Jennifer grew wary as she turned from the images of shredded trailer homes in the mud.

Chapter 3

She wasn't sure if it was an airport or a small outpost in Afghanistan. As if the red-eye flight down to Atlanta wasn't bad enough, an endless array of cute guys popping out of nowhere to vie for Scarlet's attention and all but wipe her ass for her while no chivalrous gents were anywhere to be found when Jennifer had to climb on top of her seat and jam a hand-carry nearly her own weight into an overhead compartment she couldn't reach.

Things went sharply downhill when they transferred to their connecting flight in Atlanta. Jennifer'd thought propeller-driven aircraft had gone the way of eight-track tapes. She wondered which of the Wright brothers were piloting that day, Wilbur or Orville. As the humming vibration of the propellers only seemed to keep her tequila hangover alive, Jennifer wondered whether a fatal crash might be preferable to reaching their final destination at all.

As Scarlet yucked it up with some randy Southern business yokels, as comfortable as if she were on her way to homecoming, Jennifer wracked her mind for what it was she'd ever done to piss off management enough that they'd send her on some assignment to Hooterville with Ellie May here.

But all that was forgotten when, still an hour or two before sun-up, the plane bounced to a landing in the middle of nowhere on what could only be called a cow pasture. Jennifer knew she'd better gather

her wits about her. She'd seen that movie Deliverance, well at least until she walked out with everyone else during the scene where…

Her hand-carry almost killed her when she popped it free from the overhead. Scarlet didn't have a carry-on. Instead, Jennifer watched as some toothless old man piled Scarlet's three full-sized suitcases into the trailer he pulled behind some kind of all terrain vehicle caked in mud.

Their cameraman, Charlie Green, ran ahead to scout out the rental car. Jennifer felt a bit better having Charlie along. He was a big guy, all muscle from the gym. Always impeccably dressed, he even smelled good. Jennifer could have gone for Charlie, but like most men, he'd shown no interest in her. But more importantly, like her, he was a New Yorker. She knew he'd feel as she did, like this assignment was some sort of punishment, or worse yet, that they'd been duped into signing on for some warped reality TV show, a cross between Redneck Weddings and Survivor.

But management felt the news had to give some attention to the poor victims of Mississippi. Not everything bad happened to big urban centers. They had to start getting more in touch with "the folks." They figured Scarlet was the ideal face for this particular outreach with a certain feel for the setting. Of course they sent Jennifer, low man on the totem pole, to put words in her mouth.

Jennifer recoiled from a potential abduction situation when a rusty old pickup truck stopped in front of her and the luggage, brakes squealing amid a cloud of dust. She was about to bolt when a man jumped out the other side of the truck and the driver's door slammed shut with a clank.

But Jennifer was relieved to see who it was as he came around to her side. "Charlie? What's this?"

Charlie looked at her like a teenager taking his date out in his mother's minivan. "This is our rental."

Jennifer never thought of Charlie as the joking type. "Our rental?"

"Yup. She's even got a name. Meet Bessie."

Jennifer watched as Charlie threw his equipment and their luggage in the back of the pickup and got back in the driver's seat in a huff. "Well? You two coming?"

Jennifer looked at Scarlet who didn't seem at all put out by their mode of transportation. That's only because Scarlet had probably been conceived in the bed of one just like it, she thought.

"Y'all better get in the middle," Scarlet said to Jennifer. "You're just a little ol' thing. That stick shift's bound to get frisky with someone of my stature. Need a boost, Sweetie?"

Jennifer cursed the girl with her eyes and climbed through the passenger door.

* * * *

"I think you made a wrong turn back a ways, Charlie." Jennifer always got impatient when she had to pee. And she'd already chugged her last bottled water trying to wash away her hangover. The mud they called coffee back at the airport didn't help. And since Jennifer Steele only knew of two food groups, caffeine and nicotine, she'd resumed her natural state of chain-smoking. She'd found from experience that smoking was the only remedy could keep her migraines at bay. Yet no amount of tobacco seemed to touch that damned hangover of hers.

"I'm just following the directions you're getting off your cell's GPS."

"Well I think we're lost. Not that you could tell," she added, peering out the window. "Everything looks the same. It's nothing but nothing, leading to nothing." She couldn't even find a sight to focus on. Everything was flat, just fields of hay and weeds. The condition of the road grew worse with every mile.

"I don't know what you're all complainin' about," interrupted Scarlet. "I find it kind of relaxing, like the music at the Wal-Mart. It's just mellow background. Let's a person think."

Just the thought of Scarlet Witherspoon thinking was a novel concept to Jennifer. "So what are you thinking about?"

"Nothin'."

Jennifer didn't know whether to slap her or just be content in the knowledge that the sun still rose in the east.

"We're lost," she repeated.

"Well, what's that GPS of yours say?" asked Charlie.

"It says to turn left at the next crossing."

"Another left? That's the fourth left in a row. You know what that means?"

"I don't know about four lefts," chimed in Scarlet, "but y'all know the old expression how two wrongs don't make a right, but three lefts do."

"A damn circle!" shouted Charlie. "We've been going in circles. Let me see that!" he insisted, grabbing Jennifer's phone.

"Damn it, Jennifer. That's the same crossing from over an hour ago. Your GPS is frozen," he said, tossing her phone back in her lap.

Jennifer picked it up and had to concur, after tapping a few buttons, shaking the thing, and even holding it out Scarlet's window to try and pick up a signal. "Either there aren't any cell towers out here or they're all blown down from the storms." Jennifer was beginning to miss the relative population explosion of the airport.

* * * *

"We're gonna die."

She didn't know what else to think when the truck broke down. By the time they'd driven a couple of hours, the road had deteriorated to the point where they'd have been better off without one at all. Whether the jostling from one pothole to the next had rattled some essential truck part loose was merely speculation on the part of the two city slickers and the brainless country flower. Charlie did his best man-impersonation, snooping about under the hood of the truck for something amiss, but having never actually owned a car in all his years in New York City, he'd have been as likely to find a missing proton in a nuclear reactor.

"We're gonna die," repeated Jennifer when she saw neither of her colleagues had anything to the contrary to say. They were lost, with no signs of civilization, no food, no water. And with no cell phone service, no hope.

It didn't take long for the trio to head out on foot. Jennifer's entire wardrobe, being the urban fashionista from New York City, consisted of only two colors, both black. And that Mississippi morning sun was having none of it.

Staring bleary-eyed off into the distance, they couldn't be sure it wasn't just a mirage dancing in the heat bouncing off the pavement, but they each convinced the other there was something dark off where the road met the horizon. They concluded it was either the end of the world where they could conveniently fall off, or at least some sort of tree line to shelter them from the sun. That it might represent some form of human habitation remained beyond their wildest imagination.

Charlie brought his good luck New York Yankee cap. Scarlet carried her favorite high heels. Jennifer brought a pen and notepad to be able to document their final days should their bodies ever be found.

Chapter 4

Little eight-year-old Felicity Barnes had never sold a single glass of her sweet tea to anyone other than locals before, through no fault of the tea, which was delicious, and practically irresistible. And it wasn't the fault of the sales department either. Precious little Felicity was cuter than any ol' supermodel. It was just that passersby were so few and far between. So it was a pleasant surprise to see three thirsty potential customers materialize from the dusty horizon approaching Sweet Spot.

Mikey Dunham saw things slightly differently. Then again, Mikey always did. You see, Lord love him, there was just somethin' slightly off with the boy. At least that's what everyone said. Mikey was all of 20 years old and fully grown— actually more than grown— huge in fact, with the mind of a six-year-old. Guess you could call that off all right.

But Mikey's six-year-old mind was sort o' single-minded. See, Mikey had one interest in life, and that was makin' sure nothin' bad ever happened to little Felicity Barnes. He was something akin to one o' those junkyard dogs, only Felicity was anything but junk. And when Mikey saw three small dust clouds forming off the horizon, he didn't see potential customers for Felicity's famous sweet tea. He saw stranger-danger.

So while little Felicity happily hummed a nursery rhyme in anticipation of her first sale of the day, Mikey stood up to his full height, facing the intruders, squinting to better assess a threatening situation.

* * * *

Scarlet never did much reading. So it was her fresh eyes that made out the first signs of life at the edge of the tree line up ahead.

"Told y'all we'd find help," she gloated with a Southern grin, elbowing Jennifer in the ribs.

Weary from walking, dehydration, and the general assumption she was about to die, Jennifer fell over from Scarlet's over-exuberant ribbing. Charlie righted his near-weightless associate with one hand by the back of the collar, and dropped her back on her feet, which were still automatically moving like some kind of wind-up toy.

She squinted to confirm Scarlet's claim, but was yet unwilling to rule out just another mirage. The last one she'd had about the Manhattan skyline turned out to be a family of muskrats lined up along the ditch at the edge of the road as if they were waiting on a commuter bus.

But when Charlie picked up the pace, she had to assume there was something to it this time. Without the strength to keep up, she just hoped her colleagues would send an ambulance back for her.

* * * *

A little girl selling sweet tea from behind a folding card table. What better sign of civilization, thought the three desperate travelers as they fell over themselves on their approach, dreams of hot showers and internet dancing in their heads.

Like a horse smelling hay from the barn at the end of a long journey, Jennifer somehow found her second wind and got to the stand first. But utter joy turned to apprehension when she found herself looking up at the giant's scowling countenance.

The arrival of Charlie and Scarlet didn't seem to break the ice either. It was only the little girl's voice chirping from behind the human shield that took the edge off.

"Hey, Mikey. Move aside. You're blockin' the merchandise. How 'm I supposed to make my first sale of the day with your big old butt in the way?"

There was only a moment's hesitation before Mikey stepped aside, scowling like a puppy gently reprimanded with a rolled up newspaper to the snout. In contrast to the foreboding bodyguard, little Felicity was a beam of sunlight, a welcoming glow emanating from her smiling eyes and blonde ponytail.

"Hey y'all. Welcome to Felicity's Fountain. Finest sweet tea in the land. Made fresh by the mornin' sun. Only 25 cents a glass. Will that be three glasses? Don't mind ol' Mikey. His bark's worse 'n his bite."

It wasn't until they'd consumed a second glass each that they thought to assess their situation. Their first attempts to communicate with what appeared to be the adult of the two weren't particularly rewarding. In fact, the giant with the unruly beard and overalls seemed mute.

"Can he talk?" Scarlet asked the little girl.

"Course he can," she replied. "Only he's got to get to know you first. He was taught not to talk to strangers."

"Well, how come you're talking to strangers?"

"That's different. I've got a business to run. I'd go belly up if I had to rely on locals alone. The real money's in the tourist trade. Besides, what do you think I pay Mikey for? He's in charge of security."

"Security, huh," murmured Jennifer, eyeing the mute giant warily. "Where are your parents?"

There was an uncomfortable delay as a serious look momentarily flattened out the corners of Felicity's ever-present smile. Then, after just a beat or two, the smile was back.

"Oh, they're in heaven."

Jennifer was caught off guard. The words came from her lips before she could edit them to avoid reopening a devastating wound to an eight-year-old girl.

"I'm sorry. What happened?"

"Twister came and took 'em both... directly up to heaven," she added with a skyward nod.

An involuntary gasp escaped her lips as Jennifer turned to see the looks of horror on Scarlet's and Charlie's faces. Seems like they'd fallen upon their assigned destination after all. They looked about for evidence of a tornado. Though there was nothing to see in the way of tree damage, they all knew how hit-and-miss tornadoes could be, sparing one street of homes while annihilating another. Maybe the town itself would reveal the twister's dirty work.

Back to the little orphan in front of her, "Who do you live with now?"

"I live with Miss Sarah Pritchard. She takes care of me. We take care of each other."

"And where do you and Miss Sarah live?" Jennifer inquired, thinking they'd better get on into town, whatever was left of it.

"In the school bus. Out back o' the church."

"Oh my God," blurted Scarlet to the others, tears coming to her eyes. "You hear that? Poor thing's livin' in a school bus."

"Where's your house?" asked Jennifer.

"We don't have no house no more. 'Course there's the church. We spend a lot of time there, prayin' and stuff. Miss Sarah's a big one for prayin'. But the church is for everyone. So we sleep out back in the bus. It's nice in the bus."

Charlie finally put into words what they'd all been thinking. "Maybe we'd better get on into town and see what's what." He placed a charitable five dollar tip on the little girl's card table, asking where they were and directions toward town.

"This here's Sweet Spot, Mississippi. The path behind me will take ya' right into town. But ain't that much to it so don't blink or you'll miss it," she answered, holding the Lincoln up to the sun to check its authenticity.

* * * *

And so the intrepid investigative team of reporters started down the path to town, marked only by the worn foliage of occasional foot traffic. For most, the solitude of their wilderness hike might have been a relaxing stroll. And for Scarlet, it wasn't so long ago that she used to run barefoot through similar landscapes as a child in Mississippi. But for Jennifer and Charlie, just the thought of confronting a wild rabbit crossing the path had their anxiety levels up. Perhaps the sight of a homeless person or a mugger might have been more comforting, at least remind them of Central Park. But there in the wilds at the edge of Sweet Spot, Mississippi, Jennifer and Charlie thought it much more likely to run into a tiger or a great white shark.

It wasn't long, however, before they did, in fact, run into some signs of life, such as it was in Sweet Spot. At first, they weren't sure where the sounds were coming from. They couldn't see the source of the commotion, but they knew it wasn't a tiger or a shark when they heard Jeb Clancey cursing at the top of his lungs.

"That damn redskin! Never shoulda let them off the reservation." Jeb always said that when he discovered Chief Firewater had quietly absconded with a jug of his best moonshine during the night. The chief still possessed the innate stealth of an Indian brave stalking his prey. And the sound of Jeb's snoring reverberating off the walls of the cave in which he and his prized still resided, provided plenty of cover.

Although they had no intention of wandering into a cave in the middle of the wilderness in hopes of conversing with its occupant, they did feel a certain empathy for the poor soul forced to seek shelter there, apparently driven from what was left of his home after the tornado.

It was a little ways further down the trail that they came upon the source of Jeb's current woes. The only teepee any of them had ever seen before had been erected inside the Museum of Natural History. But, while those may have been surrounded by mannequins representing various indigenous peoples of the Americas, as far as they knew, no real people actually lived in them.

Once again, although Chief Firewater was at home, sleeping off the results of last night's successful raid, the weary travelers couldn't muster up the nerve to see another unfortunate victim of the tornado, forced to construct a primitive shelter out of sticks and animal skins.

Things were looking worse than they'd imagined. And sure enough, passing through open fields as they made their approach toward town they began to see further evidence of the killer tornado. Fallen barns and nearly fallen homes patched up with sheets of plywood and plastic blue tarps serving as roofs, old refrigerators and washing machines strewn about the fields as if picked up and blown there right out of someone's kitchen.

Even the weathered fences dividing one field from another were falling down. Who knew what livestock had been liberated as a result of the storm damage? And just as Jennifer warily eyed her surroundings pondering that very question, the answer presented itself.

"Holy cow," said Charlie. "Would you look at the size of Elsie over there?"

Jennifer and Scarlet turned to see Charlie's cow.

Jennifer took a step backward simply due to the size of the beast. Scarlet stepped back as well, but for another reason. "Uh guys, that ain't no cow," she whispered.

"It's not?" Charlie replied, looking back at the animal in question.

"Uh, no. It's not," Jennifer confirmed on closer inspection, agreeing with Scarlet. In fact, she'd already started running for the woods when the bull looked up.

Charlie and Scarlet were slow to join the full-scale retreat but made up for Jennifer's head start by sheer leg-length. The tree line seemed impossibly far for Jennifer despite her short legs moving twice as fast as her colleagues'.

Initially oblivious to the field's intruders, the commotion of the sprint for the woods peaked the bull's interest. He started his charge, confident he could catch the small slow one lagging behind.

Jennifer felt the rumble of hooves through the ground upon which she ran. Through sheer panic, she couldn't help peeking backward over her shoulder, if for no other reason than to see her executioner face to face. Just when she thought things couldn't get worse, not looking where she was going, she felt her foot land on something soft and slippery, both feet heading skyward, landing on her back with a splat.

As the earth beneath her trembled from the approaching stampede, Jennifer's life passed before her eyes. Unimpressed, she was just thinking about asking for a do-over, when the earth suddenly stopped quaking.

Had the bull lost interest and gone away? Or was he standing inches from her head, simply waiting for the right moment to trounce her? Jennifer didn't know. But in the second or two that it took her to wonder, her inquisitive mind overcame her paralyzing fear and she opened her eyes.

Hooves. That's all she saw. Two sets of hooves sailing over her head and landing on the opposite side with a thud. The damn beast had jumped right over her.

Yet before she had a chance to thank the Lord, or the bull god, or whomever else she should be thanking, the fact that it wasn't even a bull registered in what little remained of her senses. It was a horse. A horse had just jumped over her. Had it been a horse the whole time? Was there no bull at all?

She sat up and looked around. No, it was a bull all right. It was still there, about 20 feet back, angrily pawing the ground, sod flying high behind it.

But between her and the bull now stood a magnificent horse, a white stallion, rearing up on its hind legs, its bareback rider sitting tall, controlling the steed with a handful of mane in one hand and gripping a golf club in the other, a three-iron, to be exact. A bronzed god, tanned and shirtless in a pair of tight jeans, a confident grin exposing gleaming white teeth, a head of long straight dark hair whipping through the air.

Before Jennifer could blink the apparition away, the horse and rider slowly advanced, facing down the bull. And just before the snorting pair of horns began its charge, the horse god swung his three-iron with one hand, the head of the club arcing through the air until it came in contact with a three-inch stone lying on the ground.

The stone flew through the air, striking squarely between the bull's eyes. The bull seemed momentarily confused by the turn of events. Only momentarily, as the bull wasn't one prone to alter its plans once made. Yet two more similar stones, again, right between the eyes, as the horse and rider advanced directly toward the animal, seemed to do the trick. Jennifer collapsed on her back again in relief after the bull fully retreated to the other side of the pasture, the horse and rider in full pursuit.

Only Scarlet's whooping cheers and Charlie's applause seemed to rouse her again. She sat up to see her bareback tanned Adonis's triumphant return, standing fully erect upon his galloping steed's back.

Slowing his approach to a trot, he smiled broadly, taking a bow, and sat once more, finally bringing his mount to a controlled halt alongside Jennifer. He looked down upon her with a curious expression. She was hypnotized by his godlike bone structure and long dark hair shimmering in the breeze. But by the time she thought to reach her hand up from the ground for assistance, he'd moved on. Moved on? Where was he going? He'd saved her life. She was ready to offer herself to him in whatever capacity an all-powerful god might desire of a willing female mortal. Yet he'd moved on.

Maybe it was all a dream. Or maybe his mount had sprouted wings and carried him back up to Mount Olympus. Jennifer sat up and turned to see where he'd gone, only to have reality douse her fantasy like a fire hose to a child's birthday candles. Her old familiar scowl quickly replaced the joyous grin that had briefly taken its place when she realized she'd been saved. She knitted her brows in disgust as she watched her god, her god, jump from his horse and gently lower his head to kiss the back of Scarlet's hand.

"Well aren't you the sweetest thing?" Jennifer heard Scarlet gush, as she approached the fawning couple.

"Such a thing is not possible, to be sweeter than the nectar from a flower as beautiful as yourself," answered the god.

"Aww, would you listen to him," Scarlet said to Charlie, her eyes never leaving her savior. Then to the man still holding her hand,

"Sugar, you're makin' me blush," she added, fanning her face with the other as if to dissipate a hot flash.

Between all the nauseatingly sweet nectar and sugar, Jennifer, still queasy from her ordeal, began to wonder if she was having some kind of diabetic attack or something.

"Hey, thanks for saving us," she stated trying to work her way into the conversation, holding her hand out. She'd meant it as a handshake, not expecting a kiss as Scarlet had received. But apparently she wasn't even worthy of a mere handshake. Instead, he didn't even acknowledge her. The man never took his eyes from Scarlet.

"Um, yeah, well, hello?" Jennifer persisted. "Listen, that was really something back there. You know, the whole Ringling Brothers PGA Tour thing and all. We really owe you." Her outstretched hand began to droop from neglect.

Not until Scarlet muttered a "Thank y'all" with a batting of her eyelashes did the man seem to hear a word.

"No, no," he began in protest. "It is I must thank you, for brightening this day, for bringing such joy to my life." He still hadn't let go of Scarlet's hand.

Scarlet practically snorted with embarrassment. "Well aren't you the charmer? You really know how to sweep a girl off her feet."

"As you wish," he replied, literally doing so with two hands about her waist, plucking her from the ground like a wildflower, and placing her on the horse's back. Then, with a deep bow, "Your chariot, my amor. Where do you wish me to carry you?"

In answer to his question, Scarlet was wondering if his bed had satin sheets.

Jennifer, on the other hand, turned to Charlie, rolling her eyes. Not the first time she appeared to be invisible to a man, she thought maybe he would have better luck.

"Charlie, could you ask our lothario here how far we are from town?"

"Hey, uh, yeah. Great job out there," he began. Holding out his hand, "My name's Charlie. And you are…"

The man still didn't turn his gaze from Scarlet to notice the outstretched hand, but at least he showed signs he could hear voices other than hers. With a deep bow from the waist, arms extended to either side, he rose again to take Scarlet's hand in his.

"I go by many names, but in this land, they call me Pedro."

"In this land? Yeah, well, listen, uh, Pedro—" Jennifer began before getting cut off.

"And what would a goddess such as yourself be called?" Pedro inquired of Scarlett.

She couldn't help bending toward Jennifer and muttering out of the side of her mouth. "Y'all hear that. He called me goddess. The man's got taste."

"Well he might have taste, but he doesn't seem to have hearing. Could you ask him to show us the way to town?" Jennifer tried.

Scarlet turned back to the admirer still holding her hand. "They call me Scarlet," she giggled, as Jennifer rolled her eyes again. "Tell me, Pedro, could you maybe show us the way to town?"

"But of course," he replied. "You have but to ask anything of me. But there is no much town for to speak of."

Of course, thought Jennifer. The tornado. Probably not much of the town was left. After all, here they were speaking to a man on horseback. Gasoline for cars was probably being rationed, saved for emergency and generator use.

"Well, who's in charge? Is there some governmental agency we could speak to?"

Pedro stood smiling up at Scarlet sitting comfortably upon her equine throne. Scarlet nodded her head over in Jennifer's direction, granting her prince permission to speak with her royal subject.

Pedro slowly tore his gaze away to focus on Jennifer. The smile left his countenance as he looked down his nose at her.

"So what about someone in charge, Romeo?" she inquired.

"No, it is Pedro, not Romeo."

"Whatever."

"Well, I guess you should see the mayor, Meester Buck."

"The mayor. Yes, the mayor. That sounds perfect."

With that, Pedro shouldered his golf club, turned and started leading the way through the fields, his trusty steed dutifully following close behind with the mounted princess Scarlet, followed by Charlie, and lastly Jennifer, scrambling to keep up with her longer-legged companions.

Scarlet momentarily tore her eyes from Pedro's butt, to turn and see if Jennifer also noticed the man's ass-ets, only to find Jennifer giving her the evil eye for receiving the royal treatment while she could barely see over the high grass.

Scarlet got the message and with a pang of guilt, turned back to Pedro. "You know, Pedro, I think there might be room for two up here."

Pedro looked up at her, smiling broadly. And with a wink, "I believe you are indeed correct, m'lady."

When Jennifer approached the horse, reaching up for a hand to mount, she was nearly kicked in the head as Pedro swung his own leg over the horse's back, settling in comfortably behind Scarlet. With a thrust of his hips to spur the horse onward, the pace increased. At first, Jennifer stopped in her tracks in indignation, only to start running to catch up lest she be left behind.

Scarlet was too busy just trying to keep from falling off the trotting horse to worry about what it was in Pedro's pants that kept poking her from behind.

Chapter 5

Buck Jones was a thinker, not a tinker. He was a big ol' boy who could swing a hammer with the best of 'em, if the situation called, but he wasn't particularly adept at fixing contraptions, not for a country boy, anyhow. So even though he wasn't sure it was the right tool for the job, there he was sticking to what he knew best, swinging his trusty ballpeen hammer at that danged generator of his, tryin' to git 'er to fire up. No generator, no air conditionin'. And that sticky ol' Mississippi afternoon heat was a bitch.

So that's how they found him, the out-of-towners, out back of his trailer home, shirtless, gleaming with sweat, swingin' his hammer like some Chink coolie layin' the transcontinental railroad.

"Meester Buck, we have guests."

Buck looked up at the sound of Pedro's voice, a drop of sweat dangling from his nose as he took in the unusual scene, Pedro hopping down from a white stallion that still carried some kind of princess/playboy bunny, followed by some big-city fella squire, maybe for security, and bringing up the rear, some sort of disheveled little page-boy. Buck tried to blink away what appeared to be a scene from some artsy-fartsy porno movie. He shook his head, not sure he was seein' just right, finally dislodging that tenacious sweat droplet. Was it the moonshine lingering from breakfast, or just that damn heat?

Pedro found it unusual seeing Buck speechless, so he tried to provide his boss with some additional information to prime the pump.

Helping Scarlet down from the horse, he tried to use the new word she'd taught him on the ride to town.

"This is Scarlet Witherspoon, my beautiful meto... meteoro... lolo olo... uh, how you say, uh, weather goddess."

"Howdy do," said Scarlet, extending a hand in greeting to the mayor.

Buck tried not to stare at her tits— unsuccessfully— as they jiggled mid-handshake.

"This is Carlos, uh, Charlie, her photographer."

"Cameraman," said Charlie by way of correction as he too greeted the mayor.

Ignoring Jennifer's approach for her introduction, Pedro continued his tale. "They come all the way from New York to see you, Meester Buck."

"Eh- hemm ," coughed Jennifer, elbowing Pedro in the ribs, looking for her introduction. She'd quickly sized the mayor up as one hell of an uncouth good ol' boy, but that didn't mean she didn't deserve a greeting.

Buck felt something was off when the pageboy approached him. He knew that gay fellas often went for soft-featured boys. Or was that pedophiles? Sometimes Buck confused the two. And Buck was anything but gay, yet, there was just somethin' about the kid, somethin' just a tad... uh... interesting.

When Pedro looked down at Jennifer, she could tell by the blank look on his face that he'd forgotten her name. So she took an exasperated step in front of him and extended her hand in greeting to the Mayor.

"Jennifer Steele, journalist with CNN."

Jennifer? But that's a girl's name, thought Buck. High voice, too. And sure enough, no Adam's apple. Buck be damned. It was some kind of female after all. What a relief. Woulda been damn inconvenient to be turnin' gay at this stage of his life. Next time Buck's nuts got to stirrin', he'd have to put more trust in the little fellas, despite the dirty skin and mussed up page-boy hairdo that looked as though it might be harboring bat's eggs. *Did bats lay eggs?* Buck wondered. He knew there was somethin' about the girl's face, her eyes, that caught his fancy.

Still flummoxed over his momentary concern about his sexual orientation, he held out his hammer when he meant to shake hands. Realizing his mistake, he dropped the hammer... on his foot, wiped his dirty hands on his dirty pants, and shook the girl's hand.

There musta' been some kind of static electricity from the hammer, 'cause they both had to step back from the shock delivered when their hands touched.

From a safe distance, Buck looked her in the eye, actually it was green, both of them were, a matching set of mesmerizing emerald green eyes, and found the words to introduce himself.

"B... B... Buck Jones, mayor, Sweet Spot, Mississippi." Something made the words come out like a nervous schoolboy's. He was still locked on her eyes when his nose began to object to something in the air.

"We're here about the tornadoes," stated Jennifer.

"You're full of shit," answered Buck.

"Excuse me?" replied Jennifer, confused by the mayor's exclamation.

"I said you're full of shit," repeated Buck.

Jennifer'd had quite a day to that point and was in no mood to tolerate rudeness. There was no call for the man to accuse her of lying. And coming from New York City, she was perfectly capable of verbal sparring with the worst of them.

"My ass," she countered.

Buck couldn't disagree. "Yeah, your ass, your back, all of it, full of shit."

Jennifer angrily turned to her crew. "We come all this way to cover the plight of the tornado-ravaged South and this is how we're greeted? What kind of bull-crap is this?"

Buck pointed at her back now facing him, then holding his nose, "I don't know how many kinds there are, ma'am. After all, I ain't no expert or nothin'. But you're up to your neck in it."

Jennifer was about to turn and pop the mayor in the mouth when Scarlet whispered in her ear, "The man's got a point, Sugar. You got bull-poo all up and down your backside."

"What?" asked Jennifer trying to look back over her shoulder.

Charlie had to suppress a grin as he finally saw where the smell was coming from.

"I believe," began Pedro, "in your country this is called, uh, the cow chips."

"Cow ch…" muttered Jennifer, realizing she'd slipped and fallen on a pile of cow dung while running from the bull. "Shit!" she cursed.

"Exactly," agreed Pedro. "This is another name, yes."

"Mother f…" Jennifer cursed, peering over her shoulder. "All the time I thought it was that damn horse making that stench. Now I know what I slipped in back at the pasture. Shit!"

"Exactly," confirmed Buck. "I knew you'd come around. You've got quite the sailor's mouth on you, little girl."

"Oh, you'll have to pardon her," Scarlet intervened. Then in a whisper, "She can have quite the potty mouth when she's havin' a bad day. And here she is up to her eyes in cow poo after all."

"Oh, that's OK," answered Buck. "I like a filly speaks her mind." Buck was hopin' she might even talk dirty in the sack.

Jennifer'd had enough of people talking about her right in front of her. "Mayor, does this town have any working plumbing? A shower?"

As much as Buck would have liked to offer his cute little stinkweed a shower, he had to reply in the negative. "Well, no, ma'am. I'm sorry, it don't."

"Wow," chimed in Charlie. "I didn't realize the damage these tornadoes could cause. A whole town with no plumbing."

"Well, what am I supposed to do?" whined Jennifer. "I can't walk around like this."

Buck didn't know what tornadoes had to do with the plumbing, but it's not like no one took baths in Sweet Spot.

"You just need a dip in the fishin' hole is all, just the other side o' town," he assured her, nodding in the general direction.

"The fishin' hole?" Jennifer knew she had no choice. "Well, Mayor, does anyone have any clothes I might borrow until you can send someone for ours back at the truck?"

"Please, Jenny, call me Buck."

Jenny? She hadn't let anyone call her Jenny since the third grade.

Buck continued, "Just tell me where you left the truck and I'll send someone to rescue your clothes. In the meantime, I don't think we got no one your size 'round these parts. Miss Sarah's too big, and little Felicity's too small. Shoot, I got a robe I borrowed once from the Days Inn you can use."

Jennifer didn't relish having anything belonging to that man actually touching her body, but anything beat the eau' de pasture she currently sported.

"Pedro, go tell the chief I got another job for him," ordered Buck. "Bring, uh, Charlie with ya, and see if y'all can find their stuff and fetch it back here."

He then briefly disappeared into his trailer only to re-emerge with a robe and a double-barreled shotgun.

Jennifer didn't notice the moth holes in the robe, distracted as she was by the shotgun.

"What the hell is that for?" asked Jennifer.

"What, this?" smiled Buck. "Oh, well, out here, you never know when you might run into some varmint, you know, bear, gator... When that happens, you always got a choice. You can *catch* dinner. Or you can *be* dinner."

By the leer he threw Jennifer's way, undressing her with his eyes, she wondered if it was her he had in mind for dinner. With that, she grabbed the rifle and cracked open both barrels, confirmed they were loaded with shells, whipped them closed, and slung the thing over her own shoulder. She felt much safer in control of the firearm than leaving it in the hands of the randy hillbilly before heading deeper into the wilderness with him.

"Ok, Mayor, let's go," she ordered, heading off in the general direction of the fishin' hole.

Buck, eyes wide with wonder over the little girl's familiarity with the 12-gauge, hustled to catch up, toting her robe over his arm like some kind of spa attendant.

"Hey, where'd you learn to handle a gun like that?" he called after her.

"Oh, we got plenty of varmints in New York City, too," she called back over her shoulder without turning around.

At least her no-good daddy taught her something after all, she thought. Who'd have imagined anything that man had to say would come in handy one day? But Jennifer was never one to wallow in the past. And that was one skeleton much better off left in the closet.

Chapter 6

The hike through town to the fishin' hole was an eye-opener for both Jennifer and Buck.

As Buck huffed and puffed to keep up a New York pace, the view from behind the gun-toting ragamuffin spitfire was surprisingly appealing. From her swan-like neck, to her tiny waist, to her dainty little feet, not to mention the rhythmic no-nonsense sway of her hips, Buck was mesmerized. He couldn't wait to try and sneak a peek at some skin down at the fishin' hole. Just something about the girl reminded him of one of them Victoria Secret models. It couldn't have been her height. And certainly wasn't her rack. Yet something about the total package placed Buck under her spell. Maybe it had something to do with her air of confidence, the impression that she never doubted, took no prisoners.

Jennifer, on the other hand, was doing her best brave-girl imitation, pretending not to be scared out of her mind. All she wanted was to get out of the soiled clothes she wore and bathe in some fresh water. Yet here she was, traipsing through the wilderness with some big sweaty Neanderthal breathing down her neck. Every time she picked up the pace to place some distance between herself and the redneck, he seemed to narrow the gap. Little alarms were going off in her head, warning her that the man was just waiting for her to get naked.

As the trail emerged from the woods along the edge of town, Jennifer was introduced to all the highlights of Sweet Spot, reminding her why she was there in the first place.

The devastation rendered by the tornadoes was overwhelming. Lines of crooked electric poles any which way but vertical, every window in the town either shattered or boarded up, old barns with caved in roofs, grain silos toppled over and lying horizontal on the ground, old cars and farm tractors stacked up in heaps along the side of the road, all signs of what must have been at one time a quaint little farm town, now flattened by a swat with the back of Mother Nature's hand. Not to mention the loss of life. She couldn't forget that poor little orphan selling sweet tea.

She hoped her news coverage of Sweet Spot's plight would gain them some much-needed national attention. Large metropolitan areas weren't the only places to suffer from natural disasters. Sure, they got all the coverage, but big cities held no monopoly on suffering. Small towns were not immune. Sweet Spot was sorely in need of some aid from the feds. That's what journalists did, after all, bring attention where it was sorely needed, shine a light upon inequities wherever they might exist, help the little people.

Jennifer would never feel that passion, that sense of accomplishment, writing cute banter for the weather bunny. But now this was her chance, her chance to garner the national spotlight and do some good at the same time. And if anyplace needed something good, it was this place, people living in caves and teepees, no electricity, no running water. This was America, for God's sake, not some third world refugee camp.

Just before the trail veered away again into the wilderness, a loud vehicle of some sort pulled up alongside them. It reminded Jennifer of one of those post-apocalyptic Mad Max movies. But that's only because she'd never been to a monster truck pull before. It was covered in equal parts rust and gray primer, with oversized off-road tires taller than Jennifer, raised suspension to clear the mud, vertical tailpipe to keep clear of the swamp, and, of course, the obligatory rebel flag flying proudly behind the cab. It pulled over next to them, launching a cloud of dust into the air.

Three men in camouflage jumped out, carrying rifles. Jennifer briefly thought to shoot first, emptying both barrels in hopes of taking one or two of the lawless looters out before they knew she was dangerous, but she quickly saw she was no match for their combined firepower. They carried AR-15's, tactical shotguns, grenades, and what appeared to be a bazooka. Jennifer thought to make a run for it, knowing it would be fruitless, but confident she'd be better off shot dead in the back than being turned into some sort of sex slave to this crew.

She was just about to sprint for the woods when the mayor spoke up.

"Howdy, boys. Watcha' shootin' today?" He seemed to know them.

"We shootin' dinner, that's what."

They were staring at Jennifer as if they'd never seen a woman before. She knew she was too small to be the main course for the three strapping men, but dessert wasn't out of the question.

"Seen some sign o' wild boar back a ways," the man continued. "You know that fresh stuff puts store-bought to shame. And sure a lot easier on the wallet."

Jennifer'd forgotten how the power outages must have left fresh food in short supply. Sounded like there might be some price gouging going on as well. So here, right in front of her eyes, was a prime example of resourceful people fending for themselves. No wonder country folk were such fanatics for second amendment rights. Without the right to bear arms, they'd only be left with the right to starve.

Never taking his eyes off Jennifer, the apparent leader of the trio continued. "And if that ol' pig gets away, well, we'll just have to settle for whatever else gets in our way.

Jennifer didn't like the sound of that, automatically stepping to the side just to be sure she wasn't "in their way."

Her movement reminded Buck of his manners.

"Gentlemen, this here is Ms. Jennifer Steele, a TV reporter from New York City. Ms. Steele, this here's the Winchester brothers, Earl, Bubba, and Eustace.

Jennifer couldn't help but jump back again as one of the brothers lunged at her, brushing back a forehead full of greasy hair.

"You say TV?" barked Eustace, upstaging his brothers, standing at an angle to favor what he imagined to be his good side.

"Now you just calm down, Eustace," chuckled Buck. "She ain't here to do no biography on you or your kin," acknowledging the other two trying to push Eustace to one side. "She's here to report on them damned tornadoes."

"Damn! Pottsville been hit?" asked Bubba, slipping off his John Deere baseball cap and scratching his head.

Jennifer turned to Bubba. "Pottsville too? Is that the next town over?"

"Too?" asked Eustace. "Whudaya mean, too?"

"You're saying Pottsville and Sweet Spot have both been hit?" she asked in clarification.

Eustace was perplexed. "Well I don't know 'bout Pottsville. You brought it up. But Sweet Spot? That's another story. Sweet Spot's the only place round never been hit."

"Well, you mean until now," stated Jennifer.

"Now?" Eustace was confused. But that wasn't uncommon. So, as usual, he looked to Earl for some clarity.

But Jennifer took the pause to continue. "That's right. That's why I'm here. To show the world what you're going through. To get you some federal aid. We need to get FEMA down here."

Buck's ears pricked up.

"FEMA?" Bubba tilted his head to one side like a dumb ol' chicken listenin' to Shakespeare.

"That's right," she answered. "You just need some air-time and I'll have the president himself down here posing for the money shot as he personally hands out the federal aid."

Bubba's turn to chime in. "But we don't need no federal aid."

Jennifer had to smile. Spoken like a true American. Independent. Self-reliant.

"Please don't get me wrong. This isn't charity. Don't be too proud to accept a little helping hand from Uncle Sam. The federal government sets aside money for just this purpose. Your town has suffered a grievous hit. No need to be proud. If anyone deserves the help, it's you people. It's your money, after all. That's why you pay taxes."

"Taxes? We don't pay no t—"

"Eh-hemm," interrupted Buck.

Jennifer continued, gesturing about her. "Just look at the devastation. The loss of life and property. The toll that Mother Nature can take when—"

Earl couldn't make heads nor tails out of the fool girl's speech, so he interrupted her to try and explain.

"Shoot, ma'am. You don't seem to understand. Ya see, that's why they call it Sweet Spot. We ain't never been hit by no t—"

"Now just hold on a minute there, Earl." Buck cut the man off like a hang nail. He'd been watchin' the back and forth goin' on between the Winchester boys and the reporter when he began to feel a tingling in his spine. He sensed somethin' was amiss. And Buck was pretty sharp so long as he was sober, which by some stroke of luck he was that afternoon. So it didn't take him too long to add two and two together. If he could just get the boys to hold their tongues long enough for him to confirm what his gut was tellin' him.

"Boys, now stop your interruptin' and let the woman speak."

With a nod to the mayor, Jennifer took the floor again.

"Why any fool can appreciate the devastation your town has suffered. Just look around. People living in caves and teepees. No electricity or running water. That poor little Felicity lost her parents…"

Buck couldn't believe what he was hearing. Could it be true? Could Sweet Spot finally be receiving its due? All he had to do was keep those damn Winchester boys from blowin' a gift from heaven. He thought about Jeb's cave-born distillery, Chief Firewater's teepee, the falling down everything that was Sweet Spot's charm. Shoot, Felicity Barns lost her folks five years ago over in a neighboring county. As Buck looked about him at the sites of Sweet Spot, he tried to see these things through the eyes of some big-city reporter. The girl's voice droned on and on in the background as Buck Jones had the epiphany of his life. Could it be? Could it really be that this silly Yankee thinks Sweet Spot's been hit by a twister? Could one man's comfortable old T-shirt full of holes be a sure sign of poverty to another? It was all too good to be true. A chance to partake in them FEMA handouts, without even actually having to pay the price? All the rewards of a bonafide natural disaster, but without all the muss and fuss?

It all suddenly clicked. These city folks were so out of touch they wouldn't recognize simple livin' even if it were explained to them on the front page of the New York Times. Buck briefly thought the Spotters should be offended by the misunderstanding. But that didn't last more 'n a second. Buck could swallow a bucket of pride for the right price. And yet, it didn't seem right, to lie and all. Well, it's not like he made up the lie. They did. After all, was he obliged to correct them? What would Jesus do?

Jesus weren't no fool. If Rome had mistakenly sent some gold to help them poor Christians, gold the Romans had stolen from them to begin with, Jesus wouldn't send it back. Now Buck Jones weren't tryin' to pretend he was no Jesus, but he was mayor of Sweet Spot after all, and he had to care for his flock. This was Buck's call to action.

"You know, we got black folk too!" he blurted out, cutting Jennifer off. This was no time to be pullin' punches, he thought. Buck was bringin' out the heavy artillery early.

"Excuse me, mayor?" responded Jennifer. "What's that supposed to mean?"

"Uh, listen boys," he resumed, ignoring the girl and turning to the three confused backwoodsmen without missing a beat. "I need y'all to go warn, uh, I mean, explain to Jefferson Washington that there's a reporter here from CNN come to discuss the needs of our black community in the wake of the horrific tornado that's decimated our beloved Sweet Spot."

The boys looked confused. "What do you mean tornado—"

Buck nipped them in the bud. "Don't y'all worry about that. Jefferson will know what I mean." Then, tapping his wrist impatiently, "Tick tock, boys. Tick tock. Now run along."

Buck used a firm hand on her back to escort Jennifer back to the path leading to the fishin' hole. Time was a wastin', and he could already taste that sweet government assistance.

Chapter 7

Pedro knew he'd better be careful. Despite the ecstasy he knew he could taste with this Scarlet goddess, she'd brought a truckload of baggage. And not just the kind Chief Firewater was now towing behind his trusty little John Deere in that U-Haul trailer he'd permanently borrowed a few years back.

Oh, there was plenty of that too, suitcases and camera equipment and such. Because of it, the trip was taking longer than expected, as the Chief had to run his little tractor in low gear to be able to drag such a heavy load of cargo. On horseback alongside the chief, Pedro couldn't complain. At least he didn't have to pull the load with his horse. Such menial labor was not fit for a mount such as Conquistador, his stallion.

But it was the baggage the camera equipment would bring that concerned Pedro. Reporters, cameras, television. Soon the whole town would be on display. He feared Sweet Spot would soon no longer be the quiet little hideout he'd so desperately needed when he showed up a couple of months ago on horseback.

Things were going so well for him in Sweet Spot. Sure it was a little sedate, no night life to speak of. No ladies, until Scarlet descended from heaven. But he had food on his plate and a place to lay his head. And his horse. He had Conquistador. That horse meant the world to Pedro. And for now, that was all he needed.

Yet suddenly it was all in jeopardy, with reporters, cameras, even something about government representatives coming to town. It seemed that in no time, all eyes would be on Sweet Spot. And after all, someone in Pedro's position couldn't have his face plastered all over national TV.

It was only two months ago that he'd crossed the border into Mississippi to lay low for a while until he could figure out his next move. These townsfolk treated him real nice, spoiling him with Southern hospitality. They didn't ask any questions. They even thought he was Mexican.

He would miss the playboy life he'd led back in Palm Beach. But that was over now. There was no going back.

* * * *

Scarlet had already been fantasizing about a roll in the hay with Buck's man, Pedro. But the peaks of ecstasy imagined at the climax of each of those vignettes were dwarfed compared to the multiple orgasms she'd experienced upon being reunited with her luggage.

She was all over Pedro, her hero, upon his triumphant return with her makeup case. She'd actually teared up when she caught her first glimpse of the little pink suitcase that held her makeup, beaming in the warm afterglow that follows the release of all that pent-up tension.

After all, a girl can't just go walking around without so much as a little foundation to smooth out the rough edges.

That was one of the first things she'd learned from the pageant. Never be caught with a naked face. Keep 'em wondering what's underneath. Dress it up first thing in the morning, and keep it dressed until the last thing at night, and even then, only if no one was around to see. And it wasn't just makeup. She'd learned everything she knew from the pageant, how to dress, how to walk, poise, take no prisoners backstabbing competitiveness…

Sure, she'd had some natural talent. Above average looks, superb skills at flirting with men, and an uncanny ability to sleep around with just the right people to advance her career. No, a girl's gotta be made of the right stuff at the start. But she needed some help, some polish. And that first announcement in the Penny Saver magazine about the Annual Miss Grits and Gravy Pageant down at the VFW saved her life.

She'd showed up like some kind of teen hooker in her Daisy Duke cutoffs and a flowered tube top, pure bred Ellie May white trash, which she was. But she was the hottest piece of teen hooker ass those judges had seen in a while. So naturally she won.

Sure she'd beat out a lot of nice girls who knew all there was to know about makeup and clothes, and posture, things Scarlet knew nothing about. She'd pissed off a lot of stage moms that day. But the girls were as nice as could be, happy to share their pageant secrets with her, and Scarlet absorbed them all like a sponge.

Oh, those other girls knew what they were doing. Unfortunately for them, however, they were, compared to Scarlet, shall we say, genetically challenged, a little long in the tooth, with plenty of underbite to go around.

So Scarlet became Miss Grits and Gravy. And having tasted the unvarnished envy and adulation of the crowd, there was no turning back. Scarlet would use every skill she could muster to climb her way up the pageant circuit, leading her further and further from her hardscrabble roots back in rural Mississippi to a spot on national television. She knew all too well what life was like on the other side of the tracks, and she had no intention of going back.

"Oh no, it was nothing," offered Pedro. "The chief, he did all the work with his little tractor. Conquistador and I were merely escorts."

"Well you can be my little ol' escort any time," Scarlet replied. "And I mean that, Sugar... day... or night," with a bat of her eyelashes. Scarlet had learned there was nothing to be gained by being subtle. Go bold, or go home. And that's how she led her life, nothing left on the table.

* * * *

Buck had promised Jennifer that he wouldn't come within 100 yards of the fishin' hole so that she could be assured of ample privacy as she discarded her soiled clothes and freshened up in the water.

Yet the view through Buck's binoculars was so clear it made him feel as though he were right there in the thick of the action, skinny dipping right alongside the girl.

At least he could confirm what to that point had only been theory.

"Yep. She's a girl all right," thought Buck as he took in the sight from his deer-blind, perfectly situated in a tree with a clear shot of the fishin' hole 101 yards away.

"No tattoos neither." He took another swig from the bottle of Jack he always kept stashed there, relieved in the affirmation of his own sexual predilections. More than relieved. In fact, he was rather... uh... excited about his discovery. There was just somethin' about the girl, somethin' Buck hadn't felt in a long while.

Oh, not that he'd missed it. Over time, he'd come to believe a man was much better off a lone wolf, master of his own fate, no silly games to play, havin' to please another, ever vigilant so as not to say or do the wrong thing. Without a woman 'round, there weren't no right nor wrong. Without a woman, the only thing mattered to a man was whether a thing felt good or didn't, whether it gave you pleasure, or pain.

Of course Buck had to admit he hadn't felt much of either lately. The pain from his past had finally seemed to fade. But the things that were supposed to feel pleasurable remained dull and muted.

Yet as he watched Jennifer Steele peel off those jeans on her way into the fishin' hole, he sure felt somethin'.

But that's just what he meant, about women and all. Here he was with the shot of a lifetime for the folks of Sweet Spot, and the mayor of the town was being distracted from his duty to the town. So as Buck sat there, enjoying the show, he tried to focus on the situation at hand, back to his master plan.

A chance like this didn't come along but once in a lifetime, and Buck had no intention of blowin' it. Weren't every day some out o' touch Yankee do-gooders come along, thinkin' your home is a disaster area, and wantin' to throw money at the situation to relieve their own collective guilt. Yet that's exactly the situation Buck found himself in, along with the whole town of Sweet Spot. And as mayor, it was his civic duty to leverage their good fortune into the life-altering phenomenon he knew it could be.

First thing Buck had to do was be sure all the Spotters were on the same page. Wouldn't do no good to have one of their own spill the beans on national TV. Tornado? What tornado? Why, Sweet Spot's never been hit by no tornado. Sweet Spot always looks like this. No, that wouldn't do at all.

Well, that was the Sweet of old. As of today, that reputation's been shattered. And folks were goin' to have to get over it. Sweet Spot was hit bad, real bad, completely tore up. Just look at the place. God help us. Send water, batteries, but mostly money, cash money, and big checks, checks with lots o' zeroes. Sweet Spot was about to be declared an official disaster area... that is if Mayor Buck Jones had any say about it.

He'd call a meeting over at the church, educate the populace about the opportunity thrown their way, the potential windfall at their fingertips. All they had to do was play the game. Even little Felicity Barnes could retire. No more long hot afternoons peddling that delicious sweet tea of hers.

There were a million details to work out. Reporters were already on site. The chief and Pedro were probably already back with the camera equipment. Only a matter of time before the national spotlight lit up the tiny town of Sweet Spot, Mississippi.

He'd best get Jefferson Washington prepped. Call it type casting, but they needed a victim, and according to Jefferson, there weren't nothin' the liberal media and the federal government enjoyed more than a black victim. Note to self, probably should check on the latest politically correct label for black folk. He knew "colored" was definitely out. But was African American back in vogue again this year? It was becoming so damn hard to keep up with all the latest terminology.

Course Jefferson barely qualified in that respect. Oh, he was black all right. But as black as Jefferson was, he was also a staunch right wing conservative with any number of vocal opinions on the founding fathers' original intent in the framing of the Constitution. Yep, Jefferson was gonna' need some extra coaching in the art of victimhood.

* * * *

Jennifer felt 100 % better having scrubbed the bull crap off her back. That dip in the fishin' hole sure was refreshing. Yet despite the mayor's assurance that there were no water moccasins or other manner of venomous snakes in the fishin' hole, she wasn't quite at ease in the murky water. She was ready to come out.

But there was just one catch. You see, the mayor's robe she'd so strategically placed hanging from that low-lying limb at the edge of the fishin' hole was farther away than she'd thought. The plan was to be able to reach it from the water without exposing herself. But now that she was ready to call it a day, she could see she'd overestimated the length of her arms. At least the upper half of her torso would have to emerge from the fishin' hole if she was going to reach that damned robe.

Yet no matter how clean she was, just the thought of exposing herself made her feel dirty all over again. Oh, it wasn't so much a matter of being naked in a public place. It was him, that mayor. She could feel his eyes on her. Jennifer Steele was no idiot. She knew he was out there, somewhere, watching her.

She wasn't afraid of the man anymore. Having spent a bit more time with him on the trek over to the fishin' hole, she'd decided he was perfectly harmless. Just a bit of a horn-dog was all. And she had possession of the gun after all. The more she thought of it, a grown man, out there hidin' behind some tree somewhere, completely under her spell, Jennifer Steele began to feel some oats of her own. Been a long time since she'd felt desired.

Probably too much time hangin' around Scarlet. Who could even see Jennifer with the gorgeous model obstructing the view? Sure Jennifer was short and her cup always seemed to be half empty, her bra cup that is, but she wasn't so bad, and what boobs she possessed were certainly still perky. She wasn't fat. She had all her teeth. She used to think she was damned cute until she started working around all the plastic amazons that populated a television studio.

And maybe this Buck Jones wasn't so bad after all. Nothing a little spit and polish couldn't overcome. He had good height, maybe six foot one she thought. Thinking back to her introduction back at his place, the shirtless mayor was broad-shouldered and well-muscled. OK, so he had some love handles. What woman wants a man thinner than herself anyway? Didn't often see that flat-topped marine haircut in Manhattan. And she could be sure there'd be no hair products found in the man's medicine cabinet.

Jennifer preferred a real man to some skinny metro-sexual anyway. A man's man. Not that she had a right to be so picky given the dry spell she'd been going through.

And now, here she was, in the buff, getting some mayor all hot and bothered. Sure, he wasn't the mayor of New York City. He was barely the mayor of anything, at least what was left of the place, but she knew the man had to have his hands full, what with dealing with a natural disaster and all. Yet here he was, doing who knows what somewhere out in the bushes, driven to distraction by the charms of Jennifer Steele. You go girl.

Buck Jones leaned further and further back in that rockin' chair he kept up in the deer blind. It had grown abundantly clear to him that the girl had quite a stretch to get to that robe. This was gonna' be good. If only those damned binoculars would stop foggin' up on him.

Jennifer resigned herself to the fact that there was just no way around it. Besides, maybe getting out of the fishin' hole and still feeling a little "dirty" wasn't such a bad thing after all.

The rocker happened to be all the way back when Buck froze, so as not to shake the binoculars. Just a little further girl. You can do it. This was going to be real good.

Jennifer was beginning to prune up. Oh, the hell with it. If she had to expose herself to the man, she might as well look good doing it. So she took her time. Grace. Poise. There. Got it. What was that noise? Sounded like a chair falling over.

Buck woke up seeing stars. It was still daylight, though. Looking at his watch he realized he was only out a minute or so. Maybe it had somethin' to do with that bump on the back of his head.

Chapter 8

She couldn't remember ever having sex that good. She woke up gleaming with sweat, ridden hard and put away wet. But the man was no jockey spurring her to a quick finish. No, he took his time, gently taking her through all her paces, skillfully leading her from one peak to another, controlling her, riding her, like the master equestrian he was.

At first she didn't remember where she was. Was it even real, or was it just a dream? Then she discovered her hair was full of straw. And so was everything else. As the world came back into focus, she realized she was in a barn. So that's what they meant by a "roll in the hay." Her lover had gone, but there was a witness that could confirm her patchy memory of those recent events. Conquistador stood quietly in the stall next to her, chewing his oats and looking her way every once in a while just to make sure she was OK.

But Scarlet Witherspoon was more than OK. In fact, she'd never felt better. Sex with Pedro was like a facial, mani-pedi, massage, and pilates class endorphin high all rolled into one, with dark chocolate and a double shot of espresso chaser. Every pore in her body was wide open and she was glowing like a firefly. Her Latin lover Pedro was definitely going to be habit-forming.

But for now, she'd best find her clothes and start plucking the straw from her hair. Charlie would have the cameras and satellite feed up and running in no time. He'd be wanting to go out and start getting background shots of the devastation.

* * * *

The meeting was already under way when Pedro arrived late to the church. After all, one had to keep their priorities in order. And Scarlet Witherspoon had definitely become a priority. He and Conquistador had lived alone in that barn for the past month or so. And it made a world of difference having a woman's touch around the place.

As he entered the church, it seemed everyone was there. Looking upward, he wasn't so sure it was a good idea to have the whole town gathered together under that one rickety roof, bowing inward from years of neglect. Too many crows come to roost at one time and the whole town could be wiped out.

Judging from Felicity's tip jar, she was making a killing with that sweet tea of hers, strategically located just inside the front door.

The mayor was addressing the small crowd.

"No no no, Mrs. Butts, you don't have to worry about straightenin' your place up just 'cause some TV folks from New York City gonna' be snoopin' around. That's just my point. They think they're touring a disaster site. And that's just the impression we want to give. Don't clean nothin' up. Now is not the time to suddenly be concerned about appearances."

"But Mr. Mayor," Mrs. Butts protested, "you know I got that busted-up above-ground swimmin' pool all over the front yard. Since the day Jimbo and his buddies drank a whole keg of Pabst and decided to have that belly flop contest, that thing been sprawled all over my place. Them things ain't built to withstand that kind o' abuse. You know I been meanin' to get that eyesore cleaned up soon as I got around to it."

Buck's frustration was growing. "Soon as you got around to it? Been goin' on two years now. Besides, that pool o' yours is exactly what this town needs. It's the perfect symbol of a town suffered the wrath of Mother Nature."

"But it weren't no Mother Nature," she argued. "Were only Jimbo and his gang's big asses destroyed that poor plastic pool."

"Now hold on there," objected Jimbo. "Weren't our big fat asses. Was Miss Piggy, that prize sow o' yours. She the straw that broke the camel's back."

Mrs. Butts was offended now. "Don't be callin' Miss Piggy no straw. She's 800 pounds of grade A ham. 'Sides, I can't imagine how you knuckle heads got her in that pool in the first place."

Jimbo had to chuckle remembering the site. "Said yourself we was havin' a belly flop contest. Who's got a bigger belly than ol' Miss Piggy?"

The church crowd had to agree, heads nodding in agreement. Even Mrs. Butts couldn't hide a little selfish pride in her sow.

But Buck was losing his patience. "You're missin' the point. Don't matter who broke the pool. Point is it's broke. Splattered all over the yard. And not just you, Mrs. Butts. Everyone in this damn town's got some kind o' eyesore over at their own place too. All I'm sayin' is now ain't the time to be sprucin' up the joint."

"We all know just who made all the mess," he continued. "But they don't. Them fool Yanks think we been hit. Just 'cause we don't give a hoot 'bout appearances, they thinkin' of sendin' us a plane-load o' FEMA money. Now why you wanna' go settin' 'em straight?"

Mrs. Butts had no answer, as she started to see the light.

But someone else did. Mikey Dunham had just whispered something into Felicity's ear, and she felt obliged to pass it on.

"Cause it's a lie!" she shouted. "That's why. That's what Mikey says. And I think he's right."

It never occurred to Buck that his plan would meet any resistance. But he certainly wasn't going to be dissuaded by some little girl and... well, Buck had nothin' against Mikey Dunham, but the poor kid was the village idiot, after all.

"Now, now, Miss Felicity... and Mikey. Ain't no such thing. There's a difference between statin' a bold-faced lie, and simply allowin' people to persist in a misunderstandin' of their own makin'. Folks ain't obliged to go around correctin' other grown folks all the time. People got minds o' their own, after all. If we was to spend all our time tryin' to correct the opinions of every misguided Yankee in the country, shoot, we'd never get nothin' done 'round here."

Little Felicity wasn't fooled. Buck could see it in those pretty blue eyes of hers just lookin' right through his little deception.

"Just don't seem right is all," she chirped.

The kid was just bein' pig-headed, thought Buck. So he was goin' to have to use all his powers of persuasion, pull out the big guns, go straight for the jugular.

"Do you have any idea, Miss Felicity, how many customers for that delicious sweet tea o' yours gonna be descendin' upon this fine metropolis, unaccustomed to our summer heat, money practically fallin' out their pockets?"

Buck was almost certain he could see little dollar signs ring up in the little girls eyes.

"Well, all right," she wavered. "But I don't have to like it."

Mikey just shook his head. He wasn't convinced.

Buck knew to close the deal while he had the momentum. "So we're all on the same page then, right? The eyes o' the world look at Sweet Spot and see a tornado-ravaged town. Who are we to argue with CNN? We just a bunch o' backward country yokels. No, them big-city reporters know better'n us. We're just here to oblige. Let's show 'em some o' that good ol' Southern hospitality?"

"Who you callin' backward?" called out Jeb, always runnin' a few paces behind any conversation.

Buck had to frown. "Ya live in a cave, Jeb. Don't get much more backward 'n that."

The townsfolk had to chuckle along with the mayor.

But Jeb was takin' things personal and didn't want to feel singled out. "What about Chief? He lives in a teepee. At least my home'll withstand a twister, we ever actually get one."

Chief didn't need Buck to defend him. Always prideful in the ways of his people, "What wrong with teepee? My people always live in teepee. Good for environment. Native Americans the original "green" people. We green before green fashionable. Very small carbon footprint."

"OK, so it's all settled," stated Buck, impatient to move on to the next matter at hand. "Now Earl, you and your brothers got that airport rental truck o' theirs over at the shop, right?"

"Yes, sir. Chief hauled it in this afternoon.

"You boys figure out what's ailin' her yet?"

Earl looked at his brothers in confusion. "Shoot, ain't nothin' ailin' her, Buck."

"What are you sayin'? There's nothin' wrong with the truck?"

"That's right," confirmed Earl.

"She just out o' gas is all," added Bubba.

Buck was disappointed. "You kiddin' me? Well, that ain't gonna do. We can't have them mobile 'til we set the hook. Least not 'til Uncle Sam's check is in the mail. Can't y'all find somethin' a little more debilitatin' wrong with their vehicle?"

Eustace was scratching his head. "Mayor, you sayin' you want us to sabotage their truck?"

"Now I never said no such thing. I simply asked if you could find somethin' a little more debilitatin'."

"But—" Bubba didn't get it.

"Shut up, boys," said Earl cutting off the discussion. "We got this, sir," turning to Buck with a wink. "That truck ain't goin' nowhere 'til you gives the say so," saluting Buck, happy to take on the mission. Earl badly missed his days in the military.

Everything was going just according to plan, thought Buck. He could almost smell the coffee and taste those glazed donuts courtesy of the Red Cross. One last hurdle remained. One last pre-performance sound check before the curtain could go up. Buck turned to Jefferson Washington.

"Now Jefferson, you and I gotta have a little strategy session before your big national debut. We gotta make you seem a lot more pathetic than you are."

"What da hell that supposed to mean?" asked Jefferson, his feathers ruffled.

"Now don't go gettin' your panties in a wad. I just mean that, well, first of all, you can't be lettin' on 'bout your college pedigree. They can't know you got that damn degree of yours from Harvard.

And even if they do somehow find out you're college educated, let 'em think it was only thanks to them, you know, through affirmative action, reparations for slavery and all."

"Affirmative action?! You know damn well I wasn't haven' none o' that. I even pretended to be white when I applied. How else would I ever know if I got accepted on my own merit?" Then, with a chuckle, "Shoot. Remember I showed you that photo of Alfred E. Newman I used on my application. You'd think those brains at Harvard would o' picked up on that."

"But that's just what I'm talkin' 'bout," countered Buck. "They can't know all that. They gotta believe you're helpless and can't survive without some o' their government largesse. And then we gotta smooth out some o' those rough edges o' yours."

"What you talkin' bout rough edges?" asked Jefferson, getting his dander up.

"Oh, you damn well know just what I'm talkin' bout," Buck began. "Your whole thing about personal responsibility and how America's succumbing to a sense of entitlement and victimhood, sucking off the teat of big government, and how it won't be long before the U.S. of A. turns into one big Marxist mess, blah blah blah. That's what I'm talkin' bout."

Jefferson wasn't ready to compromise his principles. "Well, ain't it plain as day? Can't argue with the facts. We keep electin' them damned democrats buyin' votes by givin' away shit they bought on our credit card with money they borrowed from the Chinese."

"But that's just the whole point of this little exercise. Ain't a man here don't agree with your logic, Jefferson. It's just that while we never ask for nothin', them damn politicians keep dolin' out favors to everyone else, the national debt goin' through the roof anyways. Here they come finally wantin' to spread a little our way, I don't see no good come out o' standin' on ceremony and turnin' down our own damn money. All you gotta do is go along to get along. Play the victim for just this once in your life, Jefferson. That's all I'm askin'. For the good o' the town."

Jefferson clicked his tongue and shook his head. "Go against every fiber of my being, pretendin' I need no damned government to survive. President Reagan be rollin' in his grave, rest his soul."

Buck held his tongue, lettin' it set in. He knew Jefferson was far and above the smartest fella' in the damn town, 'ceptin' himself of course. And Buck was confident wouldn't take long for the man to see the light.

True to form, you could almost see the wheels turnin' in Jefferson's head, 'til the light came on, and he began to speak.

"On the other hand, sho' would be a hoot pullin' one over on them feds up there on their thrones in D.C.," muttered Jefferson, thoughtfully rubbing his chin.

"Now you're talkin', Jefferson," encouraged Buck.

Jefferson began to show a little twinkle in his eye, a little grin like he was up to no good.

Soon, in just a few blinks of their eyes, the whole town witnessed Jefferson Washington's transformation from a lifelong card-carrying conservative republican member of the John Birch Society into a full-fledged welfare-addicted victim of a legacy tainted by the evils of slavery.

His voice got higher and his eyes wider. His spine seemed to bend under the weight of generations pickin' cotton.

Then the new Jefferson began to speak. "That's right, massuh. I's just some po' nigga in desperate need o' some gubment assistance cuz I's too ignorant to take care myself. Oh, woe is me. Please, massuh, please hep me. Lordy, someone hep me."

Buck had to roll his eyes. "All right, Jefferson. No need to overdo it. We ain't lookin' for no Academy Award."

Chapter 9

Jennifer wasted no time that afternoon once Charlie had the cameras set up. She knew the station would be looking for some footage, so she was sure to have the team hit the ground running just as soon as Charlie got the satellite feed up.

Prior to that, they'd had no communication with New York. They'd fallen completely off the grid, and for all New York knew, their plane had quietly gone down in the middle of some mysterious crop circle.

Apparently cell phone service had been knocked out by the storm, and the mayor couldn't give her any idea when it would resume. What Jennifer didn't know was that cell service would never resume because Mayor Jones neglected to tell her that Sweet Spot never had cell service in the first place. Due to the scarcity of cell towers, the worldwide phenomenon of mobile cellular technology— oh, and don't forget that new-fangled contraption called the internet— had yet to debut in the land that time forgot.

So Jennifer was amazed at how the whole town seemed to adjust so easily to what she believed to be the sudden loss of service in the primitive aftermath of a natural disaster. Her crew had never been so long without an iPhone or Blackberry, and they were beginning to go into withdrawal, the phantom twitching of thumbs making them look desperate. Yet the townsfolk acted almost as if they'd never seen a cell phone before. There was even talk of a working payphone somewhere that the town used whenever they had something important to relate to the outside world.

The crew still didn't have a vehicle to get around with, seeing as their truck was up on blocks over at the Winchester Garage, or front yard, depending on your point of view. And the Winchester truck seemed to be the only remaining working vehicle in town. The chief offered to loan them his tractor but they could walk about just as fast without all the noise and fumes. So once the camera was ready to roll, they headed out on foot, all the better to get a feel for the place.

The first obstacle that had to be confronted was Scarlet's wardrobe. She'd never really been out in the field before, out on location. The closest thing to actual weather the weather girl had ever seen was the smiley sun and the cloud with puckered lips blowing wind projected on the blue screen behind her back at the station.

But this was the real deal. So when Jennifer handed Scarlet the obligatory baseball hat that all reporters wore when filming on location at a natural disaster, Scarlet balked, whining something about mussing up her hairdo. And while they were on the subject, she made it known that she would not be donning the hip boots they found with the rest of the foul weather gear they'd packed. On screen, those things would easily add ten pounds to her hips. Not gonna happen.

So the team walked from overturned car to collapsed barn to tarp-covered shack, gathering heart-wrenching footage to send back to the station. Noticeably missing among the carnage were the hallmark mangled trailer homes. Jennifer thought the lines she had Scarlet read off the teleprompter for public consumption were true. After all, it was the mayor himself who confirmed her theory that all the trailer homes had been completely blown away by the tornadoes, picked up like so many children's toys, completely dismantled, and cast about the countryside like toothpicks.

Had she gotten to any of the other residents of Sweet Spot before that emergency meeting of theirs over at the church, she'd have learned the truth. The only resident of Sweet Spot who could afford the luxury of a trailer home was the mayor. And it wasn't that all those twisters somehow destroyed everything in the town except the mayor's trailer home. It was that the town always looked that way. There never were any twisters. And the town had never been destroyed... except maybe by neglect... and gravity.

Yet even if they'd known, no one on the other end of their camera feed living in the civilized world, let alone New York City, would have believed that such devastation could be the result of anything other than a full-blown natural disaster, an unapologetic swat with the back of Mother Nature's hand. How could all this simply be the natural state of a town in these United States of America? This wasn't some village in Haiti, or Bangladesh. This was small town U.S.A., rural Mississippi, to be exact.

So the folks back in New York ate it up. They were so pleased with the team's work and sacrifice, scooping such a poignant tale of woe in the face of all manner of personal suffering and indignity just to obtain their story. There was already some talk being bantered about concerning a possible Emmy Award.

The station back in New York was shocked by the conditions under which their colleagues toiled, the constant sound of gas and diesel generators supplying whatever electricity the town could scrape together. The sight of men openly carrying rifles about town led to speculation about the breakdown of order, lawlessness, of possible looting, every man for himself, or worse yet, a hardy people simply foraging for food, trying to fill their families' hungry bellies.

The uncut glimpses of their very own intrepid meteorologist touring the wreckage by horseback, riding bareback behind some handsome local, was almost too much to comprehend. The poor horseman was seen trying to shield his face from the camera, apparently embarrassed by his plight.

Although the team on location hadn't intended to have the horse in the shot, the sight of New York City's brave and beautiful Scarlet Witherspoon cheerfully waving from the back of a horse situated upstage from a collapsed rusted tin-roofed barn was chosen by the station as the theme for their initial coverage, the symbol of the extent to which their reporters would suffer just to bring these events into the nation's consciousness. It would be shown over and over, nationwide, every time there was an update to the horrible events unfolding in the nation's heartland as a result of the storms.

* * * *

The team was bone-tired by the time they started to lose the light. They'd been up practically all night, what with the red-eye flight out of New York, the drive, then hike, from the airport, rescuing their equipment from the broken-down truck, only to hit the ground running so as to get some initial footage off to the station.

Charlie'd been quite the trooper, withstanding Jennifer's strong-willed direction, the constant bark of commands and general oppression suffered at the hands of a Type A+ personality in the throes of nicotine withdrawal. It seemed a lifetime ago that Jennifer'd inhaled her last stick of tobacco.

Scarlet, on the other hand, had quickly begun to wilt under the pressure of her taskmaster. So it was only in the face of impending mutiny that Jennifer agreed to call it a day and head for the church.

Mayor Jones had apologized profusely for forcing them to stay at the damaged church, a makeshift shelter of sorts, that is since, as luck would have it, the town's quaint five-star bed and breakfast had been conveniently carried off by the storm. The man almost seemed to tear up when he told them the name of the Southern-themed inn, Gone With The Wind. What cruel irony.

So it was with great trepidation that the team approached the front of the church. The way the roof bowed inward and the entire frame appeared to list to the right, they weren't sure how sturdy the structure could be, obviously having been hit hard by the recent tornado. It had more the look of a condemned death trap then a shelter from the elements.

Even though they'd imagined rows of cots set up for those displaced from their homes, they weren't too surprised when they stepped through the creaky front door to find they were the only tenants of the dilapidated ruin. The residents of Sweet Spot probably felt safer sleeping out of doors.

The smell of some sort of incense brought their attention to the back of the dimly lit church where they could make out the back of a figure in a hooded cape, knelt in prayer in front of a row of candles.

Scarlet and Charlie were a little freaked out by the whole thing, clutching at each other for security, but Jennifer was way too tired to stand on ceremony.

"Eh-hemm," she coughed, hoping to grab the attention of their housemate.

The hooded figure slowly rose to its feet, hands together in prayer, and after one last bowing of its head, began to circle the room, lighting more candles to brighten the church hall growing darker with the setting sun.

As it did so, Jennifer and the team studied the mysterious figure. By size, shape, and motion, it was apparently a woman. And as it lit the last candle, it pushed back the hood of what turned out to be not a cape after all, but a hoody sweatshirt, to unveil a tricolor head of hair, blonde roots, followed by bright orange, which ultimately faded to washed-out pink tips. As she turned to look at them, the aforementioned hairdo only involved one side of her head, the other side shaved smooth. And instead of hair on her left side, she boasted a purple pentagram tattoo.

Jennifer was trying to summon what she could recall about witches and Wiccan cults but she was distracted by Scarlet's French-manicured nails digging into her arm, the taller girl cowering behind her.

When the woman, actually more of a girl, approached them, they all took an involuntary step backward, cowed by her intimidatingly dark eye shadow, topped by a barbell-shaped eyebrow piercing.

Backs against the front door, they'd run out of real estate, when the girl extended one arm and pointed a black nail-polished hand in their direction. Their first instinct was to duck, letting whatever black magic curse she was preparing to hurl at them pass overhead. But they quickly realized they'd completely misinterpreted a simple hand extended in greeting when they saw the girl smile.

The word smile didn't come close to doing justice to what they saw on her face. It was so much more than that. The change brought by a simple raising of the corners of her mouth was astounding.

The New Yorkers were awestruck. Any apprehension they'd harbored immediately melted away. The brimstone hair— shaved on one side—, the tattoo, the piercing, it all faded into the background, upstaged by the most welcoming, serene, angelic smile any of them had ever witnessed. The love was palpable.

They were completely disarmed, transfixed in the face of such a glorious site. The very sun shone from that smile. They were healed, as angels from heaven sang. At that moment, for the first time in their lives, they knew it in their souls, they felt the presence of the Lord.

It literally took Jennifer's breath away, but she was shaken from her reverie when she felt the breath of her two colleagues on the back of her neck as they noticeably exhaled in relief.

"Hey y'all," said the angel. "Welcome aboard. M' name's Sarah Pritchard and I'll be your stewardess on this flight."

Jennifer shook the girl's hand, feeling more of a comforting embrace than a shake. The current she felt through that hand was a soothing warmth, a sense of tranquility she'd never known. Jennifer felt her body go limp in rapture, her eyes involuntarily closing for a moment.

She had to shake her head to gather her wits again when she felt Scarlet poking her from behind.

"Jennifer. Y'all gonna introduce us, or what?"

"Oh. Yeah. I'm sorry. It's just—" Jennifer began.

"It's OK. I know," assured Sarah, noticing Jennifer's loss for words. "Happens all the time. You haven't let the Lord into your heart yet, have you?"

Jennifer didn't know how to answer that.

"It's OK," the girl continued. "You will. I feel the goodness in you. You'll find grace when you're ready."

Jennifer took a good look at Sarah Pritchard, just a teenager, maybe 18, and saw a girl with more miles on her than her years called for. She saw a girl who'd been through something, something no teenager should know. She saw a girl who'd been tested, tested in ways only few could survive. And yet, this girl had. She'd been through hell and back. She'd been burned by hellfire, but come through only stronger, like forged steel, carrying God's reflection in her smile.

"J... J... Jennifer Steele. CNN," she mumbled. Turning to her crew, "Scarlet Witherspoon and Charlie Green."

They each shook the girl's hand in turn, each visibly affected by her touch, left staring at their hands as though they'd never seen them before.

"S... S... So you're Sarah Pritchard?" Jennifer resumed. "Little Felicity mentioned you. You're taking care of her?"

Sarah had to chuckle. "Oh, Felicity? Yeah, she's stayin' with me. Only I'm not sure who's taking care o' who. That girl's got a better head on her little shoulders than I'll ever have. Don't know what I'd do without her."

"I still remember the day I met that little girl. She saw the path I was on, what kind o' life I led, and she saw the void in my life. Don't no one know right from wrong like she do. She's my compass. She pointed me in the right direction, and afore you know'd it, I found my Lord and Savior, Jesus Christ. As God is my witness, Felicity Barnes saved my life."

Not exactly the religious type, Jennifer was beginning to feel a little out of her element. But Scarlet's curiosity was peaked, given her own sordid past.

"Honey, I don't mean to be nosy and all, but you mind tellin' me what it was you did was so awful?"

Scarlet thought she heard the girl reply that she used to be a Methodist. Scarlet didn't know if she should be offended or not.

"Well, what's so wrong with that? Why, I been a Methodist my whole life."

"Methodist?" Sarah replied in confusion. Then covering her mouth in embarrassment. "Oh, I'm sorry. I didn't mean to offend you. But I didn't say Methodist."

"You didn't? Why, I could o' sworn you said you used to be a Methodist."

"No, no. I said I used to be a meth addict."

Scarlet looked confused, then the light came on. "Oh, shit! A meth addict? Like crystal meth?"

Sarah nodded her head. "Near killed me."

"That's some serious shit," chimed in Charlie.

Jennifer didn't know what to think. So their host for their stay in Sweet Spot was a born again ex-some kind of devil worshipping teenaged meth addict? And this is the person little Felicity Barnes lived with? In the bus behind the church? Things were growing curiouser and curiouser.

As was dinner. After getting settled in their temporary home, they were pleasantly surprised when Sarah brought them a pot of stew she'd prepared. Maybe they were just hungry, but after joining her lead in saying grace, they found the food delicious, a sort of Cajun-spiced gumbo. They insisted Sarah let them pay for the meal, but she adamantly refused to hear of it.

Scarlet asked what was in the stew.

"Don't rightly know for sure," answered Sarah.

"You don't know what's in it?" asked Jennifer, one eyebrow raised.

"Well, the Winchester boys brought it. They're always helpin' us out with vittles."

Jennifer recalled all too well the gun-wielding survivalists she'd met on her way to the fishin' hole. Apparently they'd had a successful hunt that day.

"No wonder this is so delicious. The meat must be fresh," she commented.

"Well, not necessarily," Sarah replied.

"What do you mean?" asked Jennifer. "Do they have some of their game stored frozen?" With the power outage from the storm, Jennifer assumed maybe they had to use up what supply they had before it went bad from lack of refrigeration.

"No. It's just the game 'round here's been a little scarce lately. Sometimes you gotta make due."

"Make due?" asked Charlie.

"You know. Accept what the Lord provides."

Charlie put his fork down, looking at Jennifer and Scarlet. "Provides? Where?"

"Over at the interstate."

Jennifer and Scarlet took Charlie's lead and also put down their forks.

Charlie narrowed his eyes at Sarah. "You saying they found this already dead in the highway?"

Sarah swallowed another mouthful and smiled. "You know what they say 'round these parts. Roadkill rocks."

The team from CNN didn't know whether to pity a town so devastated that they were reduced to living on roadkill... or to induce vomiting.

Chapter 10

The next morning, Buck was feeling a little queasy in the stomach himself. He couldn't quite put a finger on what the cause could be. But he noticed he only felt it around that reporter from CNN, that green-eyed vixen, Jennifer Steele. Buck hadn't been so distracted by a woman since his introduction to puberty by Daisy Duke during reruns of The Dukes of Hazard.

Yet here he was, finding it hard to concentrate on the questions the girl was throwin' at him. He hadn't messed up yet. So far, he'd kept to the story, how the storm came out of nowhere with no warning whatsoever. The fierce power of the wind, the sound like a roaring train, the feeling of utter helplessness, fear for their lives, how they'd lost everything that day, and now, how it was a daily struggle just to survive. All the usual stuff.

But the more he stared into those eyes of hers, patiently enduring her crossing and uncrossing those tight-jeaned legs in the chair across from him, the walls of what he once thought was a good-sized trailer home seemed to close in about him, becoming claustrophobic, making the simple act of breathing require a conscious effort. When she absent-mindedly brought the end of her pen to those full painted lips of hers and started sucking on it, it was time for Buck to cross his own legs.

* * * *

Jennifer was trying to be professional. She'd been sent to this God-forsaken place to get a story, gather footage for the world to see. And yet, in the confines of the mayor's trailer home, she was having trouble concentrating. When she first met him, she'd thought he was, well, a little slow. Seemed the man could barely string three words together. So what if he was the mayor. Sweet Spot wasn't exactly a teaming metropolis.

But as she'd had more contact with him, he was beginning to grow on her. The stuttering, as if something had been making him nervous, had mostly cleared up. Even now, he still seemed a bit distracted. Though maybe that could be attributed to the overwhelming responsibility thrust upon him in the wake of the storm.

He wasn't the Neanderthal she'd imagined on first impression. Even though the way he looked at her made her want to put on more clothes despite the Southern heat, she didn't find it all that displeasing. She even wondered if maybe it was she who had the problem. After all, that's how men looked at Scarlet all the time. Could it be that the man had the hots for her?

He wasn't so bad himself. Even with a shirt on, he exuded a certain masculine aura, though her mind seemed to prefer wandering back to the gleaming shirtless form that confronted her upon her arrival the day before.

He'd played the perfect gentleman so far, very respectful to her, even humorous, in a folksy sort of way. Maybe there was more to this country bumpkin than she'd imagined. Now that she thought of it, wasn't that an Armani suit she'd glimpsed upon arriving, before he'd had a chance to shut the closet door behind him? What was that all about?

* * * *

Buck could sense things were finally getting down to the nitty-gritty. He was preparing to make his pitch. But not just yet. He'd play it humble at first. Suck 'em in with the ol' rope-a-dope.

"So how come you're not receiving any help from the county, or the state for that matter?" Jennifer asked, taking notes.

"Well, we're a proud people here in Sweet Spot," answered Buck. "We don't want to be a burden on others."

"A burden? Anyone can see the town is overwhelmed, in desperate need of assistance."

"Well, we don't see it that way. We'll make do. There's always others somewhere worse off than oneself."

"Worse than this? I find that a little hard to swallow."

"You really think so?" asked Buck, just beginning to reel in a little line.

"Mayor, you have no electricity, no water, and as I found out last night, no food. It doesn't get much worse than that."

"Well, you know, ma'am—"

"Please, call me Jennifer."

"Well, you know, Miss Jennifer, Mississippi ain't a rich state. There ain't a whole lot of reserves to be throwin' money around willy-nilly. And with all the floods and tornadoes throughout the state, we'd feel bad takin' from others."

"Well, OK, but what about federal aid? There are always federal dollars set aside for places like Sweet Spot, places decimated by natural disasters."

"Shucks, I don't know," exclaimed Buck, scratching his head.

"Sure. With just a little national coverage, we can get that federal spigot opened and have aid pouring in from all over the country."

Buck was preparing to sink the hook, but didn't want to overplay his hand just yet. "Well, I suppose… if it was federal aid… you know, money comin' from rich folk in New York and Hollywood, why, I guess that might be OK."

"Now you're talking, Mayor," she replied, proud of herself that she could act the savior for this place in need.

"Call me Buck, please."

"OK, uh, Buck. I have another question for you, and it's a little delicate. I'm not really sure why the people back at the station need to know, but I've been instructed to ask you if you have any, uh, how do I put this, uh, people of color in Sweet Spot?"

Buck could take her at her word and believe she honestly didn't know why her people wanted to know, but Buck knew. He'd been waiting for them to take that bait all along. But he didn't want to seem too eager.

"Well, now, let's see. You've met Pedro and the chief."

That caught Jennifer off guard. She was going to have to come out and say it. "Well, yeah, Pedro and the chief, of course, but, um, they were thinking a little darker color." The words made her uncomfortable.

"Oh. You mean colored people?" Buck wasn't going to let her off easy. He enjoyed watching her squirm at the outdated term.

"Well, of course, um, no one calls them that anymore. They're African Americans."

Bingo. This was too easy, like shootin' fish in a barrel. "Well, now, I don't know if he's ever been to Africa or not, but we got Jefferson. Jefferson Washington. Would you like to meet him?"

"That'd be great," answered Jennifer, just relieved to move on from the uncomfortable subject of race.

"So, what kind of aid do you think is most needed up front?" she continued, shifting gears. "Water? Food? Generators? Roof tarps?"

Uh oh, that wasn't part of Buck's plan. "No, no. Sounds like that would be a hassle shipping all that stuff here. You know, planes, trucks, man-power."

"Really, I hadn't thought of that. Well, what then? What would be most useful?"

There it was. The question Buck was waiting for. This was it. Time to make his move.

"Cash, ma'am... uh... Jennifer. Cash money. That would be the most effective means to save what's left of our Sweet Spot. Ya see, that way we could distribute it in the most efficient manner throughout the town as we see fit, the local folks knowing where the need was most dire."

So there it was. Buck had made his pitch. Would she see right through Sweet Spot's little deception? He knew if he could fool the media, the war was more than half won. He found himself holding his breath waiting on her reply.

"Well, that sounds reasonable to me," she replied.

Buck felt a wave of relief.

But the reporter didn't leave it there. "Of course, that's not my call. I'm sure FEMA has its own policies and procedures in handling these things."

He knew that would be the case. But Buck Jones could be very persuasive when the call arose. He just needed a face, a target, to which he could direct those skills of his.

"Well, uh, when do you think we'll be seein' some o' them muckity mucks from FEMA? You know, the decision makers, the people with the checkbook?"

The reporter answered with a self-congratulatory smile, "Well, just so happens I have some good news on that front, Mayor. Thanks to yesterday's broadcast, my people back in New York tell me we can expect FEMA as early as tomorrow."

Buck could barely hide his glee. But there was also a strong dose of trepidation. Sure, things seemed to be going exactly according to plan. It couldn't have gone better if Buck had written a script. But would his neighbors be able to pull off their plan in the face of a swarm of FEMA reps descending upon Sweet Spot? Buck knew he'd have no trouble himself dealing with a bunch of naive Yankees, but Buck couldn't be everywhere at once.

"How many reps you think'll be showin' up? A whole team?"

"Don't really know Mr. Mayor—"

"Eh eh ehhh…"

"Oh, right. Sorry, uh Buck. I don't really know. They just gave me the one name. A Mr. Goldfarb. Simon Goldfarb.

Damn the luck, thought Buck. He knew how those people could be about money.

Chapter 11

Simon Goldfarb thought it must have been some kind of mistake when he got the order to get on a plane to some place called Sweet Spot, Mississippi. The only thing he knew about Mississippi was that some relative on his mother's side had supposedly disappeared there during a civil rights protest in the sixties. Simon Goldfarb had no desire to disappear.

At 28 years of age, he hadn't been working for FEMA all that long. But he'd grown used to crunching numbers in his little cubicle at the back of the office, and never anticipated doing any field work. He liked the idea of helping disaster victims, and felt he was doing his part. But in the same way he'd never built up the nerve to join the Boy Scouts, it was the idea of camping that was appealing, not the actual using of leaves for toilet paper.

Besides, he had allergies. Allergies to what? Just the outdoors, that's all. Anything that flowered or was green. Anything that couldn't be bathed in Lysol.

So the whole thing had to be some kind of mistake. They must have confused him with another Simon Goldfarb.

Yet when he made his way to the supervisor's office, they assured him that he was their man. With the staffing shortage due to budget cuts, all the experienced field workers were tied up with other projects. And this Sweet Spot seemed like such a tiny town anyway, they thought even Simon could handle it. After all, what was the big deal? You just fly down there, check out the story, and authorize the funds.

Simon felt an anxiety attack coming on. He was short of breath and was getting stomach pains. Of course it could have been just his asthma or irritable bowel syndrome acting up. Or both. As he rifled through his desk drawer for his inhaler, Imodium, and Xanax, he realized it was probably all three. He was having an anxiety attack about his asthma and irritable bowel syndrome... oh, and about disappearing in Mississippi. That, most of all. The whole thing just had to be some horrible mistake.

Yet despite his best efforts, Simon Goldfarb soon found himself on a small commuter plane connecting from Atlanta to the deepest darkest regions of Mississippi, places possibly as yet undiscovered by civilized man. He stared out the plane window, clutching a small carryon holding his medications and a spare pair of glasses. Besides his inhaler, Imodium, and Xanax, he wore a Compazine patch behind his ear to fend off air-sickness, and packed some Quinine tablets just in case malaria was indigenous to the area.

He'd thought to leave word with anyone back home that might wonder where he'd gone, or might care to send a search party for him, as they'd done 50 years ago, the last time a Goldfarb wandered into Mississippi. But Simon had no one. The last of dwindling family had either died off or moved to Israel. Simon hadn't the courage to up and move with them. And he'd never formed any relationships to speak of. Of course there was his shrink... and his pharmacist. But he wasn't convinced they really counted. And the people at work were the ones responsible for sending him to his death. So no one would really miss him.

The plane was apparently descending, but there didn't seem to be any signs of civilization down there, let alone an airport. Maybe the whole place had been wiped out by the storms. His mind drifted to images of carnage he'd picked up from every horror movie he'd ever seen about the end of the world. Dead bodies haphazardly strewn about the place. Zombie-like hoards of survivors aimlessly wandering about in search of food. Simon had enough trouble watching those commercials for starving children in Africa, or even the ones just about abandoned pets. How was he going to face real people, dead and starving ones?

Simon grabbed the air-sickness bag, just in case, and closing his eyes to the unwanted scenes in his head, prayed he could just make an appearance, approve the funds from FEMA, and get back home to his familiar cubicle.

* * * *

Pedro didn't like it. He didn't like it at all. The day he and Conquistador had wandered into Sweet Spot, Pedro thought he'd found the perfect hideout. Who would think anyone would run from the glamour of Palm Beach to hole up in a place like Sweet Spot? But Pedro knew it felt right the moment he came across that little girl with the sweet tea. It was the furthest thing from the international jet setters' underworld sleaze he was running from. They didn't even know his real name. And no one in a place like Sweet Spot would look twice at a man with a horse.

Yet here he was, gathering the same meager belongings he'd arrived with, throwing them back into his duffle bag, preparing to hightail it out of town before things went south.

It all seemed to start that day he'd painted that bull's eye on the mayor's roof. Oh, he knew the bull's eye had nothing to do with it. After all, the twister the mayor had hoped to lure with it never materialized, despite one hell of a dance by Chief Firewater. But the whole idea of having the town declared a disaster area was bad karma. And now all eyes were on Sweet Spot, Mississippi, as CNN broadcast the plight of small town America nationwide for all to see.

He had mixed feelings about the day those reporters showed up. On the one hand, his cover was blown. He thought he'd done a pretty good job of keeping out of sight so far. But it was only a matter of time. And now, representatives from FEMA would be descending upon the town. So he knew he had to move on.

On the other hand, there was Scarlet Witherspoon. Pedro distractedly ceased packing as his thoughts wandered to his blonde goddess. Sure she was no rocket scientist, but neither was he. And maybe the whole thing was just sex. Wouldn't be the first time. But this time it was different. This woman had no idea who he was. She thought he was just some Mexican illegal with a knack for horses. Yet she still came to his bed. She was drawn to him for him, not for the idea of him, as was so often the case back in Palm Beach. Maybe this was the one to put an end to the lonely life of the international playboy.

Who was he kidding, thought Pedro as he resumed packing. They'd never stop looking for him. And if they ever found him, they'd kill him... and Conquistador.

He'd miss this Scarlet girl. But there were always more where that one came from. Other fish in the sea. Or were there? He'd slept with all kinds of women. Old, young, rich, poor. Mostly old and rich, though. But he'd never felt anything like he did for Scarlet Witherspoon. It had to mean something. Like a sign. Maybe he wasn't meant to run. Maybe this tornado thing would blow over and they'd never find him.

He stopped packing once more. He had to pull himself together. Maybe he was overreacting. That's it. He'd stay a while longer, give it a chance, see how things went. But he'd have to be careful. He'd have to lay low, be wary of any outsiders showing up in Sweet Spot. If they ever did come to town looking for him, he'd have to see them first.

* * * *

Rocco saw him first. He never watched the news, particularly during a lap dance at the boss's strip joint near Palm Beach. But he always kept an eye on the sports channels, hoping for a good day collecting gambling debts for the boss. Yet even with his attention divided between the game and Tiffany's ass, he couldn't help but recognize the man he'd been hunting for.

They kept interrupting the Miami Marlins game with coverage of those twisters in no man's land. Must be a slow news season. Like anyone cares about a bunch of trailer trash. But there was no mistaking it. That was him. The guy on the horse with the weather bitch in back. They showed that same image every time they cut to their disaster update.

Tiffany fell on the floor as Rocco jumped to his feet. She stood up apologizing profusely, hoping she hadn't done anything wrong. She didn't want to make Rocco angry. After all, he worked for the owner of the club. She didn't even charge him for the dances.

But Rocco didn't have time to worry about some stupid stripper. He had to tell the boss the news. So he pulled out his cell phone and walked into the strippers' dressing room to get away from the loud music. He ignored the half-hearted protests from the half-dressed girls. He wasn't there to collect the money they owed him for supplying their coke habits. That was just a hobby of his. No, he was there on real business this time.

"Hello, Boss?"

"…"

"Yeah, it's Rocco."

"…"

"Sorry to bother you, but it's real important."

"…"

"No, the club hasn't been raided for prostitution again."

"…"

"No, listen. I found him. I found your spic."

"…"

"Some toilet called Sweet Spot, Mississippi."

"…"

"No, I'm not high again. Yeah, I promise. I ain't shittin' you."

"…"

"Yes sir. Right away, sir."

"…"

"No problem. I got this."

Putting his cell away, Rocco had to reflect on his mission. Rocco Buttafuoco didn't like killing people. After all, Rocco was a lover, not a hater. But business was business.

It was just a matter of time. An international playboy polo champion with the looks of a model and larger-than-life personality doesn't just disappear. Not unless the boss makes him disappear.

So what, if the guy slept with the boss's wife. The boss didn't give a shit about that. Actually considered it a favor keeping the nasty bitch occupied and out of his hair. The man didn't care about his wife, but he did care about his money. He'd only let the kid sleep with the hag so he could catch them in bed together, then pretend to be upset and use the scene as a pretense to blackmail the kid into a business relationship. But when the Latin gigolo continued winning, him and that damn horse, despite being ordered to throw matches, that was costing the boss money. No one costs the boss money and gets away with it.

At first, the boss had no intention of bumping him off. He thought it would just take a little gentle persuasion. But when Rocco went to kill the horse, that Conquistador, he didn't know the kid often slept in the barn with his beloved stallion. So when the kid saw Rocco enter the stable, he smelled a rat, mounted the animal in one smooth leap, and jumped the fence, heading off into the countryside. That kid sure could ride.

The day he'd disappeared, he not only avoided paying his unwritten debt to the boss, but now he'd stolen a valuable horse as well. At least a dead horse brought insurance money. No such guarantee with a missing one. That could mean a complete loss.

So now, the gloves were off. Nacho Garcia was a dead man.

Chapter 12

Jennifer Steel, deep-sea fisherwoman. Well, not exactly. So it was just a little fishin' hole, hoping to snag a catfish. Whatever it was, it wasn't anything she thought to find herself involved with only a few days ago. A high-powered CNN journalist from the Big Apple, perched on a log with a spinner reel trying to catch dinner. Supplies were scarce in a tornado-ravaged town.

With the initial mission of garnering national attention accomplished, all there was to do now was to wait for the cavalry, i.e. FEMA, to come to the rescue. In the meantime, a person's got to eat. Jennifer secretly prayed that she wouldn't catch anything. Just the idea of catching an animal with a bloody hook in its mouth did as much to assuage her hunger as actually eating the poor thing. Thank God the mayor was chivalrous enough to impale the slimy worm on the hook for her.

As much as Jennifer felt out of place in her new assignment as hunter gatherer, Mayor Field & Stream there seemed right at home, as if he'd done this sort of thing every day of his life. He seemed completely absorbed in his casting and reeling and whatever else he was doing that she didn't understand as she sat there with her bait hiding securely out of the way on the bottom of the fishin' hole.

Yet, for all her ignorance of fishing lore, this wasn't the first time Jennifer'd gone fishing out in the countryside. But that was a long time ago, in her childhood, a time she'd just as soon forget, a time when just being out of the house brought promise of a detente to domestic hostilities. Jennifer always took full advantage of those times when her father and mother weren't trapped together in the same place, with Jennifer in the middle. At least at the fishin' hole, her father could get drunk in peace, with no one to vent his inner demons on. And at that age, Jennifer wasn't a target herself.

So she did find a certain twisted comfort in the sights, sounds, and smells of a country fishin' hole, the water gently rippling in the breeze, the buzzing of the cicadas, a whiff of wildflowers in the air. Escape. That's what it was. Escape from a world out of control.

But Jennifer wasn't five years old anymore. What did she have to escape from? She loved her job, the city. She led the perfect life, a life most girls, uh, women, could only dream of. And yet...

Jennifer glanced surreptitiously over at the mayor, hoping he wouldn't catch her. Who was she kidding? He was looking somewhere else, as usual. He never seemed to look at her. No one ever looked at her.

He seemed to have no trouble ogling Scarlet Witherspoon. Just like the rest of them. Why couldn't someone ever look at her that way? Oh well. She had a killer job. A girl can't expect to have it all, could she?

* * * *

Buck looked away just in time, pretending to fiddle with his fishing line. She almost caught him that time. He just couldn't help himself. There was something about her. He couldn't keep his eyes off her. That cocky little spitfire really got his motor running. Sure that Scarlet bimbo was easy on the eyes, but definitely not breeding stock.

Oh, this one was a looker all right, in her way, in his way, just his type, whatever that was, but she was more than that. She was intelligent, with spirit, like a fine race horse, or a prized coon hound. This one was a keeper.

So why was he so tongue-tied around her, suddenly shy and awkward, nothing like the Buck Jones the world so knew and loved?

Go figure. He could talk circles around any number of Hooter's calendar girls, but here at the fishin' hole, home court, alone, with his idea of the perfect woman, he found himself embarrassingly mute.

Maybe his throat was just dry, from the miniature cutoff shorts she made out of those designer jeans of hers, a crucial modification in order to withstand the Southern heat. Maybe a shot of Jack Daniels would loosen his tongue. But it was still early afternoon and he was trying his best not to look like some kind of hillbilly alcoholic in front of his guest.

The girl even seemed to know her way around a fishin' pole. Buck wondered what other kind o' pole she could handle. Whoa, easy boy. You're gettin' ahead o' yourself again. Don't overheat the motor.

* * * *

Jennifer felt so relaxed watching the summer breeze tickle the leaves on the trees that she thought she could just lay back on that log and take a nap. She couldn't remember the last time she'd felt so relaxed. Life in New York City left no time for naps. And her job, she seemed to be working 24/7. This little afternoon respite really hit the spot.

It wasn't just Jennifer, either. Charlie was off somewhere learning about auto repair from his new buddies, the Winchester brothers. And Scarlet, she seemed to fill her days taking "riding" lessons with Don Juan, uh, Pedro. Seemed to fill her nights riding too.

Everyone seemed to be enjoying themselves despite the primitive conditions. Like one of those dude ranch vacations advertised in the travel section of the New York Times. Leave your troubles behind. Become one with nature. Find your inner caveman. Well, Jennifer Steele, in cutoff jeans, lying on a log projecting out over the fishin' hole, catching dinner with a worm, was about as cavewoman as it got.

All she needed now was a caveman. And there just happened to be a prime example, right out of the Museum of Natural History, just at the other end of her log. Too bad she wasn't his type. She couldn't milk a cow, she couldn't bake a pie, and she couldn't win a wet T-shirt contest. She had absolutely nothing to offer a country boy. What could he possibly see in her?

* * * *

What could she possibly see in me? thought Buck. A woman like that wouldn't give the time of day to some country bumpkin like him. He was sure she'd only have eyes for some suit-wearing, Wall Street dwelling, captain of high finance. Buck didn't even own a suit. Well, he still had the one. But he never wore it. Not anymore. It was more of a memento, something to remind him of a previous life, a long time ago, a life he had no intention of resuming.

No, Buck Jones was a simple man now. He'd chosen the life he led, and live it he would. Sweet country air, a little whiskey, and a fishin' pole. What else could a man need?

Well, there was that one thing, he thought, sneakin' a peak at the girl through the corner of his eye. But why that girl? He was lookin' for a Ford, not a BMW. That girl looked like high maintenance to him. Five dollar cup o' coffee. Fine champagne, if she even drank at all.

Besides, she seemed kind o' bossy. Even if for some strange reason he could win her eye, wouldn't be long before she had him shavin' regular and addin' a "study" onto the double-wide. No, a man just couldn't sacrifice his principles over a woman.

Or so he thought, as a cool breeze carried the scent of her perfume his way, and, losing his train of thought again, he resumed surreptitiously studying the cut of her shorts.

"Shit!" she shouted, almost pulled off her log into the fishin' hole. "What do I do? What do I do?" She'd been fishing as a kid, but never remembered actually catching anything. This was just what she was dreading.

Buck Jones looked over to see her scrabbling to maintain a grip on the log as her fishing line attempted to drag her out to sea.

"Just hold on," answered Buck, calmly wedging his pole between some branches before getting up to go over and help.

Even though she'd never hooked anything before, Jennifer knew the monster on the end of her hook was no minnow, the pole bent over double under the strain. She wrapped her leg around the backside of the log lest she become Jonah, swallowed whole by the whale. What was taking that lazy mayor so long?

"If you'd hurry up and get off your ass, we could feed the whole town with this thing!" she nagged.

"Keep your shirt on there, Admiral," teased Buck, doing his best balance beam routine, making his way over to the distressed damsel. "Looks well hooked. Little Nemo ain't goin' nowhere."

Jennifer would have taken that pole to his backside if she could only get it under control. Then, wouldn't you know it, just as the cavalry arrived, the thing gave up the fight and the line went slack. That was odd. Must have gotten away.

"Damn you, Mayor. Must have lost it. My first fish." Her line lay slack at the end of her pole.

Buck sat down beside her. "Don't pout, little girl," he said, struck by her disappointment.

"Don't patronize me!" shouted Jennifer, for whom failure was never an option, even at something as dumb as fishing.

Buck quickly withdrew the hand he'd extended to pat the girl on the back, aborting any attempt to console her, lest his hand get bitten off at the elbow.

Well, now that the mayor'd lost her catch, she thought she might as well reel in her line and have him replace the lost worm. But as she started to do so, the line seemed to snag on something. She tugged and yanked but couldn't reel in any further.

Buck went to take the pole from her and remedy the situation, but she pulled it away as though he were trying to pry candy from a child's hand.

"I don't need your help. I can do it myself," she assured him. No one was going to make Jennifer Steele look incompetent.

Buck backed off, hands raised, wondering if it was that time of the month for the girl.

Jennifer gave up attempts at brute force, deciding she'd need to use brain over brawn. So she lay on her stomach on the log, and leaned out over the fishin' hole.

"Can't see a thing," she muttered as she peered into the murky water, hoping to ascertain what had snagged her line. "Probably caught on a twig."

"More likely a Chevy transmission, courtesy of the Winchester boys," countered Buck.

Ignoring the man's helpful comment, Jennifer lowered the end of her rod to get some slack in the line. If she could only get a better grip to pull, she thought, as she proceeded to wrap the line several times around her hand.

Buck didn't like the look of things. "Uh, you probably don't wanna do that," he suggested gently, fearing the girl would do the exact opposite of anything he advised. In fact, he was just about to take out his pocketknife and cut the line before anything untoward could happen, when the girl went head over heels into the water.

It all happened so fast, Jennifer thought maybe he'd pushed her in. But still under the water, she realized it was her hand. It was caught, and something pulling the line wrapped around it had her head down in the fishin' hole.

It was a good thing Buck was already leaning her way in order to cut the line, so that when her top half disappeared under the water, he was able to reach out and grab the back of her shorts by the waist.

Now the real battle was on, only this time Jennifer was the bait. Buck hoped the girl's jeans were American made, or at least of a quality sufficient to withstand a tug of war.

Apparently they were, because Jennifer could recall two things clearly from the incident, one was being pulled out of the water by her ass, and other was... oh yeah... the other was the gaping jaws of the alligator that emerged with her just inches from her face.

Next thing she knew she was flying backward over the log away from the beast after Buck managed to swipe the line with his knife.

All she could do was flop the short distance to the bank of the fishin' hole and quickly crawl on her hands and knees to dry land.

She turned to look back and see if what she'd imagined really happened, and there was Buck Jones in waist deep water wrestling with the monster. The thing looked to be the size of a surfboard, somewhere between Jennifer's and Buck's weights, as Buck jumped onto its back, hanging on through three or four death rolls.

Jennifer was frantic. Should she go in to help? But her legs had no intention of setting even one toe back in the water. Should she run for help? No, he'd be dead by then. So she grabbed the nearest rock she could find and threw it at the thing's head.

Buck almost blacked out when a rock flew out of nowhere and hit him in the head, but he somehow managed to keep his hold.

Jennifer realized her rock-throwing probably wasn't helping. At a loss for what else to do, she thought a little sideline coaching couldn't hurt. "Mayor... uh, Buck! Get out of there!" she shouted, not knowing if that was even possible.

Buck continued riding the great reptile like some kind of bucking bronco.

"Not without my rod!" he shouted, one hand prying the tip of the nose back, the other tugging at his coveted rod and reel lodged halfway down the thing's throat. "Come on. Cough it up, ya damn overgrown salamander!"

With his legs in a scissor grip around the alligator from the back, Buck managed to yank the rod from its mouth and fling it to shore. He then closed the animal's mouth with both hands, dismounted, and flung it by the head out into the middle of the fishin' hole.

As Buck wearily trudged his way to shore through the muck at the bottom of the fishin' hole, checking for bleeding from the mysterious bump on the side of his head, Jennifer was jumping up and down, frantically waving him to come ashore before the killer could turn and come after him.

Once safely ashore, Jennifer jumped into his arms, hugging him with all her might, relieved at his narrow escape from what appeared to be a certain death.

Buck didn't know what all the fuss was about, but he certainly wasn't about to turn away no woman hangin' onto him like some rock-star groupie, especially not this woman. So he accepted the hug, and even hugged back, and she wasn't objecting. And before he knew it, he was looking down into her gorgeous green eyes, and she wasn't turning away.

The kiss started light and gentle. But like a match to kerosene, soon the whole world was ablaze, and they both were consumed by it. Both the mayor and the reporter lost all sense of themselves, becoming one, completely engulfed in an all-consuming flame of passion. They each forgot who they were, their past, their present, why they were where they were, and where they were going.

He was completely lost, lost in a place he no longer believed even existed.

So was she...

...at least at first. But then she heard it. A little voice. At first she couldn't make out what it was trying to tell her. She wanted it to go away. But it wouldn't. It continued to pester and whine, to poke at her. And with that voice, the flames began to recede, replaced by a choking smoke, and soon by chilling ice.

Before she even knew why, Jennifer Steele pushed the man with his arms about her away, and slapped him hard across the face.

Jennifer opened her eyes and saw the shirtless unshaven redneck yokel standing before her.

Buck abruptly woke up expecting to see a goddess standing before him. But that goddess was nowhere to be found. Instead, he was confronted by an angry little shrew, albeit an angry little shrew in a titillating wet T-shirt, yet a shrew nonetheless, a scowl on her face, pointing an accusing finger at him.

And Buck's cheek stung somethin' fierce.

"Hey. What was that for?" he asked, rubbing the side of his face.

"You tried to kill me," she accused.

"What are you talkin' about?"

"An alligator! There was a fucking alligator in there!" she shouted, pointing at the fishin' hole.

"Yeah. So?"

"You knew? You knew it was there?"

"Well, yeah, I seen it around. This ain't Central Park ya know. This is rural Mississippi."

He did know. She couldn't believe it.

"But I asked you about poisonous snakes."

"Ya did. And I answered you. There ain't no snakes in this here fishin' hole. Ya didn't ask 'bout no gators."

The man was exasperating. "How could you let me bathe in alligator-infested waters?"

The woman was hysterical. "It ain't infested. It's just little ol' Lizzie."

"That monster has a name? You named it?"

"Lizzie wouldn't hurt a fly."

"No? Then why was she trying to eat me?"

"Well, you antagonized her."

"I what?"

"Oh, Lizzie's more afraid of you than you are of her. She was only mad 'cause you threw a hook in her mouth. How'd you feel if someone—"

"You're defending her... uh... it?"

"You almost lost me a perfectly good rod and reel."

Jennifer was speechless.

Buck knew he'd crossed the line with that last remark.

Jennifer turned on her heel and stormed down the trail back to town.

Buck stood dripping water, watching the girl go. *Definitely that time of the mo*nth.

What was I thinking kissing that bastard? thought Jennifer.

What was I thinking kissing that bitch? thought Buck.

Chapter 13

Focus, thought Buck, going through last minute preparations with the townsfolk before the FEMA representative's arrival. He couldn't let the latest events involving that Yankee tease down at the fishin' hole distract him from the big prize. Nothin' sweeter than government money. And Buck Jones could almost taste it now. He just had to keep his eye on the ball a little longer, lest the authorities catch on to their little deception.

Standing once again at the church pulpit in front of his flock, he wondered if maybe he'd missed his true calling. But as thoughts of that CNN vixen in her wet T-shirt kept dancing around his susceptible mind, all manner of impure thoughts quickly displaced any dreams of salvation. Even if he were to be sainted for delivering his people from the land of naught, and given a free pass directly to heaven, he just knew he'd be lurking around up there wonderin' what them girl angels had on under them flowin' white robes.

No, Buck's place was right here, on Earth, takin' care o' business. And by Buck's reckoning, the man should be arriving any minute. That Mikey Dunham might be slow upstairs, but he was a quick runner. And just as soon as little Felicity, Buck's sentry at the edge of town, spotted the man, she sent Mikey runnin' to give Buck a head's up. Mikey put up a fight, not wanting to leave the little girl on her own, but he knew better than to argue with the President and CEO of Felicity's Fountain once she'd made up her mind.

* * * *

Soon as she saw the briefcase and dark suit that reminded her of an undertaker, Felicity knew she had her man. So once she sent Mikey runnin', she did her best to stall him with her sweet tea. But she was sorely disappointed. She figured that briefcase must have been stuffed with money, but that tightwad wouldn't even cough up a quarter for some of her liquid gold.

She gave him her best presentation, all big-eyed and grinning from ear to ear, but the man was cold as ice, never smiled once. Wouldn't give her the time o' day. Felicity'd never known such rejection.

That really put her off. Didn't like the looks o' the man one bit. Didn't help matters that she couldn't make out his eyes through those dark sunglasses. How could a person get the mettle of a man won't show his eyes? No, this guy was gonna be trouble.

* * * *

Soon as Mikey came bangin' on the door of Buck's trailer, Buck snapped out of his funk from the episode down at the fishin' hole and jumped into action.

First thing he did after dispatching Mikey to stand guard outside the church was send Pedro off on that stallion of his, like some kind o' Paul Revere, to warn everyone to get over to the church. Nothin' like a whole town found prayin' for their very survival to loosen up them government purse strings. And with CNN broadcastin' the scene to the whole damn world, they were all as good as winnin' the Powerball jackpot.

Not that this was a sure thing. It was touch and go for a while there, just him and the folks, before the CNN team showed up at the church preparing to air the federal government's rescue of small town America.

"Y'all just let me do the talkin'," Buck had insisted, knowing there wouldn't be much time before the reporters and the government man showed up.

"So do I gotta open some kind o' bank account now?" asked Jeb. Where my gonna stash all this cash I'm comin' into?"

"While you make a good point, Jeb, after all, you don't wanna be buryin' wheel barrels o' cash at the back o' your cave, you're gettin' ahead o' yourself. Cart before the horse, Jeb. Cart before the horse. That's what we call a high class problem. Let's just focus on gettin' the cash first, why don't we."

Then it was the chief's turn. "Do they make mount for flat screen TV can hang in teepee?"

"Slow down, Chief. You're gonna need electricity first," replied Buck.

"They ain't gonna cut off my food stamps, are they Mayor," asked Mrs. Butts.

"Shoot, Gladiola," began Buck, "we get what's comin' to us and you ain't gonna need no food stamps. Why, you can open up your own Piggly Wiggly."

That got the whole church buzzin' about potential business investments, but Buck had to herd 'em all back to the here and now. Any minute them reporters were gonna show up, followed by the man with the purse strings. Wouldn't do no good to be found discussing S-corporations, LLC's, and tax loopholes.

"Look, y'all. Let's try to focus here. Remember, y'all just lost everything you had. Try to look a little... well... pathetic. You know... like..." Buck looked around the church at the assortment of colorful characters assembled before him, lookin' for the right word.

"Oh shoot," he said, throwin' up his hands in defeat. "Just be yourselves, for God's sake."

No sooner said than the doors of the church flew open as the reporters hustled in, Charlie checking the lighting, and Scarlet checking her makeup, as Jennifer kept nagging her about crucial talking points for when the camera started rolling.

Buck looked around the church, assessing the condition of the townsfolk, who appeared to be on their best behavior. He was, however, sorely disappointed to notice that, directly ignoring orders to the contrary, everyone had put on their Sunday best in anticipation of their national television debut. Chief even wore his headdress. But as to the rest of 'em, Buck didn't think it really mattered one way or another. After all, you can put lipstick on a pig, but it's still a pig. He didn't think anyone would truly notice.

Buck's train of thought was broken when an excited Mikey Dunham burst through the church doors, quickly slamming them closed behind him.

"He's here!" he shouted, doubled over, trying to catch his breath. "He's here! Coming up the path to the church!"

There was an excited mutter from the congregation.

Buck jumped into action, standing up straight. This was it.

"All right, Mikey. Calm down and have a seat. Everyone calm down. Y'all just let me do the talkin'."

Wasn't more than a couple of ticks on the clock till the church door cracked open again and a man with a dark suit and briefcase walked in. First thing he did upon entering was to honor his Catholic faith by removing his hat and making the sign of the cross.

There was an awkward silence when he looked about and saw every face in the room staring at him. But it was brief, as the whole town chimed in. It wasn't exactly Academy Award material, but Buck was truly impressed when the whole church erupted in crying and mournful wails right on cue, just as they'd rehearsed. Buck could almost hear the director yell, "Action!"

"Buck Jones, Mayor of Sweet Spot," announced Buck by way of introduction. "We been expecting you."

The man first noticed the cameras when Charlie moved in for a close up. Quickly raising his hat to shield his face, "Hey, no cameras! No cameras!" he shouted.

Rocco Buttafuoco had no intention of having his mug broadcast all over national TV. He had a job to do, and that's what he intended to do. In and out, bada-bing bada-boom, with the utmost discretion.

Jennifer was disappointed that they wouldn't get that first shot she'd anticipated of the federal government coming to the rescue. She would have thought the politicians back in D.C. would have paid for that kind of coverage, but she would respect the man's wishes. Maybe there was some kind of government policy she wasn't aware of. After all, she didn't exactly have any experience in this sort of assignment.

Buck was disappointed as well, but the show had to go on nevertheless.

"And you would be, Mr..."

Only after confirming that the cameras were off did Rocco remove his hat from his face.

"Don't you worry about who I am. I'm lookin' for Nacho."

Buck was taken aback. The man comes all this way to tour a national disaster area, and first thing he does is demand food? Wasn't he supposed to be bringin' the food?

"Uh, we ain't got no Mexican restaurant in Sweet Spot."

"What are you talkin' about?" asked Rocco.

"Nachos. We ain't got no nachos."

"I can get you some grits if you like," offered Mrs. Butts, tryin' to show the man some Southern hospitality.

Rocco finally understood the problem. "I ain't lookin' for no food. That's his name. Nacho. Nacho Garcia. I'm lookin' for him."

Buck had to scratch his head. "Don't know no Nacho."

Then it occurred to him who the man might be looking for. Buck looked around the church, confirming that someone was missing. Where was Pedro? He sure seemed to be layin' low these days.

Finally, Bubba Winchester, of all people, figured it out. "Hey, we ain't got no Nacho. But we got a Pedro."

"Pedro, huh. This, uh, Pedro, he got a horse?" asked Rocco, smelling a rat.

Alarms were going off in Buck's head. "Now Bubba, remember, you just let me do the talk—"

But it was too late. Bubba already blurted it out. "Sure does. White stallion. And he's a beauty."

Damn it! Buck didn't like this one bit. Things were already goin' off script. What was FEMA's interest in Pedro?

Rocco had to smile. This wasn't going to take long at all. He pulled a photo from his pocket of the internationally known polo player he'd cut from the sports pages of the Palm Beach Daily News. He held it up in front of Bubba.

"Is this your, uh, Pedro?"

Bubba had to smile. "Looky here. Our Pedro in the newspaper."

Buck didn't know why Pedro would be in a newspaper. Didn't care. And what did all this have to do with their government assistance?

"Um, excuse me, Mr... uh..."

"Smith," stated Rocco with a smirk. "My name's Smith."

"OK, Smith it is," though Buck knew it wasn't. "I take it you're not here about our natural disaster relief money."

He had Rocco's attention. "Relief money? Sure. If you're handin' out money, I could always use a little relief."

"No, we ain't handin' out no money. You was supposed to be bringin' the money."

"Me? Hey, buddy, I don't hand out no money."

Buck thought he'd better take it from the beginning. "Are you from the government?"

Rocco was about to laugh at that one, but then got the idea that if they thought he was with the government they might be more cooperative.

"Sure. Yeah, I'm with the government."

Buck had to scratch behind one ear. "But you're not here about the relief money."

"Like I told you. I'm here about the spic with the horse."

That's when it finally clicked for Buck. The man was from the government lookin' for Pedro, from ICE, the immigration service, roundin' up illegals, lookin' to deport Pedro back to Mexico.

That's where Rocco made his fatal error. He may have thought those backwoods yokels would be more cooperative thinking he was from the federal government, but turns out that he couldn't have been more wrong. There ain't nothin' Southern rednecks hate more than the federal government comin' to town tellin' 'em what to do. Pedro might be an illegal, but he was *their* illegal. And they wouldn't be takin' kindly to no federale from out o' town throwin' his weight around.

Buck went into resistance mode. "You're man Pedr... uh, Nacho ain't here."

"But my friend here says otherwise," countered Rocco, pointing at Bubba.

"Well, he was. But he's gone," answered Buck.

At first, Scarlet was taken aback. Her lovers didn't usually run off that way. It just wasn't possible. Besides, she'd just been in bed with him that morning. Nevertheless, she didn't like the looks of this guy, so she kept quiet.

Buck continued. "Well, the whole town's here in church. You don't see him here, do you?"

Buck prayed, for Pedro's sake, that the folks in the church would keep their mouths shut for once and let him do the talkin' as they were instructed. Least till he could sort all this out.

Chapter 14

Simon Goldfarb detested tardiness. Especially when it was his own. So when he realized there was no other means that day of getting from the corn field— or airport— whatever it was, over to Sweet Spot, he decided, against his better judgment, to accept an offer to hitch a ride aboard a small single engine crop duster headed that way.

Maybe it was the Xanax talking when he accepted the certain death sentence, but nothing short of general anesthesia could have tempered Simon's anxiety once airborne. It probably didn't help when the feisty old pilot, introduced only as Bug, decided to show off a little, reliving his old barnstorming days in the aerial circus with a few loop de loops.

It was just about nightfall when the sardine can of a plane finally touched down near the tree line at the edge of Sweet Spot. Simon stumbled from the plane, kissing the ground as he doubled over to vomit. He would have to settle, however, for the dry heaves, as during the flight, he'd already tossed more cookies than a troop of Girl Scouts.

Once Bug sailed off again into the sunset, Simon found himself all alone in the middle of nowhere, and would have felt another panic attack coming on, had he not remained solidly in the throes of the last one that began back at the airport as soon as Bug started down the cow path— or runway— whatever it was. He was already rifling through his carry-on for more pills when he noticed the little girl at the iced tea stand about to close up shop for the night.

It was near-most unheard of for Felicity to meet two out-of-towners in a month, let alone one day. And with her security detail off on a mission, she probably should have closed up long before dark. But when she saw her mild-mannered visitor approaching, she knew she'd better keep the stand open a little longer to take advantage of a promising business opportunity. She hoped this one would be a bit more sociable than the last. In fact, as he approached, she'd already taken sufficient measure of the man to recognize an easy mark when she saw one. Seeing him gather three pills from three different bottles into his hand, she saw her opening.

"Hey mister, you're gonna need somethin' cool and wet to help wash them pills down."

She saw by the knowing look on his face, the way he looked from her to the pills in his hand, that she'd called it right. This was a man who would gag trying to get even one pill down his gizzard, let alone three at a time, even with a gallon of water. But dry? Impossible. His mama probably used to grind 'em up and mix 'em with applesauce.

"Why, thank you Miss. I'm afraid you make an accurate assessment," he admitted.

"Now, I don't even know what's in them pills o' yours, but this here sweet tea's so good for whatever ails ya that ya probably won't even need 'em."

Her reassuring smile almost had him believing it so, but he took the pills and the tea just the same... just in case.

"So what brings ya to Sweet Spot, mister? Business or pleasure?"

He looked about, clearly trying to glean what form of pleasure there was to be had in Sweet Spot. "Uh, business I guess."

"You don't say. Pretty soon we'll be needin' to erect a convention center with all the businessmen comin' through."

Simon looked befuddled. "There are others? Businessmen?"

"Why just earlier today a man from the government come through. Word was he come from FEMA. You know, somethin' about the twisters."

Simon almost choked on his tea. "FEMA? Why, I'm from FEMA." They sent someone else? He knew this was all a mistake. Maybe he could turn right around and get back on that plane home already.

"Well, if someone from FEMA's already here, maybe I can just catch a ride back to the airport."

Felicity didn't want the man to go. He seemed a whole lot nicer than the last fella. Might be a little looser with the purse strings. No, she'd better bring him to meet the mayor.

"I'm afraid there won't be no more transportation out o' town for the night. Ya might as well follow me into town," she added, finally getting the iced tea stand closed up.

Simon looked around him again as night began to fall in earnest, realizing he was at the mercy of the child standing in front of him. "Guess you're right after all," he said with an unsteady voice, wondering when the Xanax booster would kick in.

Felicity gave the man a good once over before heading down the dark trail with him in tow. She took an immediate liking to him. He seemed the nervous twitchy sort, not unlike one of them little Chihuahua dogs that always seemed to be shivering. Felicity Barnes never had no pets before, least not her own. But if she'd ever seen a lost puppy before, the poor man standing before her on the verge of tears was it. She wondered if Sarah would let her keep him.

In fact, Sarah could probably use a little grown-up companionship herself.

"You much of a religious man, mister? Sarah likes 'em religious."

"Sarah? Who's Sarah?"

"Oh, Miss Sarah? She's the one takes care o' me. She'll fix you up a place to stay for the night."

"She runs a motel, does she?"

"Seems that way lately," Felicity replied with a giggle, skipping over to take the man by the hand. He seemed less than enthusiastic about the trip through the woods, but Felicity had high hopes for this one.

* * * *

Once they realized the man wouldn't be writin' no checks, the folks sent Rocco packin'. He'd have to find his way back through the woods on his own to get back to where he'd left his car. They didn't offer him any lodging, so he'd have to head over to the next town to find a motel. But he'd be back. His gut told him Sweet Spot was the place. He had a good nose about these things and he could just smell that greasy wetback. He'd be back.

* * * *

Felicity and Simon just missed Rocco's retreat by coming down the regular path, while Rocco, unescorted, wandered through the woods in the dark, hacking his way through briar patch and bog, forging a new path back to his car at the edge of town.

Simon might have escaped a confrontation with Rocco, but he couldn't escape the one waiting for him back at the church. The folks had really worked themselves up into quite a lather over the last government man and they weren't feelin' the love should another dare to show up. After all, it was bad enough the man wasn't writin' no checks, but the nerve to show up accusin' them of harboring a fugitive, well that was not to be tolerated.

Simon didn't know what to expect when the little girl dragged him through the doors to the church. But he always expected the worst. What he didn't know was that being Jewish was the least of his problems. When he saw every head in the place turn his way with scowls on their faces, he could have sworn he heard someone mutter, "Get a rope."

Thoughts of his martyred ancestors came to mind. He didn't want to disappear in Mississippi as they had, never to be heard from again. He felt one of his dizzy spells coming on, and held onto the little girl's hand for support lest he lose his balance.

Maybe he only thought he heard someone mutter, "Get a rope," but he definitely saw more than a few making a show of loading their firearms. In church?

Simon knew he was about to keel over as his vision started to blur, sprinkled with small flashing lights. He was well acquainted with the signs of pending unconsciousness. And that's when he felt the little girl pushing him forward.

"Hey y'all. This here's Mr. Goldfarb. He's from the government. Maybe he's got a check for us."

Simon saw the weapons slowly recede into pockets, purses, or under pews, as people turned suspiciously, looking to Buck for guidance. After all, that last government man hadn't worked out so well.

Seeing a fresh opportunity for news footage, Jennifer and the crew swung into action, running forward, shoving lights, cameras, and microphones in Simon's face.

Simon, unprepared in the handling of media coverage, and thinking instead that he might be the lead actor in some kind of Southern anti-Semitic snuff film, collapsed to the floor, unconscious.

* * * *

He woke up to something cool on his forehead. He felt no pain. Was it all over? Was he dead?

He opened his eyes, but couldn't really see. He reached to check his pockets for his glasses, sorely disappointed to find that he would still need them even in heaven.

He felt a cool moist cloth pull away from his brow, followed by someone gently placing his glasses on his face. That's when he was sure... when he could see. It was heaven after all. He'd never even tried to imagine what an angel would look like. Now he didn't have to. For one was looking down upon him at that very moment.

He didn't notice the piercing, the tattoo, or the half-shaved orange doo. He only saw heaven. A smile, a light, a warming glow. And she was praying... for him.

"Is this h... h... heaven?"

Upon hearing him speak, the smile on the angel's face grew even brighter, if that was possible, expanding to her eyes.

That's when another smaller face popped into view.

"See. I told ya so, Sarah. I told ya he'd have some religion in 'im." Felicity gave Sarah a hopeful look. "Can we keep 'im?"

"Shoot, little girl, he ain't no stray cat for you to adopt."

Felicity pouted at the comparison. "I was thinkin' more of a lost puppy." Felicity was definitely a dog person. "Well, call him whatever you like, we sure could use a man around the place."

"Felicity!" blushed Sarah, "Why, listen to you. That ain't how it works."

"Well, I ain't even been acquainted with puberty yet, so I don't claim to know how it works. But I know this, Miss Sarah. You ain't gettin' no younger."

Sarah shook her head, rolling her eyes. "For heaven's sake, you fresh thing, I'm only 18. You make it sound like I'm some old spinster."

"Well, all's I'm sayin' is, if you wanna be hitched to God, you might as well get thee to a nunnery. But if you're willin' to settle for a man of this Earth with all the associated benefits, if ya know what I mean, then this here one's as good as the next. In fact, given your previous luck, I'd say a whole lot better."

"Well, given my previous luck with men, I think I'm much better off with you, Sweetie."

"That may be fine and good for now. But I ain't gonna be around forever, you know. One day, I'm gonna grow up and move out on my own into the big wide world. I'd like to know I was leavin' you in good hands."

"I'm always in good hands with our Lord and Savior."

Sarah looked back at Simon. "You hush now, girl. I think he's comin' round."

Simon recognized his little guide, and while he didn't doubt she too would be accepted in heaven, he sorely doubted the little thing's number'd come up yet.

"Uh... where am I?"

"You're on the bus," answered Felicity.

"Bus?" Simon began to realize the whole heaven thing was premature. But a bus? That sounded promising. A bus back to New York? "Um... uh... where we going?"

Felicity looked at Sarah with concern. "Going? He thinks we're going somewhere. Maybe he hit his head on the church floor when he fell out. Maybe he got one o' them concussions."

Sarah smiled and touched the girl's face, both to ease her concern and pleased to see the little businesswoman show such compassion to a stranger in need. "Well if'n he did, he seems to be comin' round just fine."

Then turning to Simon, "You're on the church bus. This is our home, Felicity and me. But you're welcome to stay as long as you need."

Simon felt just a twinge, genetically speaking, at living on church property, but it was a lot better than being kidnapped by the clan, or facing the angry lynch mob that literally scared him out of his wits. In fact, he rationalized, throughout history, Jews were often given sanctuary by gentiles during dangerous times.

Besides, thought Simon, looking up at a face dreams were made of, if he had to seek sanctuary among gentiles, this particular gentile was certainly an appealing choice.

Simon sat up, taking in his surroundings. It was a bus all right. A school bus. The girls had put up makeshift curtains and were using sleeping bags as bedding. A crucifix hung prominently from the driver's mirror.

"So I'm staying here?" he asked.

Felicity looked to Sarah, practically bouncing in her seat.

Sarah put a hand on Felicity's shoulder to calm her down. "Of course you can, Mr. Goldfarb."

Felicity clapped her hands with glee.

Sarah continued. "Long as you've got your important business here to take care of."

Important business? Shit! thought Simon, looking about for his briefcase. His assignment. He'd forgotten all about it. He began to feel faint again. Where were his pills?

"Mister?" asked Felicity, noticing the sweat breaking out on his brow. "You OK?" She gave Sarah a concerned look.

Sarah gently laid Simon back down. "There there. You'd better rest some more."

Yeah, rest, thought Simon. Anything to put off going back out there. Maybe he'd just stay on the bus... with the angel... forever.

Chapter 15

Jennifer Steele had a job to do. After all, Sweet Spot, Mississippi was not exactly her idea of a charming vacation getaway. And it was becoming less and less charming every day, what with that wild kingdom incident down at the fishin' hole involving Mayor Crocodile Hunter.

But the coverage they'd planned for FEMA's big arrival hadn't gone so well back at the church. And for a while she was beginning to believe she'd never get out of Sweet Spot and back to civilization if they couldn't get Mr. Goldfarb to venture out of the bus.

Despite the fact that he'd seemed fully recovered from his swoon at the church meeting, it was only through Jennifer's personal guarantee for his safety, Felicity tugging him by the hand, and most of all, a reassuring smile from his personal angel of mercy, Sarah, that they were finally able to pry him from his sanctuary.

Once they were convinced he was steady enough on his feet, they took him on a tour of the disaster area, fully acquainting him with the tornado-wrought devastation.

The man seemed anxious to just approve the monetary disbursement and get out of Dodge. He knew it was only a matter of time before his sinuses clogged up with hay fever and his irritable bowel became irritated by the rich food served at the church. But being a stickler for details, and never one to bend the rules, he made it clear that his instructions on the government forms required personal interviews with the affected residents.

It was Mayor Jones who advised, given Mr. Goldfarb's delicate constitution, that they stop beating around the bush and cut right to the chase. Jefferson Washington was their man.

So despite her renewed aversion to the esteemed mayor, Jennifer found herself once again tolerating his presence on the way to the interview.

Even Scarlet and Charlie were starting to grow weary of the back and forth bickering between their team leader and the mayor. There was clearly some kind of tension between the two. Charlie assumed it was just the cultural divide. But Scarlet knew better. Maybe it was just that Scarlet assumed everything had to do with sex. But, in her eyes, those two love birds just dripped with sexual tension. Charlie didn't see it. But Scarlet would have bet her Miss Grits & Gravy tiara on it. Her little Jennifer may put on an all work no play front, but still waters run deep, and Scarlet just knew there must be a molten volcano somewhere deep inside that little firecracker just rarin' to blow.

* * * *

Jefferson Washington couldn't believe how low he'd agreed to stoop, all for the benefit of the community.

First he had to scrub the place of all signs of his achievements and success. Jefferson had never failed at anything in his life. But now he'd agreed to play the victim. So if, in doing so, he had to become the perfect failure, Jefferson Washington would become the perfect perfect failure.

First thing he did was take down his diplomas from Harvard and Oxford. And those were real degrees too, not some phony affirmative action crap. Best thing he ever did, pretending to be white on his applications. Otherwise he'd never know if he'd made it on his own merit, or just the color of his skin. That way those diplomas really meant something.

Never mind he didn't make much use of them, running a barbeque joint in Nowheresville, Mississippi. But that was his choice. He never intended to join the big-city rat race. But that didn't mean he wasn't qualified. Jefferson Washington had options.

Besides, JW's Serious Bar-BQ was the only profitable establishment in Sweet Spot. And it was the pride he took in that fact that made it particularly difficult to deny all ownership in the place just to play po' nigga' for the cameras.

He had to bring in Mrs. Butts, his part-time waitress, to pretend to be the proprietor while he acted "the help." He should have seen the potential downside of such an arrangement as he watched the woman eating away his profits, downin' ribs like they was 'tater chips.

But Buck assured him it wouldn't take long. This Goldfarb guy seemed easy prey. Jefferson wouldn't need to emulate a Shakespearean tragedy to pull one over on this guy, even though he was perfectly capable of doing so.

Jefferson had just managed to hide the copy of the Wall Street Journal addressed to him when the team arrived. In a moment of artistic inspiration, he kicked off his shoes and trotted out to meet them barefoot, grinning like an idiot.

"Well, howdy, y'all! Table fo' five? Rights dis way. Yo in for some o' da best barbeque south o' da norf pole. Mrs. Butts! We gots customers!"

Buck had to do a double take at Jefferson's transformation from professor in residence to ignorant slave hand.

"Uh… yeah… uh Jefferson, this here's Mr. Goldfarb and Ms. Steele with the people from CNN I told you about was wantin' to have a little chat with you. Take a load off," said Buck, offering him a chair.

"A chat with me? What fo' dey be wantin' a chat with da likes o' me?" he asked, taking a seat. "Wouldn't dey rather be chowin' down on some o' Mrs. Butts's serious barbeque?" Jefferson thought he might as well start runnin' up the government tab right away.

Jennifer was staring up at the hand-painted sign reading JW's Serious Bar-BQ.

"Mr. Washington, that must be you. JW. This isn't your place, is it?"

Jefferson and Buck locked eyes. A problem right out of the gate.

Buck was about to change the subject when Jefferson chimed in, addressing the issue head on.

"Well, yes and no, ma'am. Oh that's m' name, all right. But that's 'bout the funniest thing I ever done heard, the idea that I might have the means to own nothin' at all, let alone a fine establishment such as this'n. Why I can't even afford to be eatin' no ribs."

Then, laying it on a little thick, "Though I sho' do go for a little fried chicken and watermelon when I can gets it."

"Then why is the place named after you?" she persisted.

Buck squinted at Jefferson, unsure where the man was goin' with this. But Jefferson just gave them all a wide-mouthed grin.

"Why y'all heard o' Aunt Jemima. This here's the same thing."

His guests all looked confused, even though Buck tried to hide it.

"My boss, Mrs. Butts, ya just gotta hand it to her. Why she a genius at marketin' her brand. She just usin' my name so's the place seem authentic and all. Ya know, real Southern barbeque. If'n she could afford it, I'm sure she'd add a likeness o' me right over the sign. Just like Aunt Jemima and that syrup o' hers. You don't think no mammy own that syrup company do ya? It's just marketin'. Why dollars to donuts Jemima some skinny white bit..., uh... lady with a degree from that Harvard School o' Biness."

While Mr. Goldfarb and the team from CNN were quietly trying to absorb the man's explanation, Buck managed to close his gaping mouth before any flies could get in. He glanced over at the others to see if they were buyin' it.

But before the verdict was in, Jefferson was sharp enough to move things along.

"So, Mr. Buck tell me y'all wants to aks me some questions?"

"Uh, yes. That's right," began Jennifer. "Well, Mr. Goldfarb does anyway. So the government can help you and Sweet Spot get back on your feet. Then Scarlet here would like to chat with you a bit to see if there's anything we can use on the news. Would that be OK with you?"

"The news?! Y'all wants to put ol' Jefferson Washington on the TV? Shoot ma'am. I don't know 'bout dat."

Buck gave the man a sharp look. "Why the hell not?"

"Well, now, like I... uh... like my boss, Mrs. Butts always say, time is money, ya know. And since I'm on company time, she gonna think it only right that I... uh... she be compensated."

Buck squinted at Jefferson again, privately rolling his eyes at the man's ability to never let a business opportunity get away.

"Oh, I'm sure the station can handle that, Mr. Washington," Jennifer assured him. "Mr. Goldfarb, are you ready to begin?"

Simon barely heard her, distracted as he was by the assault on his senses. The sights, sounds, and smells simultaneously confronting him were overwhelming.

JW's Serious Bar-BQ appeared to be in serious shape, literally falling down. It was essentially a shack, or maybe the remnants of some kind of barn, leaning precariously to one side. What roof there was to speak of was half covered by blue tarp to keep out the rain.

He wasn't convinced the place was sanitary enough to board livestock, let alone serve food to humans. Yet he could hear the clucking of chickens punctuated by an occasional rooster crow coming from somewhere out back, no doubt some sort of audible version of the menu.

The strong smell of smoking swine was making him nauseous as he tried to recall what the issue was with undercooked pork. Something about parasites.

And the black smoke billowing out of the makeshift chimney crafted out of a car muffler was choking him. He thought it best to get the interview out of the way before his asthma kicked in.

"Um, yes, uh, Mr. Washington—"

"No need to be so formal. You can call me Jefferson."

"OK, Mr. Jefferson—"

"Just Jefferson. Ain't like I no president or nothin'... even though I wears the name o' two of 'em."

"Jefferson, then, I'm supposed to find out how the storms have affected your life."

Jefferson wasn't used to whining for help. But for the sake of the entire town, he was perfectly capable of spinning a tale of woe.

"Well, sir, you should o' seen this place before the storm." He paused to click his tongue and shake his head in dismay. "This here was the finest eatery in the south."

He pointed about the place, setting the scene for the government man. "Place was twice this size, finished in fine oak."

"Really!" exclaimed Simon, finding it a little hard to envision.

"Well, we all but hauled off the debris already. Had to get back up and runnin' soon as possible. We just a small place, ya know. No reserves to carry us over 'till we can rebuild."

"So you're up and running?" asked Simon, finding that, as he imagined the food, hard to digest. "Getting many customers, are you?" Looking about, he didn't see any.

"Well, that's just it, sir. All the townsfolk, they gots their own problems, all in the same boat ya know. And that boat up a creek with no paddle. Can't afford to be dinin' out at no fine restaurants these days. Business dried up since them storms."

Mrs. Butts showed up off camera with a plate of ribs, scarfing them down as fast as she could suck the meat off the bones.

Jefferson let out a woeful sigh when he saw her.

Simon turned to see what had upset the man. "What's the matter, Jefferson? Is that your boss?"

"Yassir."

"Are you concerned about your job here?"

"Well... uh... yeah, that's it." Jefferson tried to compose himself as he watched the woman inhaling his inventory. "Why, you can see, we ain't got no customers. And with the power outage, it's just a matter of time 'fore the generator for the freezer give out. We gots to cook up all them ribs before they spoil. A man can only eat so much," he added, giving Mrs. Butts the evil eye. "We gonna have to give it all away." Real tears started to form at the corners of his eyes.

Simon reached a hand out to the man's shoulder to console him. "Well at least you weren't hurt in the storm."

"That storm might as well broke every bone in my body, left me dead and buried," countered Jefferson. "Gonna be out of a job soon, 'less Ms. Butts don't get the money to rebuild. Then what'll happen to po' Jefferson Washington. Only job I know. I'll just be beggin' in the streets. Lord might as well strike me dead here and now. Woe is me." The tears were streaming down his face as he watched Gladiola Butts scarf down another plate of ribs.

Simon had seen enough, jotting down some final notes on his clipboard as he started to tear up himself. Turning to Jennifer, "I think I've gotten all I need. He's all yours."

Buck began to relax, and even began to join the show. "Now hold on y'all. Just look at the man. Goin' through hell, he is. You sure you don't need a moment to collect yourself, Jefferson?"

Jefferson had to turn away from Mrs. Butts, wiping the tears from his face. "No, I thinks I can carry on. You know, for the folks and all."

"It won't take long," offered Jennifer. "We just need a few shots with Scarlet here, if you could maybe give us a tour of the damage. I think it could really help to grease the wheels of government. You know, cut through some red tape. Then we'll be on our way."

"Well, if you and the mayor, oh and Mr. Goldfarb here, think it'll help…" Jefferson went to get out of his chair and pretended to swoon, grabbing on to Simon for support.

"Are you OK?" asked Simon, alarmed.

Jefferson wobbled back to his feet. "Oh, I be all right. Must be my blood pressure's all. What with all this stress… and havin' to get by without. Man's liable to have a heart attack or maybe a stroke. We sho' could use some relief round here."

"I'll do what I can, Mr. Washington. But I have to agree with Miss Steele. A little national attention could only help."

Scarlet came forward to take the unsteady Jefferson by the arm.

Getting a closer look at the beauty queen, Jefferson couldn't help flirting a bit.

"Well ain't you a pretty thang," he commented, perking up a bit.

Scarlet looked down at the shorter man— most everybody was shorter than Scarlet— and gave his hand a squeeze, acknowledging the compliment with a winning smile.

"Y'all pretty darn cute yourself, Mr. Washington."

Jefferson was quite enamored with the fine example of womanhood holding his hand, but as he looked her over more closely, something about the girl gave him pause. He couldn't quite put his finger on it, but there was something familiar about her. He knew he'd never met her before, and he didn't really watch television, but Jefferson Washington never forgot a face, and he was growing more and more certain he'd seen this one before.

"What is it, Mr. Washington? You OK?" asked Scarlet, catching him staring.

Jefferson had to shake his head. "Oh... uh, yeah, I's OK. Maybe it's the stress," he added for cover. "Have we met before?"

"Why, I don't think so," Scarlet replied, still smiling at the man.

Jefferson couldn't let it go. He was missing something. He couldn't help trying to solve a mystery. So he decided to take a different approach.

"You sho' looks familiar to me. You from around these parts?"

Jefferson awaited her reply, still trying to place her face.

Scarlet Witherspoon wasn't smiling anymore.

Chapter 16

All seemed to be going according to plan, thought Buck.

He had to thank Jennifer Steel too, for supplying CNN with enough footage to fill its 24/7 portrayal of victimhood in the South. The interview with Jefferson exceeded all expectations. It didn't take long before Jessie Jackson and Al Sharpton were already accusing Congress of racism for not acting fast enough in sending relief to the poor folks of Sweet Spot.

Yeah, the girl done good. Buck felt a twinge of guilt at playin' her the way he was. He still had a thing for her, despite the fact that she was even more of a challenge than he'd imagined, so uptight and all. But Buck liked a challenge. A little challenge always made the conquest all the sweeter.

Shoot, if you just wanted a girl to lie down and let a man have his way with her, you might just as well dial up The Farmer's Daughter, that escort service over in Biloxi. Certainly a lot less muss and fuss.

Not that Buck was lookin' for anything long term. Been there. Done that. He couldn't go through that again. Some scars never seem to fade.

Besides, she'd be on her way once Sweet Spot got their dough and the media found some new victim to exploit. No, Buck was only lookin' for a little healthy short term gratification. Yet the clock was runnin' out. He'd best start turnin' on the old Buck Jones charm.

* * * *

Jennifer Steele couldn't stand the man. Everything he did rubbed her the wrong way. She'd never met a man could push every wrong button she had at the same time. Not the way this man did.

Oh he wasn't the first man that made her want to run the other way. After all, she hadn't made it to the age of 30 without one because she'd set her sights too low. Just the opposite. No mortal man could fit her job description. He'd have to be Einstein, Mother Theresa, and Mr. Darcy all rolled into one. And Buck Jones was no Mr. Darcy.

No, Jennifer Steele knew what she wanted.

Or did she?

Why was she letting him get to her? He was the type of man she normally ignored, not worth the time of day. Just walk the other way. Or, in the case of Buck Jones, run for your life.

And yet, she wasn't running. She was stuck in the middle of the road, caught in the headlights.

Jennifer Steele'd never been in love. She didn't know how it worked. She'd always imagined it was like a cooking recipe, carefully measured teaspoons of sugar and spice combined at just the right temperature and out popped a delicious cake. She didn't know things didn't work that way. Love wasn't a matter of Julia Child somewhere in heaven whipping up a delicate soufflé.

No, it was more like an evil scientist throwing together equal parts Drano and nitroglycerin, or a wart-nosed witch weaving spells over a great black cauldron of bat's blood and spider webs. Either that, or God just had a wicked sense of humor.

But whatever it was, Jennifer Steele was mesmerized by the cobra's stare. She couldn't explain why. Like a deadly pile-up on the interstate, she just couldn't look away. And she didn't like it, not one bit. She didn't like feeling out of control. She couldn't wait to get back to the safety of New York. She'd had enough hey y'alls and welcoming smiles to last a lifetime. She longed for the impersonal anonymity of the big city.

On the other hand, her strolls about the countryside between filming brought back fond memories from her childhood, which was strange in itself, seeing as she didn't know she'd had any... fond memories, that is.

Her father was a son of a bitch, and her mother didn't last very long under the man's thumb. It was a lonely, scary existence for a little girl.

But that wasn't the part she was feeling now. She was feeling the warm sun on her face, hearing birds during the day, and crickets under starlit nights. She didn't have that in New York City. Even the sweet smell of the water down at the fishin' hole had gotten under her skin, despite the giant lizard.

She guessed that she just didn't remember all the good parts of her childhood because she was too busy just trying to survive. But here, now, she could take it all in, savor all the delicacies of the countryside so completely foreign to the big city. She was beginning to think she missed it all.

She hadn't had a migraine since she'd left Manhattan. There had to be a connection. Stress, foul air, foul people. That couldn't be good for migraines. People were kinder, things moved slower, smelled better, and tasted better in Sweet Spot, where even the local fare of finely prepared roadkill was a match for the finest French restaurants in Paris. As strange as it sounded, she'd begun to wonder if the chef, Eustace Winchester, had attended La Sorbonne.

She'd often find the man with Charlie, who'd become a regular fixture over at the Winchesters' auto repair shop, fiercely debating the merits of chicory spice and slow cooking.

No, there was definitely something about the place that had begun to grow on her, like a fine wine, while the mayor had somehow gotten under her skin, more like a pesky splinter, or maybe a yeast infection.

Speak of the devil, there he was walking in her direction now. Too late for her to take evasive action, she braced herself.

He was carrying two buckets. Jennifer hoped he wasn't planning to enlist her in some cow-milking scheme.

"Hey there, little girl," shouted Buck by way of greeting.

"What's with the buckets?" asked Jennifer, not one to beat around the bush.

"Thought you might be interested in some berry pickin'," he suggested, offering her a bucket.

That's right, thought Jennifer. Pleasant as things were around the place, she'd forgotten that Sweet Spot was a disaster area. And pending that aid from FEMA, everyone had to pitch in hunting and gathering.

Noticing he was also carrying his rifle again, "Umm, what sort of berries does one shoot with a rifle?" she asked, accepting the bucket, willing to do her share.

"Oh, well, you know, people ain't the only admirers of berries. Them black bears can get a little ornery they see you movin' in on their turf."

"And what kind of berries will we be fighting bears for today?"

"You're in for a treat. We still got some blueberries and raspberries this time o' year. Hopefully we won't have to fight for 'em."

Jennifer noticed the man was wearing some sort of cologne, rather refined for bear-fighting. He'd also upgraded his wardrobe, wearing slacks and a collared shirt, a step up from the shirtless overalls she'd first met him in. The man was up to something. Could he be courting her?

"You're looking rather dapper today, Mayor. Is this standard Sweet Spot berry-picking attire?"

"Why thank you, Miss Steele. Please call me Buck. It's not often I get to go scavenging with a refined young lady such as yourself. Thought I might rise to the occasion and make a day of it. Even packed us a little picnic lunch," he added with a wink, patting the small backpack slung over his shoulder.

He was! The man was definitely courting her! Jennifer didn't know what to think. She hated the man, yet was drawn to him. The situation was ridiculous. A week ago she was sipping a latte macchiato at Starbuck's on Park Avenue, now here she was berry picking in bear country. How could this possibly go well?

Yet the man was trying. He even packed a picnic lunch. How could a girl scoff at something so cute? Besides, it's not like her dance card was full. She'd just have to keep an open mind.

* * * *

Buck thought things seemed to be going remarkably well. Not only did she seem receptive to the "date" he'd planned, but since she'd lost her footing going over some rough terrain, she'd actually been holding his arm. Was this the same firecracker that disarmed him on their first outing, insisting she carry the gun?

Well, despite her improved demeanor, she still looked the same, as he periodically stole sideways glances at her every now and again. Same tight little body he remembered so fondly since the towel incident during her first dip in the fishin' hole. The bump on the back of his head had almost receded, though he still didn't know how he'd gotten the one on the side of his head during his tussle with Lizzie.

As they rounded a bend and came to the edge of a meadow, Buck saw something big and brown standing about 50 yards off. No, it wasn't a bear. Much better. It was food. An eight-point buck about 12 hands high just waiting to dive into a nice venison stew.

Buck abruptly dropped everything but his rifle and took a bead on the deer.

Jennifer almost screamed when he dropped her arm and raised his gun. As her legs prepared to run for it, her eyes instinctively followed the barrel of the rifle to look for the bear that must have been bearing down on them.

But it wasn't a bear at all. It wasn't a threat. And it certainly wasn't dinner. It was Bambi. All grown up, but still as cute as a button. She couldn't help but smile.

Until she remembered Buck was about to shoot him in the head. Before she could say anything, her arm flew up, knocking the rifle barrel skyward. Buck's shot flew harmlessly over the treetops.

"What the…" growled Buck, scrambling to take another shot before his spooked dinner could bound for cover among the trees.

But Jennifer wasn't having it. They got Bambi's mom, but they weren't gonna get Bambi too, not on her watch. She dove for the barrel of the rifle, practically hanging from it like a trapeze bar as Buck tried to get off another shot.

The woman'd gone insane. Buck didn't know what she was trying to do. It was almost as if she didn't want him to shoot the deer. But that didn't make any sense at all. Perfectly good game, just waiting to be gutted and carved into steaks that would last all season. Maybe she'd just lost her footing and tripped.

Nevertheless, she was dangling from the end of his rifle, decorating it like some kind of human Christmas ornament. He couldn't take a shot now. So he watched in sadness as the animal escaped unharmed into the forest.

"What are you doing?" he asked, focusing back on the circus act swinging from the barrel of his gun.

"Me?! What am I doing?! What are you doing?" Jennifer countered with indignation.

"I was about to feed the whole town for weeks. That's what I was doing."

"By killing that beautiful creature? What do you think supermarkets are for?"

"And where do you think supermarkets get their meat? You think they grow it in pots?"

"Well no, but... but you saw him. That deer was amazing, with a face, and a heart. That was no package of ground chuck."

Buck wanted to scream, awed as he was by the irrationality of the woman's argument. But looking at her pretty green eyes pleading with him, he couldn't help but soften, melting like butter over warm biscuits. After all, it was just some meat. So what if he turned vegetarian. Shoot, he could be god-damned Mahatma Gandhi if it would get him into the girl's pants.

"You know," he began, lowering his rifle with a smile, "I was thinkin' of eatin' more greens anyway. You know, lower the ol' cholesterol," he added, patting his belly.

Jennifer didn't know what the man was up to. But what she did know was that he wasn't to be trusted.

"Well, that's all fine and good," she replied. "But just the same, I'll be holding the gun from here on, if you don't mind," she added, holding out her hand.

Buck instinctively hesitated a moment before relinquishing his firearm to the woman for the second time, but saw no reason not to comply with the authorities.

"Let's go get them berries," he said, handing over the rifle, with a chuckle. Then proceeding across the meadow ahead of her like some kind of disarmed prisoner of war, "So tell me, what's all the fuss these days about gluten?"

* * * *

Jennifer had to admit she'd had a wonderful day. The berry picking was a blast. Like two children, she and Buck would compete over who'd found the most and biggest berries, eating as many of the juicy little things as they'd saved.

And the mayor'd acted the perfect gentleman, even whipping a small blanket out of his backpack for a picnic lunch. Tasting the homemade biscuits he'd brought along made her glad they hadn't given up gluten just yet.

It was really just the perfect afternoon, something magical, something she hadn't had in a long time... well... ever, to be honest. She'd never had a country picnic with a gentleman caller before. And that is what he was. Even Jennifer, not the most experienced in detecting signs of attraction from the opposite sex, could tell she had a bonafide suitor.

She felt at ease with the man. Safe and protected. He was like a big ol' Teddy Bear. She knew she was a little rough on the man, but he did whatever she said. And maybe it was just the wine talking, but this Buck Jones was pretty easy on the eyes. Oh, that's right, did she forget to mention the wine? Or was it wines? How he managed to stuff two bottles in that backpack of his she couldn't comprehend, but by the time he pulled out the second bottle, she was beyond objecting to much of anything.

Thoughts of migraines and the rat race back home were completely erased from her mind. That was another time, another life. The world was just a pretty meadow of wildflowers and whippoorwills.

Until the bear showed up.

The 300-pound black bear was as surprised to see them as they were it. But it was surprised, not afraid, and had no intention of retreating back into the woods, not without some berries and biscuits first.

While Jennifer froze, Buck instinctively reached for his rifle, the very same rifle that the girl'd taken from him and was now nowhere to be seen.

"Where'd you put the rifle?!" he shouted as they both scrambled to their feet, backing away from the bear.

Jennifer could barely comprehend the words, mesmerized as she was by the giant omnivore rambling their way. But understanding Buck's question didn't help the situation. Whether it was the bear or the wine, she just didn't know. She didn't remember where she'd placed the damn thing.

"I don't know!"

"What do you mean you don't know? You had it. I gave it to you. "

"Well, I don't have it now, do I?" she asked rhetorically, holding her hands out to prove she was unarmed.

Damn the woman. There wasn't much time. That bear might just eat their food and ignore them… or not. If she had a cub nearby, she wasn't going to be too happy about any potential threats wandering about her territory. No, they'd best take some evasive action.

Buck knew their best bet was the tree directly behind them. Black bears could climb, but one this large might not be so inclined. And even if it did, he might be able to fend it off with a branch from a superior position.

He pulled Jennifer by the back of her shirt toward the tree, but saw there was no way the pint-sized reporter could reach the first branch. So grabbing her by the collar and the seat of the pants, he threw her up into the tree, praying she'd instinctively cling to the branch like a cat.

"Hey!" she shouted, still coherent enough to express her indignation over being manhandled in such a way. But she was soon climbing to higher ground leaving room as Buck scrambled up behind her.

"Hey, there it is!" she shouted, almost gleefully, when she spotted the rifle leaning up against the backside of the tree.

Buck barely managed to suppress some choice foul language. "Lot o' good it'll do us down there," he said, rolling his eyes.

Jennifer, not a big fan of eye-rolling, was inclined to throw back some choice words of her own but thought better of it. After all, they were stuck up a tree together. Might as well try to get along. Besides, much as she hated to admit it, the man kind of had a point. When she'd confiscated the weapon, she'd taken responsibility for security. Maybe she'd overestimated her skill set. Maybe she was in over her head on that one. Regardless, they were treed like a pair of coons while mama bear was having a little picnic down below. No reason to make things worse.

Despite the fact that Buck had other plans for that second bottle of wine, he couldn't be too upset when he saw the bear'd managed to pop the cork with its claws. He'd been saving that five-dollar bottle from Walmart for a special occasion, but he guessed this was as special as any. If his fine wine could get that bear as drunk as he'd hoped to get his tree mate, there was a good chance they'd be able to skedaddle on their way before nightfall.

Chapter 17

Jeb Clancey wasn't used to havin' no boarders. But in his line of work, as sole proprietor of an unsanctioned distillery, Jeb could well relate to havin' to hide from the law, live in the shadows, so to speak. So seeing a brother fugitive from the authorities, he didn't think twice about offering Pedro a place to lay low. He'd be damned if some suit from ICE was goin' to start throwin' his weight 'round Sweet Spot, thinkin' the locals would give up one of their own. 'Cause that's what Pedro was. He was one of their own.

And while Jeb didn't understand how someone could live on no rice and beans every day, he supposed it was better than his usual fare of Slim Jims and Skoal. The whole cave reeked of cumin, but that too was a vast improvement over Jeb's personal brand of stank.

The part Jeb was havin' trouble swallowin' was the damn horse. Conquistador was pretty good about doin' his business outside the cave, but havin' a full-grown stallion livin' in such proximity to Jeb's beloved still had the man on edge. One false step, and Jeb could lose his livelihood.

* * * *

For Pedro's part, he feared losing more than just his livelihood. The boss's man, Rocco, wasn't here on no peace mission. And if the man ever found them, both Pedro and Conquistador would become geldings.

So Pedro knew, one way or another, the current living arrangements were only temporary. Either Rocco would give up searching for Pedro, crawling through poison oak and venomous snakes, or Pedro and Conquistador would have to hit the road.

The only thing holding Pedro back was the girl. That Scarlet goddess had him all wound up. This wasn't the first time Pedro'd found himself in a bad situation on account of a girl. The boss's wasn't the first rich bored wife he'd dallied with. It's not like he had to go looking for trouble. To the Palm Beach socialites, Pedro was the cover of a Harlequin romance, a Latin equestrian reeking of leather and sweat. Many a night, having scored the winning goal of his international polo match, he didn't even have time to shower before some sweet-smelling painted lady would toss him into the back of her limo, ordering the chauffeur home.

Of course Pedro wasn't entirely blameless. He was always thinkin' with the small head, the one below the belt, instead of the big one on his shoulders. And when it came to giving in to carnal lust, Pedro was weak.

With Scarlet, it was different, though. Whenever they finished making love, neither one felt the urge to push the other away and pretend it never happened. Instead, he found himself believing it was his duty to make the world a more beautiful place by siring children with a combination of Scarlet's beauty and his own.

And just as he knew his feelings for her were true, for the first time, he knew a woman loved him for himself, not for his reputation on the international polo circuit. Scarlet knew nothing of his playboy life. Like everyone else, she only knew him as an illegal Mexican on the run. Mexican? Pedro had to laugh. He didn't even speak Spanish. Not that anyone would expect the folks from Sweet Spot, Mississippi to know Portuguese from Spanish. Pedro was born and raised in Rio de Janeiro, Brazil.

But Rocco knew it all, and Pedro was trying to listen to the little voice in the big head telling him it was time to hit the road. Yet he knew he wasn't going anywhere. While he may have been too easily persuaded when it came to carnal lust, he was a complete slave to romance. And what was the purpose of life after all, if not for romance? Such was his Latin curse to bear.

* * * *

Rocco cursed his Latin fugitive as he stepped in yet another heap of cow dung. The whole town seemed to be paved with the stuff. His imported Italian leather wing-tips weren't made for this.

He couldn't wait to get the hell out of the place. It wouldn't be long now, anyway. He knew he didn't have much time. The boss was not a patient man. Besides, it's not like he was lookin' to put down roots in Hooterville. He'd come on a mission. He had to set an example of what happens to someone who doesn't do as the boss says. Otherwise people would start thinkin' the boss had gone soft.

Rocco wasn't sent with a warning, or even just to bring back the man's pecker in a Ziploc. Not this time. Rocco was sent to take out Nacho Garcia. And he didn't mean to the movies. Because unlike in Rocco's favorite movie, Nacho would be wakin' up to more than his prized horse's severed head in his bed. He'd be wakin' up to his own severed head too. Well, maybe he wouldn't exactly be wakin' up, but Rocco knew what he meant.

He knew Nacho was there, somewhere. He could smell a wetback for miles. Yet the whole town seemed to be conspiring to keep the man hidden. And that would prove to be a foolish decision on their part.

These yahoo hayseeds didn't know who they were dealin' with, givin' him the runaround the way they did. Where he came from, Rocco was treated with respect. People knew what he was capable of. And he wasn't talkin' 'bout just breakin' some thumbs either.

But not these people. It was like one o' them National Geographic documentaries on some undiscovered civilization that, through lack of exposure, had never learned to fear snakes or had no word in their primitive language for murder.

Well, it was time these folks learned a thing or two.

It didn't take but a little money thrown around over in Pottsville for Rocco to confirm his suspicion that Nacho Garcia did indeed reside over in Sweet Spot. In fact, all it took was a generous tip to the portly yet sweet-faced waitress at the diner to hear more than he ever wanted of the legend of Pedro.

Short on first-hand details, yet fully acquainted with talk of a talented horseman from south of the border, there wasn't a filly for 50 miles that didn't dream of the Latin lothario. For someone on the lam, Nacho Garcia sure seemed to get around.

So now that he'd received confirmation from a second source, Rocco would have to renew his efforts to bring in his man. Only, this time the gloves were off. He had no desire to stay a second longer than necessary in the greater Sweet Spot metropolitan area, or as Rocco referred to it, that shit-hole.

He couldn't wait to get home and clean the dirt off his shoes. And he was in desperate need of a manicure to get the grime out from under his nails. He was even thinkin' of a cleansing facial just to get the place out of his pores.

Yet, to date, things weren't exactly goin' bada-bing bada-boom. These local yokels weren't givin' up the fugitive. They seemed to have some sort of problem following authority. After all, he'd told them he was from the federal government. But that seemed to be a real bugaboo with these people. Most places, that carried some weight. Round these parts, seemed just the opposite. They almost seemed to get a gleam in their eye back at that church, like in one o' them Discovery Channel specials on deadliest animals. It was like they were a herd of wildebeests circling to protect their young from a hungry hyena. No, not quite. That's not what it was. The way they'd looked at Rocco, they were more like a hungry pride of lions and Rocco was a lame goat with a broken leg. Yeah, that was it.

Not that Rocco was afraid. Things got out o' hand, his trusty old 9mm would settle any disputes. Things were just takin' a little longer than anticipated was all. Rocco Buttafuoco had no intention of givin' up his man.

* * * *

Scarlet had no intention of givin' up her man.

Like barbeque-flavored pork rinds, she just couldn't get enough. Sure, she'd had her share of Latin lovers in New York, but they were just posers. A girl can tell. But Pedro was another story. He was the real deal.

Oh, she didn't care if he was illegal. She knew as well as anyone that we all have our little skeletons in the closet. Which reminded her, that wily Jefferson Washington wasn't the fool he pretended to be. He was onto her... her sordid past that is. He seemed to recognize her. And anyone from Mississippi who recognized little ol' Miss Grits and Gravy more than likely was acquainted with how she earned the title. No need havin' all the folks from the station hearin' them gory details.

Speakin' of the other folks from the station, maybe they weren't so innocent either. Seemed just a matter of time before Jennifer and that Mayor would get down to business and do the nasty themselves. Even Brooklyn-born Charlie seemed happy as a pig in a poke in Sweet Spot, wallowin' in the mud with them Winchester boys. Whether it was fixin' cars or roadkill, the man couldn't seem to get enough. He practically lived over there. No tellin' what city boy was gettin' himself into.

But all that was neither here nor there. What really mattered was Pedro. Scarlet actually needed him. She'd never needed a man before. Oh, she'd enjoyed men, used them, broken their hearts many times. But she'd never had her heart broken before, and she had no intention of lettin' it happen now.

That's why she had to find out why he seemed to be avoiding her. Pedro'd been a bit scarce of late and Scarlet was beginning to fear he'd grown tired of her. And that would have been a first for Scarlet, a man growin' tired of her. It was supposed to be the other way around. Only Scarlet was allowed to break off the relationship. The current situation was simply not to be tolerated.

And just to show how serious she was, she found herself walkin' into JW's Serious Bar-BQ lookin' for some word on her man's whereabouts. Word was anyone still livin' in Sweet Spot had to cross through JW's sooner or later.

She'd been hopin' to avoid any further contact with that Jefferson fella. The man seemed to look right through her. But desperate times called for desperate measures. And Scarlet Witherspoon was desperate. Desperate for a piece o' that Pedro. What that man did to her was pure and simple ruination.

* * * *

Jefferson Washington didn't know how long he could put up with this charade. Mrs. Butts was eatin' him out o' business. But worse than that was the effort required of him to continue playing the victim.

He did that interview with the weather-hottie, after all. What more did they need? Typical government inefficiency. How long does it take to write a damn check?

Speakin' of the hottie though, it didn't take long to yank that skeleton out of its closet. With just one afternoon's research over in the periodicals section at the Pottsville Library, Jefferson learned all he needed to know about little Miss Grits & Gravy, how she'd earned her title, and the subsequent pictorial spreads in such fine literary fare as Juggs, Barely Legal, and, yes, even Country Beaver, magazines.

But Jefferson didn't care about all that. Shoot, a person's got to use what talents the Lord provides. Jefferson had a brain. Scarlet Witherspoon didn't. 'Nuf said.

But there was more to the story. Jefferson just knew it. There was just somethin' 'bout the woman. He couldn't put his finger on it… not yet anyway. But he wasn't gonna let it rest.

* * * *

Scarlet didn't mean to frighten Mr. Washington. But when she walked into the Barbeque shack and found him in Mrs. Butts's office reading The Wall Street Journal, you'd think by the look on his face that she'd found him ogling a dirty magazine. He threw the thing aside as if it'd burned him, as if he didn't want her to know he could read.

"I's just lookin' at the pictures," he protested.

"I'm sorry," she began. "Didn't mean to surprise ya'."

Jefferson was still all nervous and fidgety, shoving the newspaper under the table. "Oh, uh, dats all right, Miss. I's just cleanin' up some old papers someone left layin' round. Got no use for readin' myself. Alls I needs to know is how to serve up a little barbeque. What brings a pretty thing like you over here?"

"Well, I was lookin' for Pedro, and people say everyone passes through JW's. So here I am."

"Well, you know Pedro been layin' low, what with that government man snoopin' round. Don't have much use for no government men myself."

Scarlet felt relieved to hear Jefferson suggest Pedro's scarcity had nothing to do with her, that she wasn't losing her touch, so to speak. The idea that a man would dump Scarlet Witherspoon. How absurd. What was she thinking?

With a weight off her shoulders, she felt free to chuckle at Jefferson's anti-government sentiment.

"Sounds like somethin' my great granddaddy used to say."

"Remind you of your great granddaddy, huh?" Jefferson's wheels began to turn. "Well you 'mind me o' someone yourself."

"Really?" She couldn't help noticing the way the man was staring at her. "This someone must o' been a real looker," she added with a wink and a smile.

Jefferson had to chuckle. "She sho' was. Why in her day, my great granddaddy's wife was the belle o' the ball. Today, she'd probably be one o' them beauty queens."

Scarlet thought it was a little odd how the man didn't refer to her as his great grandmother but as his great grandfather's wife.

Nevertheless, she felt her stomach twist at the man's mention of beauty queens. "Well, pinch me if that isn't what they used to say about my great grannie too."

"I bet they did, she look anything like you."

"Why, thank you, Mr. Washington," gushed Scarlet, the color rising in her cheeks. "You're very sweet."

Scarlet found Mr. Jefferson very easy to talk to, but remembered how members of her family never would have allowed her to chat it up with a black man. She felt ashamed.

"No offense or nothin', but my great granddaddy, now he didn't have much use for no darkies, as he used to call 'em, less'n they was hard workers."

This seemed to peak Jefferson's interest, pieces of the puzzle finally falling into place. "Own a plantation, did he?"

Scarlet saw no reason to lie about it. "That's right. Till they lost it all through drink and gamblin'."

Jefferson always savored the feel of holding that last puzzle piece in his hand before completing the picture. "Where abouts?"

"Oh, not far from here, just over in Yazoo City, Mississippi."

Jefferson's eyes went wide.

"What is it?" asked Scarlet.

"Let me ask... uh... aks you a question. This plantation wouldn't happen to be called Old Magnolia, would it?"

Scarlet's mouth dropped open. "Now how did you know that?"

Checkmate!

Jefferson just sat back with a smug smile on his face and said, "Child, I believe your family used to own my family."

Chapter 18

With no sign of that damned FEMA check, Jennifer began to wonder if she'd ever get out of Sweet Spot.

In the meantime, she'd bummed a ride with the Winchester boys over to Pottsville in hopes of finding a meal she didn't have to kill herself. All the fresh air seemed to stimulate her appetite, or maybe it was all that getting around on foot. Fresh air and exercise. Just a week or so ago, she didn't know what the word meant.

In New York City, fresh air'd practically been outlawed. And the furthest Jennifer had had to walk was over to the next yellow cab, which, in the city, were as common as salmon headed upstream at the height of spawning season.

Yes, things were certainly different in Sweet Spot. Not that she'd never known the country life. There was that matter of her childhood she'd, until recently, completely repressed. And with good reason.

Because of it, she'd always equated small towns with small-minded people, and she'd vowed never to subject herself to that life again. Sure, anyone thinking straight would admit that bad things happen in big cities too. All the time. Lots of them.

But this was a subject Jennifer wasn't capable of thinking straight about. It was only through the eyes of a scared child that she saw the matter. Growing up under the storm cloud of her parents' marriage was a nightmare. All that was nice and sweet about the countryside was snuffed out, just as her mother had been at the abusive hands of her father.

Or was it? It seemed strange hearing the birds in the morning, the crickets at night, suppressed memories from another life, a life long forgotten. It was unlike anything she'd ever felt in the city. It felt somehow like home, a home that had faded from consciousness over the years, leaving only jagged scars from bad memories.

But maybe her childhood wasn't all bad. Maybe there'd been good times too. And by erasing her childhood, maybe she'd cut off a part of herself that left her less than whole.

Maybe that was why she was alone. Just as she'd come to associate the countryside with all that was bad, maybe she'd done the same with men. Maybe all men weren't her father. Maybe there were some good ones after all.

Like Buck. Oh sure, if she could ever confuse a man with her father it would be Buck, as backward a Neanderthal as there ever was. But there was a difference. Buck was her Neanderthal. The man worshipped the ground she walked on. And she knew it. Her father never worshipped anything except his fists and his liquor, a lethal combination.

But not Buck. Her Buck couldn't hurt a fly. Her Buck? Maybe he was... hers. She felt safe with him. And she'd never felt that with a man before.

Wait a second. Buck Jones? The same man who'd tried to feed her to alligators and bears. What was she thinking? What was happening to her? Maybe it was something she ate, the roadkill. Or maybe it was a mild case of psychosis brought on by lyme disease. You can get that from a tick bite, ya know. And this place was just crawling with 'em. Maybe she just needed to get out of the sun.

Well, she wasn't quite up to the sausage and grits at the Do Drop Inn, the Pottsville diner, but a simple cup of black coffee seemed practically decadent as she perused the Pottsville Post.

The entire publication was only a few pages, mostly ads for farm equipment and recipes. She'd read her fill of whose pig had been nominated for 4-H Club honors, and the police blotter described more than one tractor accident. Foul play was suspected in the disappearance of a coonhound named Snuf, and the international section consisted of a full blow-by-blow of Jake and Dottie Buford's trip to Hawaii.

Jennifer thought it rather odd that the local paper just next door in Pottsville had no coverage whatsoever of the disaster that had befallen their closest neighbors over in Sweet Spot. Not a word. She'd have thought that would have been big news in these parts.

Seemed like the Pottsville Post might benefit from an infusion of some fresh editorial perspective. As she sipped her coffee in the peaceful diner, Jennifer wondered what it would be like publishing a small-town newspaper. Sure, you wouldn't have the big staff and hard-nosed reporting of a big-city paper, but imagine the freedom to put the whole paper together from top to bottom without having to seek the approval of 50 different supervisors. Complete control without miles of red tape and cesspools full of office politics.

Jennifer asked the waitress if she knew where the paper was published, and found that, just as everything in Pottsville, it was just a ways down Main Street. Far as Jennifer could tell, there was only one street in Pottsville, but that was in itself a major advancement over Sweet Spot. At least Pottsville had a street.

Just a short stroll down that street, Jennifer found the door to the place. The small sign above the door had been vandalized with a pocket knife to read Pottsville Piss. She had to put her shoulder and all of her 98 pounds into it to unjam the splintered wood door.

That's when she saw it... the body. There was a dead man at the desk.

He seemed to have died peacefully in his sleep amid a cluttered desk full of papers and photographs. She wondered how long he'd been left there that way. The detective in her glanced at the front page of the newspaper she carried and saw that it was indeed published that very morning. It kinda creeped her out that, assuming the paper came from this very office, the body in front of her was probably still warm.

The man had apparently lived a full life, looking all of 85 years old, a thin frail thing, balding, with a wreath of gray. His small wire-rimmed spectacles had slipped from his nose to cover his mouth as he lay sprawled backward in the worn office chair.

Whether this was the janitor or the night watchman, Jennifer didn't know. But apparently he died on the job. Good for him in a way, no extended loss of dignity in some nursing home.

Well, before heading out to find the police and report the death, with the investigative instincts of a journalist, Jennifer thought to check his pockets for some identification. Bravely approaching the little old man, she saw no signs of trauma or foul play. He looked so serene, no wrinkles over his brow. She could just tell he'd died a happy man, at peace with the world.

It was only when Jennifer reached into his pocket and grasped his wallet that all that changed. It all happened so fast, she had no idea how she ended up on the dusty wood floor with a knee on her chest and the barrel of a 38 snub nose to her head.

"Pick-pocket, eh? Well we'll just see about that."

Jennifer couldn't find her voice as she looked up at the dead man threatening her life.

"Damn kids. What do you got to say for yourself 'fore I call the sheriff?"

"You're alive!" She just couldn't imagine how he sprang from a dead sleep to subdue her so decisively. He must have slept with that damned revolver in his hand.

"Course I'm alive. Do I look dead to you?"

"Well…"

"Don't answer that, girlie. I may be old but I still got some fight left in me. And I got no intention of lettin' you kids run roughshod over this town."

"You're hurting me," was all Jennifer could whimper under the weight of his knee.

The man seemed to ponder the situation before standing up with a creak of his knees. The gun remained leveled at Jennifer.

"Well, alright, you can get up while I ring up the sheriff. But I'm warnin' ya, no funny business. We don't take kindly to no criminals in these parts."

"I'm no criminal," Jennifer replied getting unsteadily to her feet. "I thought you were dead."

"That's even worse, robbing a dead man. What's wrong with you kids? Must be them damned video games."

"This is silly," she responded, brushing the dust from her pants. "I wasn't robbing you. I was looking for some identification to report your death."

The man was not amused. "In the immortal words of Samuel Langhorne Clemons, reports of my death are greatly exaggerated."

"You can say that again," added Jennifer, noting how spry the old man really was. "I guess the investigative reporter in me got the better of me."

The man squinted and peered at her over his spectacles. "Reporter ya say?" tentatively beginning to lower his gun.

"Yes sir," she answered, "using the term loosely. Well, mostly writing copy for television coverage."

The man threw his gun on the desk and plopped back down in his chair. "Well I'll be. Ain't often I get to chew the fat with a brethren in the business. Sit down. Take a load off," he directed, leaning out of his chair just enough to throw the clutter from the only other chair in the room. "You ain't from around these parts."

"New York. I'm here from New York," she said, wiping the dust from the chair before sitting down, her knees still a little wobbly from the incident with the gun.

"Oh, the big league, eh? Where'd you train, hot shot?"

"Columbia School of Journalism," she answered, holding her chin high, unable to completely hide just a pinch of arrogance.

"Woo woo! Not too shabby. A mighty big fish in my little ol' pond." With that, he gestured over his shoulder with a simple jerk of his head.

Jennifer squinted at the back of the room wallpapered in all manner of tacked, stapled, and taped yellowing documents. But right there in center of all the clutter, in a plain black frame, hung a diploma. A diploma from none other than The Columbia School of Journalism, 1930. William J. Miller, PhD.

"Is that you? You're a journalist?" asked a skeptical Jennifer. "I thought you were maybe the night watchman."

"Night watchman, chief bottle-washer, editor-in-chief, and sole proprietor of the Pottsville Press. Folks call me Doc. Doc Miller," extending a hand in greeting.

Jennifer's mouth was in danger of catching flies as she shook the man's hand. When words finally came out, all she could come up with was, "What are you doing here?"

"What am I doin' here? Why, I'm running a newspaper, young lady", he answered, unable to mask a taste of insult. "Bringin' the world to Pottsville."

Jennifer hadn't meant to insult the man. "What I meant was, with your credentials, you could have landed a position in a major metropolitan market."

"Oh that. Been there. Done that. Ain't all it's cracked up to be. I carried other people's water long enough. No, I like runnin' my own show."

Looking at the man, Jennifer couldn't help thinking of the wizard from the Wizard of Oz. Maybe Doc Miller'd been blown to Pottsville by a twister all those years ago, and decided to stay when he realized he could be the big man on campus.

Jennifer finally spoke up. "I was just wondering myself what it might be like running a small town paper."

Doc's eyes lit up. "Want in, do ya? Well, we sure could use an infusion of some new blood. And these old knees can't get around like they used to. Why, you can start right away. What's minimum wage these days?"

"Minimum wage?" she replied with a chuckle.

"See, that's the problem with you kids these days. Everybody expects instant gratification. No one wants to put in their time, pay their dues."

Then, with a twinkle in his eye, he took another tack. "Maybe you'd rather not work your way up the ladder. Maybe you wanna run the whole shebang yourself. Maybe you'd rather buy me out. A man can't live forever. Don't worry. I'll help you through the transition period. Ol' Bessie can be a little cantankerous at times."

"Old Bessie?"

"My printing press," he answered with a toss of his head toward a door to the back room.

"Oh, I don't know," replied Jennifer, more out of courtesy than actual consideration. "I don't think I have that kind of money. Besides, what with the internet and all, I don't know if print media's got much of a future."

The man threw her concerns aside. "Oh, nonsense. First of all, I ain't lookin' to make a killin' here. Secondly, people will always like the feel of a newspaper in their hands along with their mornin' java, even at your Starbucks. Besides, lot a places round these parts still don't have no internet."

"Like Sweet Spot?" chuckled Jennifer. "Spent the past week or so over there."

"Oh, roughin' it, are ya?" he smiled. "How's my friend, the mayor?"

Jennifer had to wonder how an educated man from a place like New York could even communicate with a backwoods bumpkin like Buck Jones, let alone befriend him.

"Oh, Mr. Jones is a little rough around the edges for my taste," she finally replied.

Doc Miller raised his eyebrows and clucked his tongue. "Now, now. You call yourself a journalist. You're supposed to have keen powers of observation. Sounds like the man's got you fooled. I'd think twice 'fore underestimating the likes of Buck Jones."

Jennifer was taken aback. "How do you mean?"

"Oh, I'm just sayin' I wouldn't sell ol' Buck short. The man is much more than he seems."

"Well, that's not exactly saying a whole lot because he certainly doesn't seem like much," she smiled.

"The lady doth protest too much. Sounds like maybe you're a little sweet on the mayor."

"Who? Me?" she coughed with indignation. "Not if he were the last man on Earth."

Doc raised his eyebrows with a smile. "Ooh. You got it bad. Well, good for Buck."

"What?!" Jennifer was mortified.

Doc ignored her protestation. "That's right. The man deserves a good woman in his life, someone to get him back on track since losing his way a few years back.

"Losing his way?"

"Now I've said too much already. Not my place. You're just gonna have to unravel that one on your one."

Jennifer held her hands up. "Believe me. Mr. Jones is one tangled mess I plan on leaving fully raveled."

Doc sat back and smiled. "Well, we'll just have to see about that. Love works in mysterious ways."

Chapter 19

Felicity Barnes couldn't be happier with this Simon fella. Oh, it wasn't for herself. She wasn't hankerin' for no daddy. It was for Sarah. Sarah needed a man in a bad way. Sure she'd found her Lord and Savior, Jesus Christ. And that was all well and good... least compared to where she'd been. But the Lord could only go so far.

Felicity may have been young, but she wasn't naive. After all, a girl like Sarah's got needs. Felicity wasn't exactly sure what those needs were, but she knew you needed a man to fill 'em.

And anyone with eyes could see Simon was that man. He was nice. He was clean. He didn't drink no alcohol or chew no tobacco. What more could a girl ask for?

Besides, she could see the way he looked at Sarah. It was just like in that movie, Bambi, with that girl deer, Faline. The man was twitterpated, head over heels. Now if only she could open Sarah's eyes for anything but her Lord and Savior, for an actual flesh and blood man of this earth.

Felicity didn't give a darn about the mayor's tornado scheme, but if it was responsible for bringing Simon Goldfarb to town, maybe the whole thing was meant to be after all. Who was little Felicity Barnes to fight fate? She could put up with defrauding the federal government for a little while so long as it brought a chance for a little sorely-needed romance to her beloved friend, Sarah Pritchard.

* * * *

Simon Goldfarb certainly didn't know what he'd gotten himself into. He kept thinking he must have fallen asleep during an episode of the Twilight Zone, fallen through a wormhole into some sort of alternate universe.

He'd hoped at best to get in and get out, approve the aid money, and skedaddle on back to his cozy little cubicle waiting for him back at work. But the wheels of government were about as efficient as jacking up a house and spinning it in circles just to screw in a light bulb. He didn't know how long it would take for them to follow his recommendation and release the disaster funds.

So there he remained, stuck in purgatory, still waiting for the word to go home. He could have sworn he'd have been dead by now, whether from a hoard of pointed white hoods, or a lethal case of hay fever. Though the jury was still out with respect to his hay fever, in the face of an ever-dwindling supply of antihistamines, he hadn't seen a single pointed white hood. In fact, the folks of Sweet Spot could not have been sweeter.

Especially that Sarah Pritchard. She'd been nurse, cook, and spiritual life coach all rolled into one, all things desperately lacking in Simon Goldfarb's world.

Simon didn't know what to do with himself while waiting for an official decision from headquarters. He was so accustomed to slaving away, pushing paper nine to five in his little cubicle, that a little free time out in the country left him disoriented.

So he found himself tagging along with the church angel wherever she went, like some lost puppy. Sarah Pritchard fed him, housed him, even did his laundry, and all with a smile. Simon hadn't been cared for so well since the day his father forced his mother to cut the cord and kick him out of his room in the basement, out into the cold world.

Well, maybe Sweet Spot, Mississippi wasn't the world any of them had in mind, but Simon had to admit it was beginning to grow on him. There was just something he found calming about being outdoors, gathering fruits and flowers, and working in Sarah's garden behind the church.

At first, he was terrified that germs lurking in the soil would be the death of him. But when Sarah urged him to try it, he just couldn't say no.

He was so under her spell, he'd have done anything for her, even convert to Christianity, if she'd asked him to. Of course, she had no intention of asking him to do that. Sarah said she didn't really care what faith a person chose, so long as they believed in God, though she had to admit she still had some reservations about Islam. She didn't really know too much about it except that there seemed to be entirely too much talk of something they called jihad, and Sarah didn't abide no fighting.

So after the first Xanax just to get over the idea of handling dirt, Simon soon felt right at home. Not only did he find gardening to be soothing in a Zen sort of way, he soon found he'd forgotten to take any of his medications. Both his nerves and his bowels had quieted down. Even his allergies had gone into hiding.

Everybody remarked at how well he looked. Of course, maybe that was just the new tan he was sporting. Simon Goldfarb never had a tan before. Even that year he'd attended, he'd followed his mother's strict instructions on applying sunscreen.

He never would have imagined giving gardening a second thought, but Sarah's enthusiasm was infectious, and Simon soon couldn't get his nose out of the Farmer's Almanac. Recalling a special he'd seen on The Discovery Channel, Simon was already wondering if it would be cost effective to increase the productivity of Sarah's vegetable patch by employing hydroponic technology. He'd have to discuss it with the boss, though. That Felicity Barnes wasn't one to throw money around injudiciously.

But farming wasn't the only world Simon's mind was beginning to open to, as he soon began having thoughts of sowing an entirely different sort of crop... like maybe some wild oats. And try as he might, he just couldn't get those less than pure ruminations about Sarah Pritchard out of his mind. According to his dreams anyway, the girl had a wild side, an ungodly one, smoldering just beneath the church veneer she wore for public consumption.

Sure, she'd found another path, left her sinful habits behind, but like a volcano, just because the spout was capped didn't mean the molten lava wasn't still smoldering below. And Simon could sense it. Just as a single grain of pollen could wreak havoc on his sinuses, he could feel Sarah Pritchard's sensuality burning in his loins. Once an inert bowl of Jell-O, Simon Goldfarb was awakened. He'd never imagined what could drive a man to write poetry or die in battle for a woman. Yet now he knew. Simon Goldfarb was horny, horny for the church girl.

And that church girl soon had Simon Goldfarb praying... praying he could stay in Sweet Spot forever... praying that damned FEMA check never showed up.

* * * *

They were all in the church when the check finally showed up. Buck was trying to be patient, waiting on that government check. But the townsfolk were beginning to get on his nerves. They'd become unruly children, like the night before Christmas, fighting over gifts they hadn't even received yet.

"No, Chief, we ain't gonna build no gamblin' casino with that government money. This ain't no Indian reservation. Shoot, you're the only Native American we got. Now if you wanna spend your share on a casino, that's up to you."

"NASCAR track? Really, Earl? Much as we all love NASCAR, seems like an awful lot o' noise for a town our size."

"Sure you can buy a yacht with your money, Jeb. Don't know where you're goin' to put it, seein' as we ain't got no navigable waterway within' a hundred miles. Be a little tight over in the fishin' hole."

"Now Mrs. Butts, you really wantin' to put Smith's Hardware over in Pottsville out o' business by building your own Home Depot?"

"Don't care what Mikey and Felicity said. We ain't got room for no Disney World here in Sweet Spot. No, not even a Dollywood."

"Pedro, what the hell you gonna do with a polo field?"

"You know, you all got these big plans. But how about thinkin' a little smaller. Like how about, oh maybe, electricity or runnin' water? Wouldn't that be luxurious? Maybe a paved road. How about roofs that actually keep out the rain?"

Looking anxiously heavenward at the warped ceiling, "Maybe a church ain't settin' to crash down on our heads any second?"

Sarah couldn't hold back an "Amen!"

"How 'bout a little somethin' put aside for a rainy day, anyone?"

"All right. I know. I know. Maybe a new mayor's mansion shouldn't be right at the top o' the list."

"Meanwhile, we ain't got squat. So let's just all try to remain patient. Don't be countin' them chickens just yet. Y'all know how the federal government works. Poorly, if at all."

That's when Mikey Dunham burst through the front doors of the church carrying little Felicity on his shoulders. The little girl was holding something over her head with both hands.

"What ya got there, Miss Felicity?" asked Buck.

"It's a check," she chirped, grinning from ear to ear.

"Now that don't sound like our Felicity. Since when you takin' personal checks at your sweet tea stand. Thought you learned that lesson long ago. That things only gonna bounce on ya."

The church crowd was nodding in agreement, disappointed in little Felicity's lapse in judgment.

"Well, I sure hope this one don't bounce. It's kinda big." the little girl countered.

"Tsk tsk girl," continued Buck. "I hope you didn't give away your whole day's supply of sweet tea for no rubber check."

"Didn't give up nothin'. Even sold the man in the suit what brought the check a glass of tea for a whole dollar, cash money."

Buck was confused. "Then what's that check for?"

Felicity lowered the check to her eye level. "Says here it's from the Federal Government."

Every heart in Sweet Spot skipped a beat in unison.

Mrs. Butts was the first to find the words. "That's our check! The disaster funds!"

Buck had to quiet the excited crowd. "Now, now. Calm down. That can't be no FEMA check. You tellin' me the feds just hand off a check like that to some little kid sittin' at a sweet tea stand at the edge of town?"

Jefferson didn't miss a beat. "No one ever said the federal government was very bright. Better off given our tax money to some little girl sellin' sweet tea in rural Mississippi than to government cronies buildin' windmills, or to middle eastern countries what hate us."

Buck wasn't ready to believe it. "Felicity, didn't they want to bring it on into town?"

The girl gave that some thought but replied, "Well, frankly, the man seemed a bit put off that he had to come so far off the beaten path. He was in a hurry to get over to some big city like Biloxi to buy a convertible."

Buck was confused. "A convertible? He said that?"

"Yep." Felicity tried to recall the man's exact words. "He said there was a topless place in Biloxi where he could max out his generous government expense account."

"From the mouths of babes," muttered Jefferson as the rest of the town cleared their throats and tried not to make eye contact with each other.

Buck had a sinking feeling in his stomach. The salacious details aside, the check couldn't have amounted to much to be left in the hands of an eight-year-old.

"OK, OK, Miss Felicity. So exactly how much is this check for?"

Felicity hadn't seen very many checks before, but she did her best to read the number, still swaying about on Mikey's shoulders.

"Well, let's see. There's lots of zeroes."

The church filled with excited chatter. Their ship had come in. Visions of easy street, paved in gold, danced in the townsfolks' eyes.

Buck wasn't so quick to jump to conclusions. "Exactly how many zeros we talkin' 'bout here."

"Well there's three zeros after the comma."

The whole town groaned in unison, emotions falling from the mountain top to the valley floor.

"A thousand dollars? Is that all?" Buck was insulted.

Jeb tried to put a positive spin on the news. "Well, it could be nine thousand, right?"

"I think it's more than a thousand," interrupted Felicity, still doing the math in her head.

"See. I told you so," accused Jeb.

But it ain't nine thousand," countered Felicity. "There's no nine here."

"Oh," replied a disappointed Jeb. "Eight thousand? Seven..."

"Nope," continued Felicity. "There's only ones and zeros."

"Then how can it be more than a thousand?" asked Buck. You said there was only three zeros after the comma."

"That's right. But there's two commas."

You could have heard a cricket fart while the whole town did the math.

Finally Mrs. Butts, her mouth suddenly dry, was brave enough to ask, "You sayin' you're holdin' a check for a million dollars?"

People were grabbing each other's arms to keep from falling off the pews.

Felicity's reply didn't seem to quite settle the issue. "No, it ain't a million. A millions got six zeros, right?"

Earl Winchester had to object. "I ain't no Einstein, but I know if you got two commas, there's gotta be three zeros after each one, and that's a million bucks.

"I don't mean to be disrespectful Mr. Winchester," Felicity replied, "but you're right and you're wrong."

"She lost me," whined a frustrated Bubba Winchester, scratchin' his head. "She said six zeros."

Buck was about to go grab the check in question out of the girl's hand when she protested. "I never said there was six zeros! I said there was two commas!"

"Speak plain, Miss Felicity," instructed Buck, losing patience.

"Well, there's two commas with three zeroes after each one..."

"Geronimo!" shouted the chief, jumping up and starting a dance thanking the spirits. "It is a million dollars."

"...and another zero before the commas," added Felicity. "How much is that?" she asked, looking at the crowd.

Everyone was muttering to each other in confused whispers as Buck slowly walked up to Felicity to put an end to the game of 20 questions. His hand trembled as he accepted the check from the little girl.

All eyes were on the mayor as he studied the check.

Buck felt faint and had to take a seat.

"Is it that bad?" asked Jeb.

Buck found it hard to breath. "It's ten," he finally answered, swallowing hard, still looking at the check.

"Ten?!" shouted Eustace. "Ten measly dollars?!"

Buck had to wipe a tear from his eye and take another deep breath.

"Ten... million," he replied, slowly shaking his head in disbelief. "Ten million dollars."

Buck exhaled through puffed out cheeks, closed his eyes, and dropped his head back in a prayer of thanks to heaven above."

More than one pew fell over backward as the whole town jumped to their feet in a chorus of cheers.

Chapter 20

Jefferson was much too busy to even consider the concept of guilt in defrauding the U.S. government out of ten million dollars. JW's Serious Bar-BQ was to be the venue for a celebration such as Sweet Spot had never known before. And Jefferson was up to his ribs in ribs.

That's not to say, given the time, that he'd have felt the slightest twinge of remorse. Far as Jefferson could tell, the sole purpose of the federal government was to waste the people's money, so Jefferson was only fulfilling his patriotic duty to help in any way he could. If the government was so all fire bent on throwing away money, why not throw it away on the people? And what better people to waste it on than Jefferson Washington and his neighbors, the venerable citizens of Sweet Spot, Mississippi.

With the whole town's help, JW's was being transformed into ground zero for Sweet Spot's collective celebration commemorating their much-anticipated financial windfall.

Jefferson and the chief were up early loading up the trailer pulled behind the chief's tractor with every available rib from the neighboring Pottsville Piggly Wiggly. In anticipation of the evening's festivities, the ribs were already slow-cooking out back under the watchful eye of Mrs. Butts. And, in turn, Jefferson kept his own watchful eye on Mrs. Butts, lest there be nothing left for the evening's guests.

Mikey was helping Sarah and Felicity hang Christmas lights to add a festive air to the normally simple but utilitarian shack. Despite the summer heat, Mikey couldn't help humming Christmas carols, and everyone soon got caught up in the merriment.

Jeb grew a little teary-eyed as he watched Pedro and Conquistador hauling his latest batch of hooch from the cave to JW's. He'd never left the place completely dry before. But an event such as this one don't come but once in a lifetime. Besides, now he could afford to ramp up production as much as he liked. Shoot, he could even afford the regulatory fees to go legal and all.

Eustace Winchester was using every culinary trick he knew coming up with a few nouveaux hors d'oeuvres to supplement JW's main course of ribs. He could guarantee no one had ever eaten the likes of what he was preparing to serve.

Meanwhile, his brothers were shredding the field nearby JW's with their four-by-four before watering it down to lather up an impromptu mudding course. Nothing like a little mud to liven up any celebration.

* * * *

The team from CNN had mixed feelings about the whole thing, now that their assignment was coming to a close. Of course they were happy for Sweet Spot. They could even feel a certain pride in the knowledge that it was thanks to their crackerjack reporting in bringing the plight of Sweet Spot to the world that the town had finally earned its government salvation.

Yes, there was pride and joy. But there was something else as well. Having taken the trouble to hand wash the best of their limited wardrobes down at the fishin' hole to honor the significance of the evening's celebration, they couldn't help but acknowledge a certain sadness as well.

They'd all come to feel strangely at home with their new friends, the Spotters, including their caretakers, Sarah and little Felicity, and the government man Simon that the two girls had taken under their wing. There were their evening's hosts, Jefferson and

Mrs. Butts, helped by Jeb and the chief. The Winchesters had become family to Charlie. Certainly Scarlet and Pedro's relationship had become more than just physical. And yes, even Jennifer and Buck. Whatever their love-hate thing was, it was apparent to everyone but Jennifer.

She had no idea why she found herself borrowing some of Scarlet's lipstick and perfume. She'd convinced herself it was only out of respect for the enormity of the event they'd been invited to attend. On the other hand, she knew the mayor would be there, ogling her as usual, and she planned to make him suffer, give him one last look before she hightailed it out of town, back to civilization in the Big Apple.

That's right, civilization. Hot water, electricity, Starbucks. Television, internet, cell phone service. A place where everything you needed could be found within a block of your apartment, where you didn't have to hike through wilderness just to find another human being. You had so many neighbors you couldn't avoid them.

And yet... none of them knew your name. It was a place where Jennifer would go back to being just another lonely, nameless resident of the concrete jungle, writing words to put in other people's mouths.

What was all that nonsense about running her own newspaper? What was she thinking? Who did she think she was? Randolph Hearst? No one does that anymore.

Except Doc Miller. Sure, it wasn't the New York Times. But he enjoyed a loyal local readership. And he loved what he was doing. Maybe it wasn't about the size of the audience, or the paycheck for that matter. Maybe it was a matter of doing what you loved. And being loved.

Jennifer had to shake herself back to reality, staring at her reflection in the bottom of a tin plate to check her hair and lipstick. Sure, no one knew who she was back in New York, but who was there to love her in a place like Sweet Spot? That ridiculous Buck Jones? Please. She'd rather be sold into white slavery.

* * * *

Maybe he could just tie her up and keep her in his trailer, thought Buck, as he realized she'd soon be leaving town with the others. Now that that damned check had arrived, Jennifer Steele would be heading back to New York. As proud as he was over the windfall he'd procured for the people of Sweet Spot, he felt more like a failure than a success.

The money was great and all. Well, frankly, the money was beyond his imagination. And Buck certainly enjoyed a healthy imagination. But what did it all mean if he lost the girl in the end.

The woman had really gotten under his skin. He didn't know why. It's not like she was some kind o' centerfold pinup or anything. And he certainly wasn't looking for a relationship. Things had been just fine as they were. He'd vowed to stay clear of love all those years ago when it'd just about killed him. No, Buck Jones needed a woman 'bout as much as he needed an appendix.

And yet... he just couldn't stop thinking about her. Those green eyes, the sway of her caboose, the spitfire attitude. Damn her. He couldn't let her leave now, not before he'd had a chance to work that old Buck Jones magic on her.

He'd only been kidding about tying her up in his trailer. After all, everyone knows your business in a small town. Wouldn't be long 'for the neighbors caught on anyway.

Well, there was still the party tonight. Ever the optimist, Buck could feel it in his bones. He just knew the girl was about to come around, to succumb to his irresistible charms. It was just a matter of time. Buck finished buttoning up his good white shirt and slapping on a little extra smell good. That oughta do the trick.

And if not, maybe an underground bunker... Those pesky neighbors would never hear her cries for help.

* * * *

Simon Goldfarb couldn't believe his eyes. Sure, he'd imagined Sarah Pritchard was an angel the first time he'd laid eyes on her. He was a little disoriented that time he awoke from his swoon at the back of the church bus.

But he'd never seen a real angel before. Yet there she stood, asking him what he thought of the party dress she'd made all by herself in honor of the day's special occasion. Gone were the hoodie, jeans, and high top sneakers, all replaced by a little yellow sundress significantly tighter than the church girl'd intended, and a pair of high heels she'd borrowed from a mannequin over in Pottsville that wasn't putting much mileage on 'em anyway.

Simon was so mesmerized by the legs he never knew the girl had that he didn't even notice the court-mandated ankle bracelet she was required to wear for another six months yet, a temporary vestige of her former life.

Her half-shaven head with its Technicolor locks persisted as well, but Simon wouldn't have cared if she'd been completely bald. It was her eyes, her face, and most of all, her smile. He was completely lost in her smile. His anxieties, his allergies, even his irritable bowel. All lost, lost at sea in a tidal wave of love. Simon was drowning in Sarah Pritchard's smile.

But then there was that damned check. What had he done? Simon had only himself to blame. Now that the check had arrived, he'd have to return to New York.

But how? How could he leave? Who'd have ever thought Simon Goldfarb would find salvation in a Southern Baptist Church? But he had. Whatever had been missing in Simon's life was found in Sweet Spot, Mississippi. Whatever hole had existed in the fabric of his small pathetic existence had been filled, mended better than new, by a woman who smiled sunbeams.

What would he ever do without her?

Not to mention the kid. While Sarah made him feel loved, little Felicity Barnes made him feel needed, a feeling Simon had never felt before. He'd always felt completely disposable, like a paper cup, or a Kleenex. No one had ever needed Simon Goldfarb. And he couldn't be sure why Felicity made him feel that way. The kid was so darn smart that Simon seemed to rely on her more than the other way around. And yet, she was just a kid after all. You never knew when a grownup might come in handy. And Simon wanted to be little Felicity's grownup. He wanted to be there for her.

Simon was just beginning to crave a Xanax when that other woman in his life popped out from behind the dressing curtain at the back of the bus.

"Ta daaa!" shouted Felicity, arms spread, batting her eyelashes, as she modeled the first dress she could ever remember wearing. It was a miniature version of Sarah's.

Simon felt a pain in his chest as his heart shattered within it.

Felicity saw the discomfort written all over his face and looked down at her dress. "Don't ya like it?" She looked back up at Simon wondering if she'd done something wrong. "Is it too grown up? I know I'm just a kid, but I wanted both your women to be a matching set."

She took a step closer and looked up at Simon who was wiping his cheek with the back of his hand. "You got somethin' in your eye?"

Simon had to turn away to hide his tears. "Yes, that's it. Something in my eye. The dress is perfect, Sweetie. Perfect," as he knelt down and squeezed her in a bear hug.

The little girl burst out in giggles. "Sarah! Help!" she squealed. "I can't breathe."

And that's when Sarah Pritchard fell for Simon Goldfarb.

At first, she thought Simon was a little too bottled up for her, too emotionally constipated. But that all changed when she saw the scene that played out right in front of her. The man was full of emotion. But like lava boiling below a volcano, it needed to find its way to the surface. The man just needed a little coaxing was all.

Sarah couldn't turn away as she covered her mouth and began to shed a few tears of her own.

"Sorry child, but you're on your own. That's what happens when you flirt with men. Playin' with fire, girl. Playing with fire. Get too close and they just up and take your breath away."

Chapter 21

Scarlet couldn't seem to catch her breath, as she stared at her face in the mirror. What was wrong with her? She'd never felt this way about a man before. Just the thought of seeing him sent her all atwitter. She couldn't wait to get to the party. Pedro'd promised to be there.

She hadn't wanted to put him in danger, and told him not to come, but he'd insisted. Said he wouldn't miss it for the world. No one had seen that man from immigration since he'd appeared out of nowhere that day at the church. Maybe he fell for it when the town sent him on a wild goose chase.

She still shouldn't have let him come. She didn't know what she'd do if something happened to him. She didn't really want to move to Mexico. Her Spanish wasn't so good. But when Pedro said he thought it would be safe to come to the party, Scarlet got so excited she couldn't think straight.

So she spent all morning in front of a mirror working on her makeup, pulling out every last trick she knew, as if she were competing in the Miss America Pageant. Only, she wasn't looking to win no tiara this time. She was going for a much bigger prize. This time, Scarlet wanted to win the whole enchilada. Her enchilada. She couldn't go back to New York without her Pedro.

She didn't know what skills the man had other than... well... you know. But she knew there were plenty of Spanish speaking illegals in New York City. Didn't know if they were Mexicans or Puerto Ricans or what. Didn't care. But she didn't see why Pedro couldn't maybe blend in. Now Conquistador might be a problem. Scarlet couldn't picture the stallion pullin' no tourist buggy through Central Park. They'd have to figure that out later.

She only knew she couldn't live without her man. Push come to shove, she'd go back to Mexico with him. Shoot, she'd move to Spain if she had to. That's just how crazy things had gotten. The hell with showing up fashionably late for the party. She didn't care if she was the first one there. She just had to see him, touch him, drink him in like some fancy cocktail at the beach, you know, the ones with them little umbrellas in 'em.

Scarlet couldn't wait another minute. And that Pedro had better show up early.

* * * *

That Pedro, however, would be unavoidably detained.

He'd suffered more than one concussion playing polo, but recovering from head trauma wasn't necessarily one of those skills that improved with practice.

So it took quite some time clearing out the cobwebs and getting what was left of his head screwed back on before he could recall just how he'd ended up with his hands tied and mouth taped shut in the trunk of someone's car.

He'd just emerged from the woods on his way to JW's, looking forward to seeing his blonde goddess, when he recognized the smell of garlic and cheap cologne. He didn't actually see who'd hit him on the back of the head with what felt like a sledge hammer, but there weren't a lot of folks these days drove a car with such a spacious trunk.

Spacious or not, Pedro intended to speak to the management about the facility's climate control. It was probably the life-threatening 150-degree temperature of the locked black trunk baking in the hot Mississippi sun combined with Pedro's resultant thirst that dragged him kicking and screaming back to consciousness.

He didn't know how long he'd been there or when he'd be let out. In fact, it soon occurred to him that he might never be let out, that that was the plan all along, to die in the trunk of a mobster's car. Even if that wasn't the case, and he was indeed intended to be freed at some point, he wasn't sure the alternative would be preferable to being slow-roasted like a rack of JW's ribs.

Pedro'd never been a big fan of Rocco Buttafuoco. Unfortunately, Rocco was never a big polo fan either. Whatever Rocco had planned for Pedro that day was certainly sure to be no walk in the park. In fact, any walking at all would be questionable at best with two broken legs, or next to impossible with no legs at all, as being drawn and quartered, his dismembered limbs buried over four separate state lines, was not out of the question.

So when Pedro began to pray, he didn't know whether to pray for his release or pray to be left alone to die in peace while still in possession of all his body parts.

Regardless, no sooner had he begun to pray, than he saw the light... a blinding eye-piercing light, as the lid of the trunk flew open.

"Well, look what we got here," said Rocco. "Damn wetbacks. They'll do anything to sneak into the country. Were you hopin' to bum a ride all the way to Palm Beach?"

Pedro still hadn't quite focused enough to see his captor, but the voice was enough to confirm the man's identity. All he could think to do from his fetal position in the trunk of the car was to suck in some fresh air through his nose and shake his head "no" to the suggestion that he wanted to go back to Palm Beach. That's where the boss was, so that was the last place Pedro wanted to turn up.

"No? Well we'll have to see about that. You don't really need to go if you don't want to, well, not all of you anyway. No, I only need just enough so he knows it's you, like maybe your finger. Oh, and enough to know you're dead, like maybe your head."

Moments earlier, Pedro wanted only to get out of that trunk. Now he only wanted to retreat deeper into it.

He then felt the trunk of the car dip under Rocco's weight as he put one foot up on the bumper and leaned in to place a hand on Pedro's shoulder.

"Of course, there is a way out for you."

Pedro was all ears.

"There's a little matter I need your help with. So maybe if you cooperate, I can put a good word in for you."

Pedro couldn't imagine what he could possibly help Rocco with. He didn't think he'd be very good at anything Rocco needed. After all, Pedro was a lover, not a killer.

"See, there's still a matter of a missing horse."

Oh no. Conquistador. Pedro shook his head "no" again.

"Maybe the spic don't understand English so good."

Rocco reached out and ripped the duct tape from Pedro's mouth. "Why don't you tell me exactly what about give up the damn horse you don't seem to understand? It's that horse or your life."

Pedro's mouth burned from the pull of the tape, but he was way too hot and thirsty to dwell on it. "The horse, he is gone."

Rocco pulled the gun from his shoulder holster and tapped Pedro on the nose with it. "You think I'm stupid, don't you. I'm just a little tired of getting my Ferragamos full of shit wandering all over this barnyard of a town lookin' for you and that glue factory of yours. So why don't you just tell me where your smarter half is and I'll let you live."

Pedro never claimed to have much going on in the thinking department, but of one thing he could be certain. He'd be a dead man as soon as they got their hands on Conquistador. They wouldn't need Pedro anymore after that.

"OK, Meester Rocco, you win. You found us. Now let me go and I will bring Conquistador back to Florida for you. After all, you cannot drive a horse home in your car."

Rocco enjoyed a good belly laugh. "What makes you think I was taking the animal back to Florida? Believe me, that's the last thing the boss wants. He's already convinced the insurance company to pay up. He don't want no horse no more."

Pedro squinted at the man, not wanting to think the worst.

"That's right, I've been instructed to make sure that horse don't show up nowhere… ever," he added, fondling his gun.

Pedro would have spit in the man's face if he'd had any saliva left after his afternoon dehydrating in the trunk of a car. So he did the next best thing, uttering two of the first English words he'd ever learned on the streets of Rio.

"Fuck you!"

That's when Rocco turned out the lights.

Chapter 22

First thing Buck did when he arrived at JW's was to tack that ol' FEMA check up on the wall over the bar with his bowie knife. That way everyone could get a gander at her. It bein' a Saturday and all, Buck would wait 'til Monday to officially deposit it in a bank. 'Til then, it surely was a sight to behold, a sight most folks would never see in five lifetimes.

And as befitting such an occasion, the town certainly seemed to have gone all out. Buck had to hand it to the folks of Sweet Spot. Give 'em any reason whatsoever to party and you got yourself a regular hoedown on your hands. Well, take a handful o' po' folk and stir in ten million dollars, you got yourself ten million reasons to party.

Things were already in full swing by the time he'd arrived. The air was thick with the smell of smoked pork, and Mrs. Butts had already won the bobbing for pigs' feet contest. Jeb Clancey's impromptu bar, an eclectic collection of old barrels and a horse trough hauled out only for special occasions, was open for business, and his late summer brew was a big hit.

The Winchesters wasted no time at all breaking in the mudding course they'd designed special for the event. Scarlet sat snug as a bug between the boys, knowing full well the only way to keep the mud off her outfit was to be right inside the very vehicle splashing it everywhere else.

The out-of-towners were floored by Mikey's prowess at the ivories. It was custom in Sweet Spot to haul the old church piano to wherever a gathering occurred. Once set up, they couldn't tear Mikey away from it. The boy couldn't read or write, but he could play anything he'd ever heard on that damn piano. Anything from a nursery rhyme that Felicity might have whistled to a concerto by Bach he'd heard once on a radio over in Pottsville. Some would call him a savant, but the folks of Sweet Spot just called him a miracle.

Yes, the party appeared destined to go down in the annals of Sweet Spot as a fitting launch to the town's newfound prosperity.

And yet, Buck had something more important on his agenda. His selfless mission on behalf of the town apparently accomplished, he could check that one off his list and move on to the next challenge on his horizon.

After a couple of quick shots of Jeb's white lightening to bolster his mettle, Buck turned from the bar with a fire burning in his belly to go on the prowl for his little northern spitfire.

He quickly spotted his prey perched on a folding lawn chair next to the water-wheel slowly turning on the side of JW's, a relic that used to power the old grist mill in days past. She was sipping on a little something Jeb had prepared special for her sensitive northern palate, employing just enough of Felicity's sweet tea to hide the true nature of Jeb's high octane fuel.

The proprietor of Felicity's Sweet Tea herself sat next to Jennifer in a matching chair, her shiny new patent leather shoes swinging high above the ground. She was sporting her favorite sunglasses, the ones with lenses shaped like frogs' heads.

Felicity had been asking Jennifer if she thought there'd be enough FEMA money left, only after rebuilding the town, of course, to launch a national advertising campaign for her sweet tea.

Buck could tell by the look on Jennifer's face that she didn't know if she was dealing with an eight-year-old orphan or Donald Trump. Despite the Norman Rockwell beauty of the scene, Buck knew if he was gonna make his move he had to displace the kid.

"Hey there, Miss Felicity, Jeb tells me he's runnin' low on his stock of sweet tea mixer. Maybe you ought to start workin' on another batch."

Felicity wasn't falling for it, and didn't even budge from her chair. She was always keenly aware of her inventory. "That's impossible, Buck...uh Mayor. I left him enough tea to supply all of Pottsville as part of my contingency plan, in case we had crashers to our little soiree. Didn't want to seem unneighborly."

Buck saw he'd underestimated the kid, again, and would have to appeal to the girl's feminine instincts, at whatever stage of development they might be.

"Hmmm. Don't know why he'd say such a thing then. But apparently Jeb's not the only one in need of your services. The entertainment says he needs someone at the piano to turn the music pages for him."

That was the signal that let Felicity know something was up. Everyone knew Mikey Dunham didn't read no music. He played everything by ear. So when she looked up through squinted eyes at the mayor to see what kind of game he was playing, she saw Buck give her an exaggerated wink of one eye, a jerk of his head away from Jennifer, and a pleading frown on his face.

Felicity looked over at Jennifer, quickly assessed the lay of the land, and beamed a smile back at Buck.

"Oh Jeeze, Mr. Mayor, I'd better get over there lickety split... uh... you know... to... uh... help Mikey turn those pages." She jumped to her feet and held out her hand toward her chair like a theater attendant. "Why don't you take my chair, sir, and entertain Miss Steele in my absence?"

Despite the touch of overacting, Buck was appreciative of the girl's support.

Plopping down in the newly vacant chair next to Jennifer, they both watched the little girl skip away.

"That FEMA money sure is gonna make a difference in that girl's life," remarked Buck.

"Something tells me, money or not, she plans to make good use of her humble beginnings in her memoirs when she runs for president," Jennifer replied.

"Well, she has you to thank, we all do, for getting our story out. Otherwise we'd have never seen a dime from the government. I don't know what we'd have done without you." Nothing like a little flattery to grease the wheels of romance, he thought.

Jennifer knew what this was about. She could practically feel the man pawing at her. And yet, she appreciated the effort. If nothing else, he was persistent. She didn't want to encourage him, but she could at least return the compliment, out of simple courtesy.

"Oh, don't be so modest, Mayor. You seem to have kept things in order, despite the disaster suffered by the town. Everyone seems well cared for, in good spirits, almost as if this was their natural state of affairs."

Buck almost choked on his cocktail at that last remark, but quickly threw the thought aside as he saw the girl was clearly encouraging his advances. Nothing like a lady complimenting a gentleman to let him know he's got an all access pass into her panties.

And nothing like a shot or two of Jeb's rocket fuel in your belly to get a man's courage up.

"Please, I told you, call me Buck," he responded, gently touching her hand.

* * * *

Sarah didn't need any inspiration from the kind of spirits Jeb Clancey was peddling. She was strictly on the wagon these days. But it wasn't some ankle bracelet, a reminder of her former meth-fueled existence, that kept her clean. It was the Lord. Sarah Pritchard was high on Jesus.

Yet now, just when she thought the Lord was all she needed, that same Lord saw fit to bring her to even higher heights. No, it wasn't the money. She didn't give a hoot 'bout no check from the government. It was the deliverer of that check. Not the Lord, but a man of this earth. A man in the form of Simon Goldfarb.

Speaking of Simon Goldfarb, try as she might, Sarah couldn't keep from snorting in laughter, snorting like the little baby piglet narrowly evading capture at the hands of her government man. It seemed little Felicity had Simon Goldfarb wrapped tightly 'round her little finger, and Felicity couldn't possibly go rolling around in the mud herself to catch the little piggy, not all gussied up in her new dress she couldn't.

The pig was Mrs. Butts's contribution to the party entertainment. Nothing like a pig-catching contest to break the ice. Well, Simon Goldfarb had broken the ice and fallen clear through it. Most folks managed to remain on their feet, but Simon hadn't fully acquired his mud legs yet. Still, if Miss Felicity Barnes asked Simon to catch that piglet for her, Simon had to catch that Piglet. If only the slippery critter would cooperate.

Simon's Jewish mother always told him to stay away from pork. Well, so far, Simon had nothing to worry about. He hadn't even come close to the damn squealing football. If nothing else, the whole town was thoroughly entertained. Most of all, a giggling Felicity Barnes, and, for the second time that day, a teary-eyed Sarah Pritchard.

There was a reason Simon Goldfarb was chosen for this assignment by FEMA, a reason this man was brought into Sarah's life. Despite being at complete peace with her life in service to the Lord, her Lord had other plans for her, plans that went beyond himself. The Lord saw fit to open Sarah's eyes, and heart, to another.

Sarah had no idea what tomorrow would bring. Would Simon return to New York? Would he take her with him? Or would he stay? She didn't know where they would be, but she knew they would be there together. Of that she was certain. She knew it in her heart. She had faith in the Lord, and would leave the driving to him.

* * * *

Simon Goldfarb was never one to have much faith in anything, least of all himself. So here he stood, at the crossroads of his life, with no signs to guide him. He'd feared for his life when he boarded that plane for Sweet Spot. But he really had nothing to fear, for he had no life to lose, not one worth speaking of. Turns out it was only upon arriving in Sweet Spot that he'd finally found his life. He found it in Sarah Pritchard's smile.

But now what? He had to leave for New York in the morning. His desk must be overflowing with backed up paperwork. Simon Goldfarb needed guidance. Yet he didn't feel the guiding hand of the Lord as Sarah Pritchard did. Simon Goldfarb would have to turn elsewhere for divine inspiration.

That's when Simon turned to Jeb Clancey's brew.

And before he knew it, he was covered head to toe in mud, chasing pork rinds 'round a pig pen. A couple of weeks ago, just the thought of touching mud would have sent a shiver through his irritable bowels and clenched his allergic airways closed. No amount of medication could have saved him. Yet here he was, wallowing in it with the best of them, all at the behest of his two ladies.

And he loved it.

Medication-free, symptom-free, anxiety-free. For the first time in his life, Simon knew he was where he was supposed to be, doing what he was supposed to be doing. The stars had all aligned, and Simon Goldfarb had hit his groove.

Now it was just a matter of time. Damn his mother and her chosen people. That pig was as good as his.

* * * *

Despite a decidedly pork-themed soiree, everyone knew the Winchesters would never presume to serve any themselves. That had always been Jefferson's department. But whatever it was the Winchesters were serving as hors d'oeuvres was an undeniable hit. It teased the palate with an elegant pairing of delicate French cuisine combined with bold strokes of inbred American hillbilly.

As always, however, Eustace Winchester never revealed the source of his ingredients, maintaining that essential air of mystery to the Winchester fare. But ambiance wasn't the only reason. There was a more serious element to this secrecy.

After all, all true hunters possess an innate sense of the conservationist. And by nature, that delicate ecosystem of backcountry roads in close proximity to native critter habitat, so essential to the ready procurement of fresh roadkill, was a critical element of fine backwoods cuisine, and had to be protected at all costs.

And yet, despite the unabashed success of his first stab at catering, all was not well in the Winchester kitchen.

Charlie Green was not happy. But it wasn't the ingredients that offended Charlie's delicate city boy sensibilities and had him bickering with Eustace like an old married couple. It was that all too natural progression from backwoods master chef to the fine art of taxidermy that got Charlie's dander up. It was one thing to create gastronomic masterpieces from their hunter's bounty, but why anyone would want to immortalize, for the sake of posterity, the rat-face of an opossum, or its armored cousin the armadillo, escaped him.

As quickly as Eustace strategically displayed the little fellows among the other party décor, an embarrassed Charlie would fetch them back to the truck. Whenever he confronted Eustace with his concern, Eustace would simply answer as any true artist, that it wasn't a matter of choice. He did it because he was compelled to do so, just as one is compelled to breathe. It had gotten to the point where Charlie was barely on speaking terms with the man.

Yet, despite the chilly atmosphere at Winchester Catering, it wasn't long before the party began really heating up. As the sun began to set, the crowd grew excited in anticipation of the renowned Winchester pyrotechnic fireworks show. Folks were still reeling from the boys' Fourth of July effort. Assorted minor burns had healed, and most had fully recovered their hearing. Word about town was that this show, in honor of the occasion, would make the Fourth look like the candles on little Felicity's eighth birthday cake.

Fueled by bellies full of that highly combustible combination of Jeb's high octane lighter fluid and that wonderful Winchester cuisine, it was time to kick things up a notch.

And what better way for small town USA to celebrate than gettin' all liquored up and hauling out a cache of heavy explosives sufficient to take out a midsized Middle Eastern country.

Chapter 23

"That can't be safe," offered Jennifer, taking another swig of liquor from her red Solo cup, as she watched Bubba Winchester run detonating wire from the battery of the truck to a stack of rusty metal drums piled at the edge of the woods.

"I can certainly understand your concern, Sweetie," Buck replied, surreptitiously refilling her cup from his own, "but them boys served two tours in Iraq as ordinance experts, so if there ever was a group of fellas qualified to blow shit up, it's them."

"Is it even legal to possess that stuff?" she countered, watching them hauling barrels of gunpowder across the field?"

"You don't want to go there, young lady," answered Buck, strategically placing an arm about her shoulders.

"What's that supposed to mean?" she countered, feeling her head spin a little.

"Of course it's legal."

"Says who?"

"Says the Constitution. Maybe they never heard of a little thing called the second amendment up in New York."

Buck knew Jeb's love potion was taking effect when he noticed that the normally argumentative Yankee let that one slide. In fact, Buck's whole master plan seemed to be progressing nicely right on schedule.

With one arm around the girl, he couldn't have timed things any better for the opening salvo from the Winchester's show. The concussive shock wave from the very first detonation seemed to carry the skittish little filly completely off the ground and right into Buck's waiting arms.

The girl may have been shivering in fear, but ol' Buck was in heaven as he relished the feel of her face nuzzling his neck for shelter.

Buck would have to remember to thank the boys for this, he thought, gently stroking her hair and breathing in her scent.

* * * *

Felicity was jumping up and down in ecstasy at the flashes of light and deafening thunder provided courtesy of team Winchester. Sarah held her hands firmly over the child's ears to protect her hearing.

Simon lay prostrate under one of JW's picnic tables reliving crippling flashbacks of the horrors of war, which was odd, given that Simon had never served. He was apparently reliving someone else's horrors by proxy. Besides, given Simon's lifelong issues, if he suffered from post-traumatic stress disorder, it was probably attributable to that rough voyage of his through the birth canal.

As if the staccato pop pop pop from the Winchesters' fully automatic machine guns wasn't enough to make someone think they were smack in the middle of a war zone, it was the 50 caliber turret-mounted to the back of their truck that let you know you were on the losing side.

And just when the combined firepower of all three Winchesters in unison could have led professional reviewers of the event to criticize the evening's performance for an overabundance of sound to the detriment of sight, the boys dropped their firearms in unison only to don their tanks of gasoline and nitrogen propellant to paint the sky in what could only be considered flamethrower art.

Yet no sooner had the light show concluded than the boys reverted back to good ol' gun powder, advancing to the heavy artillery. The accuracy of their bazooka and mortar attack on the kegs of gunpowder placed at the edge of the woods was truly impressive.

Whether under a picnic table or on it, the combination of sights, sounds, and altered mental states— that part, courtesy of Jeb Clancey— transported all the New Yorkers to a place no Blue Ray with Dolby surround sound could ever recreate.

Mikey's accompaniment on church piano only added to the other-worldly ambience of the event. During each lull in the full-on military assault, one could appreciate Mikey's exhaustive repertoire of military-themed ditties. Always happy to reprise his Independence Day playlist, the crowd, excusing Simon's incapacitation, couldn't help standing up a little straighter to Mikey's rendition of John Phillip Souza's Stars and Stripes.

But it was during the Winchesters' perfectly placed temporary halt to hostilities to wheel out Grandpappy's old Civil War cannon, that Mikey began a flawless rendition of Tchaikovsky's 1812 Overture. And just as if they'd rehearsed it a million times, the cannon fire commenced right on cue at the overture's climax and continued until Earl Winchester fired the final volley making a direct hit on the old Chevy El Camino wreck the boys had been saving for just such an occasion. Strategically placed among their last kegs of gunpowder, the Chevy's full tank of gas brought an incendiary conclusion to the boys' shock and awe campaign.

With only the four-story flames and oily black smoke of the gasoline fire remaining, the ensuing silence was broken only by the whole town's ears ringing in unison, a fitting soundtrack to a crowd of wide eyes, open mouths, and thumping hearts.

* * * *

Jennifer hadn't seen a thing since the opening explosion, her face buried in Buck's shoulder. Scarlet held her hands over her heart, not in any sort of patriotic fervor, but only to keep it from leaping from her chest.

"Is it over yet?" moaned Simon from under the shelter of the picnic table.

"Let's do it again!" cried Felicity, shaking Sarah's hand as she bounced up and down in glee.

Other than the chief, it took some time for anyone to move. The chief, however, had been immediately inspired to begin a ceremonial dance about the inferno at the edge of the field. The image of the chief, caked in mud, dancing about the bonfire, combining mouthfuls of Jeb's fuel with a makeshift torch to blow flames ten feet in the air, led many to question whether the pagan ritual represented a war dance or one of thanks to the spirits of FEMA.

Buck, however, observing the chief's silhouette gyrating about the redneck version of a bonfire, thought the dance looked strangely familiar to him. Although he tried to convince himself that many of the chief's dances appeared similar to the untrained eye of the white man, he couldn't help but notice a little pick up in the evening breeze.

* * * *

It was not without a fight that Sarah finally convinced Felicity it was past her bedtime, and time to retire for the evening. It took both of them to convince Simon it was safe to emerge from the cover of the picnic table.

It was only the residual shock of the show that kept everyone's emotions distracted enough to hold it together at the departure of one of the first guests to leave. Knowing Simon would be leaving for New York in the morning, the man was barraged with a bevy of bear hugs, pats on the back, and heartfelt tears of thanks for the essential role he'd played in securing their financial salvation.

As mayor, it was Buck's idea to throw together an impromptu ceremony honoring Simon Goldfarb and presenting him with the keys to the city.

"Shoot," complained Jeb, taking a closer look, "that's just the key to your trailer home."

Buck was annoyed. "Well what better represents the key to a city than the key to the mayor's mansion?"

"But you don't even lock your door. You might as well give him the key to my cave."

"Well you just ought to be thankful we have ol' Simon here to get you out of your temporary storm domicile and back into a real home," countered Buck, throwing Jeb a wink and a warning glare simultaneously.

More than one sleeve was dampened watching Simon and Sarah walk off into the night holding Felicity's hands between them.

* * * *

But Simon's absence wasn't the only one evoking tears that night.

Scarlet Witherspoon was a mess. She never would have imagined she'd have needed waterproof mascara.

Yet, once she was no longer in danger of being thrown from a monster truck or being incinerated by a flamethrower or being caught up in a mortar barrage, Scarlet's thoughts immediately returned to her troubled love life.

Where was Pedro? He said he would be there. This was all uncharted territory for the beauty queen. She'd never been stood up before. And she wasn't taking it well.

This was no simple case of tardiness. The man was the only one in the whole town missing. No, this was something serious, or so her woman's intuition told her.

Charlie found her drowning her sorrows over at Jeb's watering hole, black mascara smearing her cheeks.

"What's wrong, Sweetie?" he asked.

"Oh, hey, Charlie," she replied, pouring another shot into her plastic receptacle.

"You look as if it's the end of the world," he said, taking the stool next to her. "Don't tell me you're gonna miss little ol' Sweet Spot. The Big Apple misses you. And you know you're long overdue for a manicure, if you don't mind me saying," he added taking her hand in his.

"Well, of course I mind," she laughed, yanking her hand away, hiding her less than pristine fingernails. "What kind of gentleman are you?"

But as she pulled her hand away, Charlie saw her bring it back to her face to wipe away some persistent tears.

"Whoa, what's going on?" he prodded, putting his arm around her.

"It's Pedro," she squeaked, barely able to get the words out.

"Oh, this is serious. Matters of the heart. Tell me about it," he added, glancing fondly over at Eustace.

Scarlet meant to explain her concerns to Charlie in a well-thought-out and coherent fashion. Yet when she opened her mouth to speak, something stuck in her throat and all that came out was a heart-wrenching wail of sorrow.

Charlie took her in his arms, letting her sob freely into his chest.

"It's OK Sweetie, let it out. Everything's going to be OK," he assured her, patting her on the back.

Her words came out in pieces, shattered between moans and gasps of air. "He's dead! He's dead! I just know it!"

"What?! Who? Pedro? Pedro's dead?" Charlie held the sobbing creature out at arm's length, looking her in the eye. "What are you talking about?"

Scarlet just went limp, shaking her head back and forth. "He's dead. I can feel it. If he weren't, he'd be here. I just know it. He wouldn't let me leave tomorrow without him."

Charlie had to support the woman's full weight as her legs gave out from under her.

"Whoa there. Hang on a minute. That's impossible."

But Charlie wasn't so sure about that. Over the years, he'd seen ample evidence of Scarlet's hold on men. Not a man alive could walk away from Scarlet Witherspoon. Not this beauty queen. No, a man would have to be dead... or crippled, if one were to place a positive spin on things.

"He's dead," she persisted.

"Now hold on. Have you looked for him?"

Scarlet was momentarily confused. After all, she'd never had to look for a man before. She blew her nose on some toilet paper from the roll she'd commandeered for her personal emotional needs.

"Well, no. But what are you sayin'? Y'all want me to go traipsin' 'round the woods in the middle o' the night till I trip over a dead body?"

"Stop saying that. He's not dead," he answered.

And yet, her choice of words gave Charlie an idea as he looked over at Eustace and his brothers thoroughly embroiled in a friendly buffalo chip skeet shooting competition. The night vision goggles they'd given each other last Christmas rendered the night time light conditions irrelevant for target shooting.

"Hey Euee!" he shouted.

Eustace flipped up his goggles and trotted over to see what Charlie wanted.

"Howdy, Miss Scarlet. Wonderful night, ain't it?"

Scarlet tried her best to smile for the man, but her heart wasn't in it.

"Why what's with the long face, ma'am? You ain't havin' a good time? How 'bout another lap around the course in the mud buggy?"

"No, no," she hastily responded. "Thank you very much for the offer, Eustace. But I think I've had my fill."

"Oh, well is there somethin' me or the boys can get for ya? Anything at all? Your wish is our command."

Scarlet didn't know what to say. But Charlie did.

"In fact, there is something you can do, Euee. How'd you like to go hunting?"

Eustace was briefly taken aback. Miss Scarlet didn't seem the huntin' type. But, he and the boys were always game for hunting, day or night.

"You lookin' to come a huntin' with me an' the boys? We always love a little company. And I'm not speakin' for myself now," he added, smiling at Charlie, "but I know my brothers would be tickled pink to have a pretty girl along for the ride."

Charlie saw the look of dread on Scarlet's face and saw fit to correct the record.

"No, Euee, Scarlet isn't looking to come along. She has a big day ahead of her tomorrow and all. But she was hoping you might go hunting for her."

"Oh, OK. Sure. And what is it we huntin' for the little lady?"

Scarlet looked at Charlie, not sure where this whole thing was going.

"Well, frankly, Euee, it's Pedro. We need you to hunt down Pedro."

"Pedro? You want us to shoot Pedro?" Eustace turned to Scarlet. "You don't need to say if you don't want, but what did Pedro do to you, ma'am? Must o' been somethin' bad if your wantin' us to kill him and all. I mean, not that I'm opposed. After all, it ain't every day we get to go hunt and kill a man."

Scarlet's eyes went wide and her mouth dropped open as she slowly turned from Eustace to Charlie.

"No, no," Charlie objected. "She doesn't want you to shoot him. She just wants you to find him."

"Oh. Oh. I see. Phew, I mean, Pedro seems like a nice enough fella. Seem a shame to kill 'im. Well, OK. When you want us to start?"

Charlie looked at the mess that Scarlet had become.

"Would it be too much to ask to start tonight?"

"Tonight? Shoot. Yeah, sure. We just about blown everything up here anyways. Always got everything we need for huntin' right in the truck." He then flipped his night vision goggles back down and smiled. "Even get to use the new toys what Santa brought."

Eustace swung about to gather up the posse. "Hey boys!"

But Charlie grabbed him by the hand before he could get away. "You be careful now."

Eustace gave Charlie a wink and darted over to his brothers like a six-year-old school boy let out for recess.

"Hey, boys! Git the truck! We goin' huntin'!"

"Huntin'? This time o' night?" asked Bubba.

"What we huntin' fer?" added Earl.

Eustace couldn't contain his glee. "We huntin' the baddest of 'em all. The king o' beasts."

"Shoot," scoffed Earl. "Ain't no lions round these parts."

"Well, I ain't talkin' bout no lions." Eustace was practically jumping up and down. "We huntin' human."

Earl and Bubba's mouths dropped open as Eustace nodded his head in confirmation. This was too good to be true. It had been quite a spell since they last hunted human.

Just to commemorate the importance of the event, the boys quickly applied some of Chief's war paint before firing up the truck to go fetch the dogs.

As the truck flew past the remaining revelers kicking up mud, a groan of disappointment could be heard coming from the cab of the truck, and Eustace could be heard defending himself in reply.

"Well don't blame me. It was Miss Scarlet said we couldn't shoot him."

Chapter 24

Jennifer didn't remember how she got into the hot tub.

She still had just enough of her wits about her to know that everything was beginning to get a little fuzzy... a lot fuzzy. At least she still had her clothes on... well, most of them anyway. She should have known she was in trouble when Jeb's jet fuel lost its bite and began to faintly resemble something that was actually meant to be taken internally.

The last thing she remembered before her momentary lapse was that the party seemed to be winding down. The mayor, however, was not. He seemed as fresh as the minute he'd arrived. And he never left her side. As sticky as pine sap, and persistent as herpes.

Yet, maybe it was just the fermented grain talking, but she wasn't entirely grossed out by the man anymore. Maybe she'd been a little too hard on the mayor. She had to admit she'd found all the attention more than a little flattering. Old Buck was clearly driven to distraction by her feminine charms, caught in her web, so to speak.

On the other hand, looking about, she wasn't sure who was caught in whose web, or tub, to be exact. If not for her ever-rising blood alcohol level, Jennifer might have realized it wasn't an actual hot tub she was soaking in. Further gone than she'd imagined, perhaps the kiddie pool's Sponge Bob motif should have given it away.

Buck knew he had to take things slow. The filly was skittish, so the couple of extra bucks he'd given Mikey to keep the cocktails and romantic music coming was money well spent. But having the boy continually top off the kiddie pool with water buckets heated up on JW's grille was sheer genius. The girl never even noticed as Mikey discreetly kept things nice and steamy. Buck was beginning to think the boy understood much more than he let on.

The seduction seemed to be a slow motion affair, but as every good fisherman knows, patience is a virtue. Well acquainted with this particular prey, Buck never imagined she'd peel off all her clothes and willingly come bouncing into a hot tub sporting just her birthday suit. So Buck wasn't dissuaded by the fact that she still had her shorts and shirt on. She had, however removed her shoes, and, accepting his hand for support, stepped daintily into the steaming hot "spa" with a shirtless Buck.

It may not have been much, as he couldn't even appreciate some wet T-shirt action on account of the dim light conspiring with the girl's modest chest, but it was a start. And Buck, ever the optimist, remained confident that it was just a matter of time until Mikey's romantic serenade and JW's soothing hot spring, along with a little nudge from Jeb's jungle juice of course, made the rest of her clothes fall off.

The steaming hot water seemed to melt the stress right out of Jennifer. She soon forgot all about the fact that she was getting on a plane in the morning headed back to work and the rat race of New York City. No, for now, all that big-city stress and pollution had been washed right out of her mind, all the soot and noise flushed away, courtesy of a therapeutic dose of Jeb's brain Drano.

Her mind was completely decontaminated, squeaky clean, and open for business, unfettered by fear and doubt, open to experience life fully and completely. Jennifer Steele was ready for something big to happen, something good.

She may have been more than tipsy, but she wasn't completely blind, not yet. She knew the man at her side was up to no good, was leading her astray. Yet something was telling her that was OK. Buck Jones may have been a redneck pig, but he seemed a good man, and a girl couldn't be too picky these days. Besides, judging by the way he kept stealing glances at her from the corner of his eye, he was, for better or worse, her redneck pig. And at the end of the day, each time this little piggy leaned over the edge of the tub to fetch another cocktail that kept magically appearing, she couldn't help but appreciate what a cute butt he had. And a cute butt's gotta count for something.

Jennifer was completely relaxed, from the hair on her head to the tip of her painted big toe. A high end health spa, or a Sponge Bob kiddie pool, none of that mattered. She was right where she was supposed to be.

The smoke from the fireworks had cleared, replaced by a different kind of light show, a country sky full of twinkling stars.

"Isn't it beautiful?" she sighed, leaning her head back over the plastic rim of the kiddie pool to take in more of the view.

Buck couldn't agree more, taking advantage of the astrological distraction above to sneak a long hard look at the view just 12 inches to his left. From her silky hair, to her graceful neck, to her perfect little ears, to her full kissable lips. He couldn't see her eyes as they gazed upward, but Buck Jones was already well acquainted with those spellbinding green orbs. He'd been drowning in their depths from that first moment back at the trailer when he'd looked up from his broken generator wondering what smelled like shit.

He'd been lost in the cobra's stare ever since.

How did this happen? Buck Jones was done with women, at least for anything other than sport. He'd been there, done that, but things hadn't exactly worked out so good. Hadn't worked out so good? That had to be the understatement of all time. Shoot, it damn near killed him. There was a time Buck was in so deep that, when it ended, he almost couldn't climb his way out. Those were the forgotten years, a part of his life ripped from his chest and buried six feet under.

But that was a long time ago. He didn't really think about those days anymore. He couldn't. If he did, he'd never be able to get out of bed. So he didn't. He just automatically woke up with the sun each day out of habit, and lived each day only in the present. There was no point in dwelling in the past. Buck Jones didn't believe in ghosts.

Yet here he was, haunted, haunted by an angel, not in heaven, but right here on earth, just inches away, sharing his Sponge Bob hot tub. And just as he thought he might be the only live person he'd known to see the face of an actual angel, she arched her back to get a better look at her celestial home, and Buck's heart stopped.

He was sure he could finally make out, through her wet shirt, those ever elusive nipples straining to break their earthly bounds and rise heavenward in the cool evening breeze.

"What's wrong?" she asked, when she heard him gasp for air.

Busted. Buck had to think fast.

"Oh... uh... it's just so beautiful," he agreed, trying to cover.

When she turned to look fondly at the man next to her, so sensitive as to appreciate a beautiful starlit night, she saw him looking at her, and not just at her, but right through her. It wasn't a look Jennifer Steele'd seen very often, or ever, for that matter. She couldn't help but soften under his gaze and wonder what might be going through the man's head at that very moment.

Buck, on the other hand, wasn't so worried about the head on his shoulders. It was the other one, with a mind of its own, that had him preoccupied at that particular moment. Buck had to cross his legs as a set of nipples wasn't the only thing rising heavenward from the steamy water of the hot tub.

Buck's dry spell was over. He hadn't meant for it to happen. He didn't think it was possible. He thought he'd placed his heart securely in a box and buried it along with his past all those years ago. But Buck wasn't thinking of the past. He wasn't even thinking of the future. He was only thinking of now. And right now, all he knew was that he couldn't let her go. He couldn't let her leave for New York in the morning.

"Do you really have to go back to New York tomorrow?" he began.

"Who's asking?" she countered, playing coy.

"I am."

Jennifer paused, taken by surprise. Was he really asking her to stay? Don't be ridiculous.

"Yep. I guess," she responded with a sigh.

There's hope, thought Buck at her less than enthusiastic reply.

"Don't sound so excited. You don't mean to say there's a chance you might actually miss our little piece of paradise here in Sweet Spot?" He looked out the corner of one eye for any sign of encouragement.

She chuckled, then thought she'd try to use terms someone like Buck might understand. "Sweet Spot's kinda like that runt of the litter you can't help but love."

Buck wasn't exactly sure whether that was good or bad. Normally you euthanize the runt.

"Growin' to love Sweet Spot, are ya?"

"Ya know, I used to think I was married to New York City," she mused. "Wherever you've come from, once you get to New York, it's hard to go back home. Now I'm not so sure," she added, wiggling her toes at the far end of the tub.

"So you were married to New York, huh? And now you're not so sure. Thinkin' of a divorce, are ya?" he asked with a wink.

She thought about her unfulfilling dead-end job and smiled. "I guess you could say I'm a free agent. You never know when the right opportunity might present itself."

All Buck had to do was come up with the right opportunity. But as much as he'd like the opportunity to move her into the mayor's mansion posthaste, he somehow thought being the First Lady of Sweet Spot wasn't exactly what the girl had in mind.

Then it came to him. An opportunity right here, and in her chosen profession. Well it wasn't right here in Sweet Spot. But it was just a short stretch up the road.

"Ya ever think about a career in print journalism?"

She turned to stare at him, wondering how he could know what was in her head. "You mean over at the Pottsville Post? With Doc Miller?"

"Oh, already met old Doc, did ya?"

"He spoke very highly of you, Mr. Mayor. Don't know why that would be," she kidded.

"Oh, did he now? Salt o' the earth, ol' Doc is. Wasn't so long ago I first came to town. I wasn't born mayor of Sweet Spot, ya know. Doc was the one helped ease the transition. Maybe he can do the same for you."

Jennifer couldn't imagine what kind of transition Buck Jones would have needed to fit right in here in Sweet Spot. In fact, she had a hard time imagining him fitting in anywhere else.

"Just so happens, Doc is thinking of retiring. Asked if I might be interested in running things over at the Post."

Buck couldn't believe his luck. First it was ten million dollars from FEMA. Now Jennifer Steele was considering taking a job in Pottsville. He prayed this wasn't some strange hallucination courtesy of Jeb Clancey.

"So it's all settled. You're movin' to Pottsville. That's wonderful. And here you never said a word."

"Whoa there, cowboy. I never said any such thing. I only thought it might be nice to run my own show at a small publication for a change. You know, get to be the boss, instead of just another peon taking orders from on high. But that's just a fantasy. I can't just up and leave my job."

Buck wasn't letting go. "Why not?"

She laughed. "Don't be silly. I make good money back in New York. I'd starve here. You've seen my fishing skills."

"Oh, I don't know. Doc ain't starvin'. The cost of living here is so low, it's practically free. Besides, won't take but just a little practice down at the fishin' hole with the right coach and..."

She burst out laughing, remembering their last encounter down at the fishin' hole.

At least she was laughing, he thought.

"Yeah, well, this isn't some Hallmark movie" she continued. "Tempting as it might be, in real life, people don't just up and leave their high-paying jobs in New York City to come run a small town newspaper."

"Real life? New York City is real life? That's no way to live."

"How would you know, Mr. Mayor?"

Buck almost answered the question. He was more than qualified to do so. But it didn't matter. Her question was merely rhetorical. So he held his tongue.

"Besides," she continued, saving him from his thoughts, "where would I get the money to buy Doc out?"

Just as Buck thought his dream up in flames, hope rose from the ashes.

"Oh, Doc? Shoot, how much could he want for that ol' termite ridden office and that antique printing press? Believe me, he ain't got no other offers. He can sell it to you for a song, or he can take it to the grave with him. And if I know Doc Miller, he put way too much of himself into that old paper to see it up and fold when he's gone."

Jennifer couldn't deny she was tempted to be the big fish in a small pond. On the other hand, working at CNN might present the type of opportunity she might not get anywhere else. After all, look at the difference her coverage had made to a place like Sweet Spot.

"You know, Mayor, if you're going to steal all of CNN's employees, who's going to spread the word about all the Sweet Spots in this world in need of a little publicity? I mean there are certainly no end of places competing for limited government assets. And I know this might seem cynical to you, but most of those places are complete frauds, just politicians and con artists looking to swindle the government out of precious disaster funds."

Buck thought he lost a lung as Jennifer's remarks sent Jeb's liquid fire down the wrong pipe.

"You OK?" asked Jennifer, concerned over Buck's sudden convulsions.

Buck tried to pull himself together.

"Yeah, yeah, I'm OK. It was just the shock over your last remarks. Do you actually mean to say there are people so low that they would try to swindle the government out of disaster relief funds?"

"Oh, you'd be surprised," she confirmed.

"Oh, these days nothing surprises me anymore," Buck choked, taking a good-sized swig of his drink.

"Well I can't imagine anything as repulsive as someone that would steal aid meant for those suffering victims truly in need. That's got to be as low as it gets."

"Oh, I don't know," protested Buck, trying to think of something worse. "What about... oh... uh, you know... them pedophiles?" he added proudly. "Can't be lower than that."

Jennifer just looked at Buck kind o' funny, not exactly sure what the man was trying to say. But Buck was never happier to see Mrs. Butts approaching with a tray of food.

"Mayor, Ms. Steele, I was just getting' ready to turn in and I thought you might want this here last tray of snacks to help wash down that Jeb's brew you two been throwin' back."

"Why, thank you, Mrs. Butts," replied Buck, taking the tray in hand, grateful for the change of subject. He handed one of the meat-filled fried delicacies to Jennifer and took one for himself.

They each tried a bite while Mrs. Butts waited around to see how they liked it.

"Wow!" exclaimed Jennifer, eyes wide. "Maybe it's just Clancey cocktails talkin', but this is phenomenal."

"Not too shabby," agreed Buck. "Just like Momma used to make."

Mrs. Butts had to smile. "I thought you'd say so. That's why I saved this batch for ya. They was goin' like hot cakes and I didn't want y'all to miss out."

"Seriously," moaned Jennifer, grabbing seconds, this is as good as any fine French cuisine you might find in New York, or Paris for that matter."

"Hat's off to the chef," added Buck. "That Eustace Winchester truly outdid himself with this one."

"What is it, if I may ask?" inquired Jennifer, licking her fingers.

Mrs. Butts had to shake her finger at Jennifer. "Now, now, you know Eustace ain't gonna give up none o' his secret recipes, but I know it's made from gator tail."

"Hooey, that sure is some tasty gator, right there," marveled Buck, reaching for another.

Jennifer, however, had nothing to say. In fact, she'd stopped eating mid-bite, and feeling suddenly ill, turned to spit out what she'd had in her mouth.

Buck had to chuckle. "Come on now, darlin', don't tell me you don't eat no gator."

Jennifer suddenly turned to look him in the eye like she was about to give him a good whuppin'. Then just as suddenly, she looked as if she was going to cry.

Buck saw it was serious. He stopped chewing and swallowed what he had. "What? What is it?"

"Gator?" she squeaked, barely able to get the word out.

Buck didn't know what was happening but he knew it wasn't good. "Yeah, sure. Gator. Taste like chicken, right?" He saw a tear run down her cheek. "Or not. What? Don't tell me you're goin' vegetarian on me."

"How could you?" Jennifer replied, the tears flowing freely now. "Poor Lizzie."

Buck didn't know what was going on. He wrapped the sobbing girl in his arms, trying to console her. "What about Lizzie?"

Jennifer pushed him away. "What about her? You're eating her, that's what."

Buck frowned, looking at the tray of hors d'oeuvres. Then it hit him. "Oh, I get it! You think this is Lizzie?" He started laughing. "Shoot. This ain't Lizzie."

"It's not?" asked Jennifer, hopefully.

"Don't be silly. O' course it ain't. Why that tough ol' lizard would never be this tender."

Jennifer didn't appreciate the insult to Lizzie.

"Besides," added Buck, "when did you suddenly grow so fond of your fishin' buddy?"

Jennifer wasn't sure how to answer that. Maybe it was just the alcohol talkin', but she'd somehow developed a bond of some sort with the monster. Maybe it was just her first experience, harrowing as it was, with the man she thought she might be falling for.

"You sure it's not our Lizzie?" she asked again, wiping the tears from her face.

Buck wasn't exactly sure when the temperamental reptile became our Lizzie, but he saw he'd better work fast or the rest of the evening would be a bust.

"Don't be ridiculous. Lizzie's practically a pet 'round here. Everyone knows that."

Jennifer wanted to believe him, but she wasn't convinced, and the tears started to fall again.

Buck would never understand women, yet his eyes were beginning to water a bit themselves as he watched the target of his affections fall apart right in front of him. He took her in his arms again, trying to calm the freely sobbing girl.

She was too weak to push him away, so she just moaned into his shoulder between gasps for air. "You're lying to me. She's dead. I just know it."

"I would never lie to you," he answered, barely appreciating the irony in the heat of the moment.

"Prove it!" she demanded.

"What? How?"

"Show me. Let's go see if she's OK."

"What? To the fishin' hole? You want me to take you to the fishin' hole, in the middle of the night?"

"That's exactly what I'm saying," she replied, pulling herself together and standing up, albeit a little wobbly, to exit the spa.

At first Buck thought all was lost, the evening ruined. But when he looked around at the lingering revelers still about, he thought again. Maybe this was his chance, his chance to get her all alone, just him and the girl. Buck always did his best work one on one. All thanks to that damn gator. Who'd o' thunk the girl'd grown so attached to the beast? Shoot, at this point, Lizzie could be the girl's maid of honor for all he cared, as long as he got in her pants before sun-up.

Buck stood up to follow Jennifer, two drunk wet fools heading off into the dark of night to go find a full grown pet alligator. Buck filled his flask with a fresh pint of inspiration as he passed the bar, just in case they got thirsty. Oh, and the check. Buck pulled the

FEMA check down from its place of honor over the bar. He wasn't gonna let that baby out of his sight.

Chapter 25

As if it wasn't bad enough that Scarlet Witherspoon got stood up by her man Pedro, now she was forced to endure watching a giggling Jennifer Steele, escorted by a randy Buck Jones, stumbling off to some illicit midnight interlude. The whole thing was more than enough justification to find herself drinking all by her lonesome, trying to drown out the pain.

But even Jeb's cure-all elixir couldn't cure a terminal malady such as this. Watching little ol' Plain Jane Jennifer traipsing off into the moonlit night with the mayor in tow seemed a bridge too far. Granted, judging by their unsteady gate, both well beyond the legal limit for walking, there was a good chance they knew not what they did. But they seemed to be having a good time doing it, howling in laughter at the moon as they helped each other stagger on down the trail into the backwoods of Mississippi. They made quite the picture of common-law connubial bliss, Jennifer insisting on leading the way while the mayor had his hands full just keeping her upright.

Scarlet never thought she'd be jealous of Jennifer Steele. But that's how upside down life had become. Since when did Jennifer Steele catch a man before Scarlet Witherspoon? This was a first. Jennifer Steele getting laid before Scarlet Witherspoon signaled something unnatural was afoot. It seemed the basic laws of nature no longer applied. What was next? Would gravity reverse itself? Would tomorrow's sun rise in the west?

That's when Scarlet Witherspoon knew her life was over.

Scarlet had never even seen the end of a party before. She'd normally had the pick of any number of eligible young men to escort her home well before closing time, while the pickin' was still good. She didn't even know what proper end-of-party etiquette entailed. Was she supposed to start clearing dishes, emptying ash trays? Whose job was it to put away the leftovers, turn off the lights? This was all uncharted territory for her, and Scarlet found it all frankly overwhelming. How did people live this way? That was all normally left to the help.

Speaking of the help, Scarlet just couldn't seem to shake that Jefferson Washington.

Charlie had turned in long ago, looking out of place without his Eustace, while Jeb and the chief were still yuckin' it up over by the glowing embers of the Winchesters' shock and awe extravaganza. They showed no signs of fading as Jeb stripped down to his boxers trying to master the chief's fertility dance.

So Scarlet had been fairly confident that she could count on remaining undisturbed to wallow in self-pity. But no sooner had she just poured herself another red plastic cup of Jeb's liquid painkiller than her inebriated bliss was shattered.

What did Jefferson Washington want from her now? Was he looking for some kind of formal apology for his ancestors? Planning to sue for restitution? Scarlet didn't see what the big deal was all about. After all, slavery was perfectly legal at the time.

It wasn't that Scarlet disliked the man, or that she was intentionally trying to avoid him. It's just that things had become just a bit awkward since learning her family used to own his.

Given her own humble beginnings, Scarlet could only feel terrible for someone raised even lower on the socioeconomic ladder than her, though even some racist folks considered white trash lower than black in their warped hierarchy. After all, white trash chose to be trash, while others couldn't help bein' born black. They didn't have no say in it.

But unlike Scarlet, Jefferson didn't possess the, uh... assets to work his way up that ladder. Least not the kind she'd used.

Seeing Jefferson Washington headed her way, she knew it was too late to escape. Despite her praying that the man would just go away, Scarlet couldn't suppress her inbred Southern hospitality. So, throwing him her best pageant smile and a hey y'all, she pulled something out of her hair that could have been either mud or manure, and patted the chair next to her.

The poor man. His plight hadn't seemed to have improved all that much since his ancestors' days back on the plantation. Here he was still slaving away, only this time, for Mrs. Butts. And judging by his communication skills, he'd probably never benefited from a single day of formal education in his pathetic life.

Just this morning, Jefferson Washington had already researched the latest NASDAQ initial public offerings. He'd also made sure to check his Wall Street Journal for the most current price of Krugerrands and had already been to Pottsville to make some calls concerning the establishment of an offshore bank account in the Cayman Islands. After all, Jefferson's sudden impending inflow of assets would need to be appropriately sheltered from the sticky fingers of the IRS.

Now that the check had finally arrived, Jefferson wasn't sure he needed to keep up the poor black victim charade, but he still had some unfinished business with little Miss Grits and Gravy, some loose ends to tie together.

Seeing her all alone at the bar, throwing back one cocktail after another, he thought maybe this would be a good time to break the good news.

"Well howdy doo, Miss Scarlet. You sho' is lookin' mighty beauty queen-like tonight," he started, breaking the ice. "Mind if I rest my weary bones with you a spell?" he asked, taking the seat next to her.

"Why don't be such a silly goose," she smiled, Southern hospitality trumping her desire to shoo him off like a pesky horsefly.

"What's a pretty Southern belle such as yourself doin' all by your lonesome, unescorted at the bar? Now what would your momma have to say 'bout that?"

The sad truth was that if her momma'd still been alive, she'd a' been renting her daughter out for beer money. Yet, even as poor of an excuse her momma was for a momma, Scarlet was feeling particularly fragile tonight. Shoot, since her momma'd died, Scarlet was no less an orphan than little Felicity. No family at all to speak of. And now she'd been abandoned by Pedro too.

"Momma's gone," she replied, her voice shaky with emotion. "And she was the last of 'em. I ain't got no family no more."

Jefferson truly hadn't meant to upset the girl, and yet he saw the line of conversation as the perfect opportunity to discuss their shared roots.

"Oh, I'm so sorry, Miss Scarlet. Didn't mean to upset you none. I know how important family can be."

"You know, Miss Scarlet, ain't a day go by I don't think about my great grandpappy. The man passed before I was born but everyone always said I took after him, you know, my attitudes about things, about how people need to stand on they own two feet and not be dependent on others."

Scarlet took the bait, thinking maybe the conversation might take her mind off her own troubles. "Really? Sounds like he was ahead of his time. Was he a big supporter of civil rights?"

"Great grandpappy? Lordy, no. That fo' sho'. He always used to remind us that it was black folk in Africa made they own people slaves, not the whites, how they was already slaves when the whites showed up to buy 'em. He certainly never would a' gone fo' none o' that affirmative action balderdash. And don't get me started on the way he used to go on about that uppity Martin Luther King."

Scarlet was shocked. "Wow. If I didn't know no better, I'd o' thought you was talkin' 'bout my great grandfather, you know, the slave owner. People always said he never got over losing the plantation. Worse yet, he never forgave President Lincoln for ruining a perfectly good way of life. In fact, just between you and me," she began, leaning in a little closer and checking that no one was in hearing distance, "I'm embarrassed to admit, word is my great grandfather was a founding member of the Ku Klux Klan," she whispered.

She looked at Jefferson, guilty as a five-year-old caught with her hand in the cookie jar.

Yet the look she saw on the man's face showed anything but disdain, not a hint of disgust concerning the revelation of her ancestor's scandalous behavior. In fact, had she not known better, she would have thought from the smile on Jefferson's face that he almost seemed to admire the man. But that was impossible. How could the descendent of slaves admire a slave-owning member of the Klan? More likely, the smile on Jefferson's face was one of smugness, a condescending acknowledgement of Scarlet's ignominious heritage.

"What are you smiling at?" she asked, confused by the expression on Jefferson's face. "I know. It's horrible. I'm so sorry."

Jefferson seemed to take the high road, unwilling to rub salt in her wounds. "Oh no, child. You don't need to be 'shamed o' your family," he assured her, placing a comforting hand on her shoulder.

"Oh please," she objected in embarrassment, amazed at Jefferson's forgiving attitude. "My great granddaddy was in the Klan."

But Jefferson's reply only shocked her more.

"So was mine," he retorted.

Scarlet was confused. "Your what?"

"My great grandpappy."

"What about him?"

"He was a founding member of the Klan."

Scarlet was astounded by the lengths the man was going just to make her feel better. "Jefferson Washington, what are you talking about? You're being ridiculous. Even if he wanted to, they didn't allow no black folk in the Klan. You're not makin' no sense. Weren't no family o' yours in no Klan."

Jefferson was not deterred in his conviction. And the smile on his face seemed to only grow wider when he replied, "Well, my great grandpappy was."

"But that's impossible. How could that be?"

Even without a belly full of Jeb Clancey's influence, Scarlet Witherspoon had never been the sharpest tweezers in the makeup kit.

But Jefferson couldn't wait a second longer for her to figure things out on her own. He couldn't hold his revelation back any longer.

"Cause my great grandpappy weren't black. He was just as white as you, Miss Scarlet."

There. He'd said it. Now he could sit back and watch the truth settle in on the girl's face.

And yet, it was like looking into the face of a Hereford cow, blank as could be, as confused as a hound dog taking a college entrance exam. She still didn't get it. Lord, he was going to have to spell it out for her, take her out of her misery.

"Miss Scarlet, your great granddaddy was my great grandpappy. They one in the same. Shoot, girl. We kin!"

Scarlet would surely have choked on her drink had it not come spraying out of her mouth. She dropped her cup and would have fallen backward off her chair had her newly-acquired relative not caught her.

"Whoa there, girl," laughed Jefferson. "I know it's a lot to take in. But I knew it from the moment I seed you. Why you a dead ringer for great grandpappy's beauty queen wife I seed in old family photos."

"But this is impossible," countered Scarlet.

"Now why you say that, cousin?"

Scarlet didn't know how else to say it. "Because you're black! That's why!"

"And so was my great grandmomma."

"But you just said great granddaddy's wife was white, like me?"

"White as new fallen snow. But your great grandmomma weren't my great grandmamma. My great grandmomma were the slave our great grandpappy cavorted with."

When Scarlet closed her eyes, it wasn't clear whether she was hoping it was to help her understand the situation, or to simply make it all go away. It was one thing to feel bad for black folk, but that didn't mean she wanted one for no relative. Kind o' like bein' all in favor of somethin' just so long as it weren't in your own back yard.

Jefferson wasn't stupid. He knew the news must have been devastating to the Dixie belle blonde with the cracker roots. Shoot, the silly way some black folk behavin' these days, many a time Jefferson wished he coulda pruned some branches off the ol' family tree himself. Heck, he certainly wouldn't have chosen no white trash as relations neither. But Jefferson Washington weren't no racist. Stupid is as stupid does, and Jefferson didn't tolerate ignorant white folk any more than ignorant black folk. But then again, family was family and you loved 'em all just the same, no matter the color, or the IQ for that matter.

So he reached over to his newfound relation and took the dazed debutante-wannabe in a comforting hug, patting her gently on the back.

"There there. It's OK. Sure we a few shades apart on the color wheel. But look on the bright side. You got family now, cousin. And family takes care o' family. You ain't got nothin' to worry about."

Scarlet still hadn't taken it all in just yet. But what with her Pedro missing and all, Jefferson's hug sure felt mighty good. It felt like... well... like home.

And as only family can, Jefferson knew just what was really weighin' on the girl's mind.

"Don't you worry 'bout Pedro, girl. Them Winchester boys will find your man. Shoot, them rednecks could track a three-legged Mississippi tick."

Chapter 26

Buck Jones had many skills, but tracking wasn't one of them. He could find his way to the fishin' hole blindfolded, even blindfolded and blind drunk. It was only the girl he had to worry about. Whether it was her inebriated state, or just her city slicker's natural poor sense of direction, was unclear, but the shit-faced filly was all over the place. And in the dark of night, Buck was going to have a hell of a time tracking his prey through the woods should he let her out of his sight.

So it wasn't long before he'd scooped up the wisp of a girl and threw her over his shoulder for safe keeping. Jennifer didn't seem to notice as her mouth continued issuing orders just as if she were still leading the way.

That was something Buck knew he would have to get used to were he successful in his plan to win her heart. Taking orders. He knew this one was going to be a handful. But that was OK. Sometimes a man knows when he's licked, when it's time to throw in the towel. It had been a long time since Buck had given in to a woman. But this one had gotten under his skin good as any Mississippi hookworm. And hooked he was.

Buck honestly thought he was over the fairer sex. Yet here he was takin' orders from the 98-pound keg of girl gunpowder slung over his shoulder. Given how unlucky in love Buck had been to this point, he never thought he'd be so quick at the trigger. But there was just no helpin' it. When it comes to love, you're either in or you're out. And when Buck Jones went in, he went all in. When he surrendered his heart, it was complete, and unconditional.

So if he didn't get Jennifer Steele on the same page before sunup, Buck Jones was gonna be left in a world of hurt.

Jennifer never planned on ending up with someone like Buck Jones. The man could have been the poster child for everything she'd ever promised herself she'd avoid, an uncouth, chauvinistic, troglodyte. Yet here she was, slung over his shoulder, being hauled off into the woods like some kind of caveman conquest. At least he hadn't hit her over the head with a club.

Oh, who was she kidding? She may have been the one being man-handled, but she was beginning to wonder, deep down in her heart, if that wasn't just what she'd wanted all along. And now, hanging upside down, bouncing backward down the path to the fishin' hole, Jennifer Steel had Buck Jones right where she wanted him.

No matter he was a card-carrying redneck, he was her redneck. It was plain as day that the man would do anything for her. He couldn't help himself. He was hooked, unconditionally.

But maybe she was too. Maybe it took several doses of Jeb Clancey's truth serum to make her epiphany plain, but if she were honest about it, she'd probably known it since the first time she'd laid eyes on him swinging that ballpeen hammer, sweat dripping off his muscular torso as he took his frustrations out on that uncooperative generator.

But, most of all, it was the way he looked at her that made Jennifer want to surrender completely. That look in his eye of brazen desire made her forget all her insecurities, about her job, her childhood, even her tits.

What would Gloria Steinem say, letting some man carry her off into the woods to have his way with her? Well, maybe that's just what ol' Gloria needed, a good ol' fashioned roll in the hay, a dripping with sweat, loins pounding, eyes roll up into the back of your head, scream out loud, fuck.

Whoa! Where did that come from? Better sound the alarm. This girl was on fire.

Jennifer couldn't really say what Gloria Steinem needed, but she knew what Jennifer Steele needed. Oh, she needed it bad, all right. And Buck Jones was just the man for the job. So even though all she could feel at this point was Buck's shoulder prodding her bladder as she bounced her way to the fishin' hole, she fully intended on feeling more than just the man's shoulder pounding into her before the night was done.

The stroll to the fishin' hole that night was anything but a quiet introspective communing with nature. Instead, the two happy fools could be heard for miles around stirring up quite a ruckus tripping over logs and cursing at spider webs impeding their progress. With serum alcohol levels so high their blood was probably flammable, the pair were making quite the spectacle of themselves.

Hanging upside down behind Buck as he lumbered down the trail, Jennifer could be heard humming Aretha Franklin's "You Make Me Feel Like A Natural Woman," while Buck whistled Disney's "Hi Ho, Hi Ho, It's Off To Work We Go." If there'd been any dangerous wild beasts out there lying in wait, they'd have surely been scared off by that improbable duet.

So distracted were they in their rabble-rousing midnight jaunt that Buck nearly walked them right into the fishin' hole as the trail abruptly ended at the clearing.

Sensing they'd reached their destination when he stopped, Jennifer was kicking her legs like a toddler wanting down, and Buck was only too happy to oblige.

As if she weren't unsteady enough on her legs as it were, the blood rushing back down from her head where it had pooled during her top down journey made her forget whatever it was she'd been thinking about. Why were they even at the fishin' hole?

Lizzie. That was it.

"So where is she?"

Buck was having a little trouble himself remembering the pretense under which he'd lured the girl out to the fishin' hole.

"Lizzie?"

"That's right," answered Jennifer, picking up right where she'd left off before they'd hit the trail. "You assured me that that wasn't my Lizzie served up on a platter back at the party."

"Oh, yeah. That's right. Your Lizzie." Frankly, Buck's thoughts had moved on. He was hoping Jennifer had done the same. No such luck. So he thought he'd take a load off and sit down on a log at the edge of the fishin' hole, pulling his flask from his hip pocket.

"Well, she's not my Lizzie. More like our Lizzie," she conceded, enjoying the idea that she and Buck shared something in common, almost as if they'd adopted a child together.

"I'm sure our Lizzie's just fine," ventured Buck, hoping to change the subject and move on from the cold-blooded leathery reptile to something more warm and soft.

"Well I don't see her," Jennifer argued, squinting into the darkness, only the surface of the fishin' hole visible in the moonlight.

"Well, she ain't your goddamned pet, you know. It ain't like she's some kind o' Labrador pup gonna come bounding up to you, welcoming you home with a lick on the face."

Jennifer stood up straight, hands on her hips, trying to control her inebriated wobble best she could. "I don't think I like your attitude, Mr. Mayor. No need to get your panties in a wad."

Buck had to smile. That was the spitfire he loved.

"And wipe that smirk off your face, young man," she giggled, seeing his grin.

"Come here," he ordered, patting a spot on the log next to him.

"You want me to sit with you? Well I don't know. What are your intentions?" she squinted down her nose at him.

Buck never knew she had a playful side. She'd already had him wrapped around her little finger. Now there was a playful side too? Just another nail in the coffin, he thought. Well, Buck Jones was certainly ready to play, all right. Only he didn't need to make no jokes. To Buck, this was as serious as a heart attack.

So he looked her in the eye and calmly laid out the evening's agenda.

"My intentions? My intentions, madam, are to make sweet jungle love to you so long and hard that you ain't gonna wanna walk for a week."

Whoa! Jennifer heard him all right. Every word. And it left her speechless. Where was the clever comeback, the witty retort? Was it the sudden dryness of her mouth that rendered her mute? Was it because she just as suddenly found she couldn't catch her breath? Or was it a combination of both those things along with the fact that she'd inexplicably gone all weak in the knees and had to sit down before she fell down?

So sit she did, next to the man who'd just indelicately propositioned her. Well, he hadn't exactly propositioned her. There was never any question in his pronouncement. It was more a bold statement of fact. He couldn't have been more clear.

She knew where this was going. And there was no turning back now. The launch sequence had been initiated, which was just fine with Jennifer Steele. She was looking forward to a turbulent ride.

But when Buck Jones reached over and brought her hand up to his lips for a gentle kiss, she saw this was going to be even better than advertised. Judging from the man's choice of words, she'd never imagined foreplay would play any part in the deal. Not that she needed any. She'd been ready to board this train for quite some time now. But when his lips moved from her hand to her wrist, ultimately beginning a slow accent up her arm, she began to think there was more to the man than she'd imagined.

"This isn't just about sex, is it?" she ventured, barely able to speak. "You really like me, Buck Jones."

"Ever since I first laid eyes on you, Sugar. Well, at least once I realized you weren't no boy."

Uh oh. Buck felt her arm tense up.

"You thought I was a boy?"

Shit! Buck tried to cover. "Well, you know, I didn't really get a good look at you... and you were all covered in manure at the time."

"You thought I was a boy?" Her voice was rising.

Oh no. Things had been going so well, Buck couldn't believe it was over just like that. No, he could fix this. He could still salvage the mission.

"Yeah, but, don't you see? Even when I thought you were a boy, I knew I loved you. Scared the shit out o' me too. Thought maybe I'd gone over to the other side, if you know what I mean."

"A boy?" She'd taken her hand away by that point.

Buck knew well enough, the first thing you do once you realize you're diggin' yourself into a hole is you put the shovel down. Things had veered off in the wrong direction. He had to redirect.

He knew he only had one last chance or it was all over. He had to give it everything he had, leave nothing on the table. So he bypassed the hand this time, placed one arm around her waist and the other behind her head so she couldn't escape, and threw his best Hail Mary. He kissed her hard, full on, mouth to mouth, do or die, no turning back.

Jennifer hadn't seen it coming. She'd been too busy picking at some silly scab that was meant to kill the mood. Only now, she suddenly couldn't remember what it was. The light in her mind, the one she used to illuminate all that was wrong with the world, and all the flaws she saw in herself, that light, the harsh light she'd focused on her whole life, had suddenly been extinguished, short circuited by a kiss, a kiss from Buck Jones.

Yet, when that light went out, it wasn't darkness that Jennifer saw. Anything but. Because that harsh white light of self-doubt and discontent had only been replaced by another. Only this light was different, like nothing Jennifer Steele'd ever seen before. It was softer, and warmer, made of all the colors of the spectrum, but more than that, more than just colors. It was a veritable rainbow of senses. It was fresh cut grass, warm cookies right out of the oven. It was the churning of the ocean just before a storm, the sound of thunder rolling over a mountain range. It was peaceful tranquility and confused chaos all rolled into one.

It was a thing heretofore unknown to Jennifer Steele. And yet, she knew, she just knew, it was a thing she never wanted to be without ever again.

Buck didn't know what hit him. He'd fallen off a bucking bronco in his younger days. He'd been knocked out with a tire iron in a bar room brawl. Shoot, he'd even been shot once. But he'd never felt nothin' like this. None of that compared to locking lips with Jennifer Steele. He might just as well have French-kissed a high voltage wire. He'd never crossed anything as deadly lethal as that girl.

For just as soon as his lips touched hers, Buck Jones dropped dead and went straight to heaven. There hadn't been any time for goodbyes, no chance to get his things in order before his untimely demise. It was all so sudden.

At first, he thought he'd miss the life he'd known on Earth, fishin', drinkin', and something he vaguely recollected about a fine specimen of a woman he'd been chasin', the girl of his dreams. But now, in heaven, it seemed none of that mattered anymore.

It soon had him thinking, had he known how it would be, he'd have died long ago. And yet, he knew somehow that that wasn't how things worked. This was nothing a man could plan out, no color by numbers. No, things like this just happened, that is, if a man was lucky. And just now, Buck Jones was feelin' mighty lucky.

As some point, neither one knew when, completely oblivious to the world around them, they'd rolled off the log and into the mud at the edge of the fishin' hole. They'd been slipping and sliding in the stuff for quite some time, locked in a kind of lover's death spiral, before coming up for a breath.

Gasping for air, covered head to toe in muck, they looked like something only seen at the drive-in movies, a pair of swamp monsters from the black lagoon.

But that's not how Buck and Jennifer saw it. Their eyes were wide open, taking in the sight of each other as if for the first time, and they didn't see a speck of mud. Nothing of the kind. What they did see, however, would have, only a short while ago, been much scarier to them both than any old swamp thing. Yet now, somehow, it didn't seem scary at all. It was the future they saw. Their future. Together. For as they looked deeply into each other's eyes, all they could see were a diamond ring and a wedding band, a tuxedo and a white dress, maybe three or four children, and a dozen or so grandchildren.

"What the hell was that?" gasped Jennifer hoarsely.

"I wanna have your babies," answered Buck, still dazed.

Jennifer smiled and laid her head on Buck's chest. "You're crazy."

"Crazy about you," Buck replied, wrapping her in his arms again.

"What are we going to do?" she asked, feeling so at home in his embrace.

"Damned if I know," he said. "I'm hardly the brains of this outfit."

Jennifer laughed again. The man sure could make her smile.

"But I do know one thing," he continued. "I want you to stay. Don't leave me tomorrow. I'm begging you."

Jennifer Steele pulled back, putting the smiles and jokes aside, and looked long and hard into Buck Jones's eyes. And that's when she knew.

"I'm not going anywhere."

* * * *

A pair of eyes glowing in the dark from the other side of the fishin' hole watched the two love-birds part as Buck scooped Jennifer up into his arms and got to his feet with the intention of adjourning to someplace a little more comfortable.

Well, good for them, the eyes thought. Lizzie would normally have paid her two friends a visit, but cold-blooded animals didn't get out much at night. Lizzie became pretty much a homebody in the chill of evening.

But she'd observed, with great interest, the mating ritual begun across the fishin' hole. It seemed a touch and go affair at times, but everything seemed to be working out just swimmingly in the end.

Lizzie never knew it was her they'd come to find. But had she known, she would have been tickled pink to have played a pivotal part in the creation of what emerged from the mud at the edge of the fishin' hole. She'd known all along, ever since her last run-in with the pair, that those two kids were destined for each other.

Maybe they didn't find Lizzie that night, probably didn't even remember what they'd come searching for. But they sure enough found something. Something bigger than any ol' overgrown lizard. Buck Jones and Jennifer Steele found each other.

Chapter 27

Nacho Garcia, aka Pedro, sure wished someone would find him.

Rocco's demeanor'd showed no signs of improvement when Pedro'd awakened from his second coma of the day. The medieval inquisition picked up right where it'd left off in Rocco's quest to dispose of Conquistador.

No matter. Pedro would never give up the stallion. Conquistador was like a brother to him. They were a team, on and off the polo field. Pedro knew that horse would willingly walk through fire at the click of Pedro's tongue. If Pedro asked, Conquistador would die for him.

Well, Pedro would do the same. So what did a few bumps and bruises mean? Nothing at all, a minor inconvenience.

And so it was in the waning hours of night that Pedro found himself handcuffed to that tree in the woods, his vision obscured by the blood dripping from his head, while Rocco caught some shut-eye in the back seat of his car. After all, beating people senseless sure could wear a man out.

Pedro figured he had maybe one last sunup coming to him before Rocco put an end to the ordeal with a bullet between his eyes. The man wasn't going to wait around forever. He'd probably just lie to the boss and tell him the horse was dead. Besides, it wasn't likely anyone around these parts would ever decipher the horse was a world class polo pony. Conquistador would probably spend the rest of his days pulling some farmer's plow.

But that was OK. The horse would land on its feet. Pedro wasn't concerned about Conquistador's future. And what of the girl? What about his goddess, Scarlet? He presumed she would soon forget all about ol' Pedro and get along just fine without him, taking her pick of suitors back in New York to replace him.

But what about Pedro? Pedro didn't want to be replaced. All well and good that his loved ones would carry on without him. But Pedro wasn't ready to concede defeat. He was a professional athlete, the crème de la crème in the world of international polo, a fierce competitor who never gave up until that final gun sounded, in this case, right between the eyes.

So he went back to scraping his handcuffs back and forth along the back of the tree. He had no idea how many days it would take to saw through the mature hardwood that way, but Pedro would never give up. Never.

* * * *

Rocco Buttafuoco was having that same recurrent nightmare he'd been having every night for the past week or so. He kept dreaming he was lost deep in the middle of some Mississippi backwoods looking for a horse. Imagine? Rocco Buttafuoco going native and taking up ranching. It was a ridiculous dream. Worse than a nightmare. It was one of them night terrors. Rocco wondered what it could mean. Probably just a bad batch of cannolis.

But it wasn't just the nightmares he was afraid of. Rocco Buttafuoco was a city boy, through and through. He didn't like being out in no woods at night. Between the gators, snakes, and bears, Rocco would have much preferred the worst gangland, crack den, flea bag hotel in New York City to sleeping under the stars in some Mississippi swamp.

But as it turns out, it wasn't no wild beasts that Rocco had to worry about. It was something much worse. Seems the biggest badass beasts wandering the woods of Sweet Spot, Mississippi walked on two legs. And them Winchester boys was on a mission.

So tonight Rocco's dream seemed to take on a new twist. There'd never been dogs before. Yet now, he could clearly make out the baying of hounds hot on the trail, only growing louder as the pack of hunting dogs closed in on their prey. Maybe those damn dogs would find that stupid horse for him, he thought.

But it wasn't the barking of the dogs closing in on his Ferragamos that woke Rocco up. It was the flash of lightning. Well, it wasn't lightning exactly, but it was a blinding explosion of light that lit up the sky over Rocco and Pedro for a good minute or so.

The Winchesters' night vision goggles were all fine and dandy, but once they found their target, before launching a full on assault, the boys preferred flares to properly reconnoiter the field of engagement.

And under the light of those flares, once the boys got the lay of the land, it quickly became evident that this weren't no simple case of no Mexican lost his way crossing the border. No, this were something much more nefarious.

As Earl put it, "What we got here is a bonafide alien abduction... an illegal alien abduction."

So now that the hounds had done their job, the celebratory fireworks show they'd started back at JW's was about to resume, only this time, the live ammo had a live target.

Rocco Buttafuoco may have known his way around a 9mm semiautomatic, but he'd never served in the military. So when the percussion bombs began raining down amid the confusion of strobe lights and blasting Lynyrd Skynyrd music, Rocco quickly determined the pea shooter he held in his hand wasn't gonna be up to the task, not against an entire army.

They could have easily turned the enemy vehicle and its inhabitant into dust with a single well-placed mortar shell. Well OK, so maybe Pedro was a little too close to avoid collateral damage tethered to that nearby tree, but Bubba was fairly confident he could have pulled it off.

Nevertheless, Earl didn't want to risk it. After all, their assignment was to bring Pedro back in one piece. Besides, it was always more fun bringing the enemy in alive. That way the games could continue long after the shooting stopped, creating the potential for several days of entertainment, depending on how hardy the captive proved to be.

Rocco had no idea what form of hell was raining down on him, so it was entirely on instinct that he fell out of the car and started scrambling along the ground for his life. He didn't know where he was going, but he knew it had to be better than where he was.

He didn't know what to make of the voice from a bullhorn ordering him to give up the hostage. What hostage? What the hell did they want from him? Shit, he'd have given up his mother if it would save his skin.

In his confusion, he thought he was done for when he crawled into a pair of legs. He rolled over onto his back preparing to fend off the blows from whoever stood over him. That's when he recognized Nacho, or Pedro, whatever the hell he called himself, still handcuffed to that tree.

The hostage! That's it. What luck, he thought. A human shield. Rocco quickly jumped to his feet behind Pedro and pulled the 9mm from the waistband of his pants.

"I'll kill him!" he shouted into the simultaneous blinding lights and black of night. His hand shook in fear as he held the gun to Pedro's head.

It must have been the right move to make, as he heard an order over the bullhorn to stand down, and the assault abruptly came to a halt.

In the ensuing silence, Rocco could feel his heart beating… and his urine soaked pants. He couldn't remember the last time he'd pissed himself.

Then he could hear hushed voices arguing among themselves.

"But we promised her."

"Don't be a retard. I ain't gonna shoot Pedro."

"Shsh."

Then, back to the bullhorn, "Give up the hostage, and we'll let you live!" came a voice from the darkness.

"Who are you? Are you the law?"

Rocco could hear a few chuckles of laughter at his question before the reply came.

"Naw, we ain't no damn law. But we're as close as it gets in these parts. And we might as well be, far as you're concerned. Now put down the pea shooter."

Rocco may have dropped out of eighth grade, but he wasn't stupid. "I put down this gun and I'm a dead man."

"You're a dead man either way."

Then back to the hushed whispers.

"What'd you say that for? You're supposed to lie to him. Give him a reason to give up the prisoner."

"Well, fuck that. I ain't no liar."

"Well you certainly ain't no hostage negotiator."

"I don't believe in negotiating for no hostages. That's only a sign o' weakness. Besides, when did Mom make you the boss o' me?"

Rocco thought briefly that maybe they'd forgotten about him and he could just walk away while they were distracted, but then the bullhorn came on again.

"Don't listen to my stupid brother. We got no truck with you. Just let our man Pedro go, and we can all go for some breakfast. Ya like bacon?"

Whispers again. "Don't be stupid. Everyone likes bacon."

Rocco began to wonder just what he was dealing with. "I like bacon fine, though I prefer a little prosciutto. But I know if I let the spic go, the only thing I'll be eatin' is a bullet."

Whispers. "Hey Earl, all this talk of food's gettin' me hungry. Can't we just shoot 'em both and go eat?"

"I'm bored. Let's go blow up some more stuff."

"You two are unbelievable. Can't you just focus on the mission for a change?"

Bullhorn. "Listen fella, we're all out of patience here. Give us our man or we'll let the dogs loose. Racoon or human, it's all the same to them. Just somethin' to tear into itty bitty pieces."

"Do that and you'll have a dead spic and dead dogs too."

"At this point it don't matter to us if you kill the dogs and the Mexican. There's more dogs where they come from. Maybe you heard Bubba. We're gettin' awful hungry. It's time to wrap this up. Sooner you kill the hostage, the sooner we can kill you and go get somethin' to eat."

Earl knew he was only bluffing. Bubba would never let him get the dogs killed.

But Rocco didn't know it was a bluff. Didn't care. His 9mm held 16 rounds plus one in the chamber. He'd kill the spic, all those damned dogs, and still have at least one bullet left for himself. He'd seen that messed up Deliverance movie and he had no intention of being taken alive only to be subjected to no hillbilly vigilante justice. Fuck that.

Rocco tightened his grip on the gun. Sweat was dripping down his forehead as he pulled the trigger halfway in preparation for the coming onslaught and shouted.

"Looks like we got us a real Mexican standoff here!"

Chapter 28

The bullet must have entered through the left eye and exited the back of the head.

At least that's how Jennifer felt when she awoke the next morning with the worst hangover of her life, if you could even call her current condition living. In fact, at that moment, she wished she weren't. She prayed for a quick death, rather than lingering in pain.

She didn't know where she was, but feared that if she opened her eyes to find out, her brain might ooze out through the sockets. No, she'd better keep her eyes shut while she worked it out in her head.

As she took inventory of the rest of her parts from the neck down, she quickly realized it wasn't just her head that was sore. It reminded her of the night she got thrown from that mechanical bull after chugging margaritas all night, only worse. Come to think of it, the way things were feeling below the waist, she might just as well have been riding a bull all night. What the hell could have caused...?

Oh shit!!! Jennifer's eyes shot wide open. Damn the pain. She had to see for herself. Could the dreams have been real? No, not with Buck Jones, she prayed. God, just say it isn't so and I'll never drink again.

It was a dog house. Jennifer woke up in a dog house. At least that's all she could think of when she opened her eyes and saw the little wood roof overhead. It was a tiny wood house of some kind. Maybe a chicken coop.

And speaking of chickens, did she mention she was naked as a plucked one? She'd been so preoccupied wondering where she was that the whereabouts of her clothing seemed only a secondary concern.

Naked in a chicken coop. Oh my Lord.

She tried closing her eyes once more in the hope that when she opened them again, she'd find herself ordering room service at the Ritz Carlton, Manhattan.

And that's when she heard it. She wasn't entirely sure what it was, but it was alive, an animal of some sort. And it was close, very close. It was right next to her.

With one glance to her right, all her worst dreams had come true, because that's where she found a snoring and equally plucked Buck Jones. He was spooning her from behind.

There was no getting away from it. Jennifer Steele'd done the deed with Buck Jones.

Oh no. It was true. Jennifer thought she was going to be sick. Her life was over. Her first panicked thought was to run for it. Where? Anywhere but where she was.

But when she went to bolt from the chicken coop, she realized he was holding her. No, not like a prisoner, but gentle and sweet, his arm softly draped about her waist, their fingers intertwined like lovers.

Whoa. Some strange sort of ache in her chest made Jennifer pause before she could flee for her life.

She looked at the big ol' hairy forearm cradling her even as he slept, his rough and stubby fingers caressing her smooth and slender ones. Then she looked over at the big ol' bear lying next to her and almost laughed out loud at the little line of drool hanging from the corner of his mouth.

The snoring wasn't so bad. It wasn't loud like a chainsaw. It was more like the purring of a cat. A big cat. She actually found it kind of soothing.

Up close this way, she was able to get a good look at the man beside her.

Strong chin, a little stubbly, but in a good way. Full lips with a sexy smirk even in slumber. Small ears, probably not very good for listening. Not a wrinkle to his brow as he slept as innocently as a baby. A full head of dark shimmering hair with just a dash of salt to its pepper.

Jennifer had to hand it to him. The man was cute as a button. She didn't know why, but just looking at him almost made her want to cry.

Yet as she gazed at the angel lying next to her, she was reminded of his devil's side. Even his smell turned her on. What exactly was it? Gardenia? Fresh baked cookies? Bacon? She couldn't be sure, but whatever it was, it was making her horny again.

Speaking of bull riding, that soreness she'd felt down under had somehow evolved into a beautiful thing, a thing a girl could easily grow to miss once discovered. And from the feel of things, this bull ride had lasted considerably longer than the minimum eight seconds. Oh boy.

But Jennifer's sweet afterglow was soon interrupted by angry shouts approaching from a distance, reminding her how much her head hurt. She gently disengaged from Buck's embrace and, unable to find her own clothes, wrapped herself in Buck's muddy dress shirt before going to investigate.

It was still pretty dark out that early in the morning as Jennifer poked her head outside the chicken coop. She couldn't see much, and when she stood up and took her first step all she felt was air.

If not for Buck's arm shooting out the door and grabbing her by the shirt tail, Jennifer would have fallen straight down to her death from the duck blind.

Holy shit! She'd slept 30 feet up a tree. How the hell did Buck...? Good thing she wasn't a sleep walker.

Maintaining a firm grasp on Jennifer with one hand, Buck pulled his boxers on with the other and joined her out on the ledge of the duck blind.

"What the hell?" he remarked, looking out into the woods.

It reminded Jennifer of that scene in Frankenstein where the mob of angry villagers all light torches and go off in search of the monster. She wasn't sure who the monster was, but it seemed the entire village of Sweet Spot was emerging from the woods and approaching the tree that bore the duck blind. And yes, they were still bearing torches in the first hint of sunup.

The residents of Sweet Spot were not happy.

"There they are!" shouted Jeb Clancey.

"Well, howdy Mayor. Miss Steele," added Gladiola Butts.

"Well, I'll be damned," remarked Scarlet and Charlie in unison, taking in the scene at the duck blind above.

Scarlet couldn't resist. "I see someone never made it home last night. Just what do you have to say for yourself, young lady," she joked with a wink.

This evoked sniggers from the mob.

Mikey couldn't resist, singing, "Buck and Jen, sittin' in a tree, k-i-s-s-i-n-g."

Buck figured he'd better get to the bottom of things. "What's all the fuss got the whole town up and about disturbin' the peace?"

They all started shouting at once.

"Whoa, whoa! One at a time," yelled Buck, raising his hands.

After a moment's pause, Jeb jumped in first, "I'd like to register a complaint!"

"And what do you got to complain about?" asked Buck.

"Well, before I get to my grievance, we'd all like to get somethin' straight."

"And just what is it that couldn't wait 'til sunup?" asked Buck rubbing the sleep from his eyes with one hand and absentmindedly scratching the crotch of his boxers with the other.

"Is it true the feds are gonna want half our winnin's to go to taxes?" asked Mrs. Butts.

"Now why would you think that?" asked Buck.

"You know," Jeb continued. "Like them Powerball lottery winners. Them what takes a lump sum check gots to surrender 'bout half."

"But this ain't no lottery winnin'. This is different," answered Buck.

"That's what I tried to tell 'em," interjected Jefferson, shaking his head in disgust. "They just won't listen. Also wouldn't hear o' no financial plannin' advice. Talked myself a blue streak tellin' 'em about irrevocable trusts and tax free annuities... you know... for the sake of asset protection, but I might as well been talkin' to the wall."

Scarlet looked at her newfound cousin in a new light, but felt, as did most everyone else, that he might just as well o' been speakin' in tongues.

"Anyway, now that that's all settled," resumed Jeb, "I'd like to proceed with my grievance."

"I'm all ears," yawned Buck.

"Well, we was all just talkin' 'bout how we was goin' to spend our share o' the FEMA money, and Gladiola here says she's plannin' on openin' her own Piggly Wiggly right here in Sweet Spot."

Buck was a little confused. "And what's wrong with that? I thought you'd all like the idea not havin' to run all the way to Pottsville for vittles."

Jeb jumped back in. "And I got no truck with vittles. But she says she's also plannin' to sell alcohol. Shoot, the fool woman's gonna put me out o' business with that cheap factory liquor. And here I was thinkin' of usin' my share o' the money to expand my facility beyond the confines of the cave."

There were general nods of agreement through the crowd.

Jeb was glad to see no one was disputing his claim. "Besides, I thought Sweet Spot's supposed to be a dry town. Ain't that so mayor?"

Buck couldn't quite get his head around the irony of Jeb Clancey askin' the mayor to enforce a law barring the sale of alcohol. "Seems to me, Jeb, you should be the last one pointin' that out. Seems your livin' in quite the proverbial glass house."

Jeb was unfazed. "You know damn well, Mr. Mayor, ain't nothin' like prohibition to support a healthy black market. No offense, Jefferson."

Jefferson had to roll his eyes at Jeb's apology, but took the opportunity to add his two cents. "And word is, Jimbo here talkin' 'bout buildin' a MacDonald's."

All eyes went to Mrs. Butts's brother Jimbo who could o' been her identical twin exceptin' that Gladiola had more facial hair.

Jimbo jumped to his own defense. "Shoot, Jefferson, what you complainin' bout. McDonald's ain't sold no McRib in years."

Jefferson wasn't having it. "But still, this town ain't big enough for two fine dining establishments."

Mrs. Butts jumped in. "Well who gave y'all no monopolies on things 'round here?"

That gave rise to a round of raised voices going at each other until Chief suddenly broke it up with some kind of war cry.

Once he had their attention, he said, "Peace, my people. We have lost our way. Cannot let Uncle Sam's money corrupt us. Better to continue living off land as our ancestors did in moons past."

"First of all," began Mrs. Butts, "last time I checked, we ain't your people. Secondly, I don't see you growin' that big ol' flat screen TV out o' the ground behind your teepee. And don't make like you don't know what I'm talkin' 'bout. I heard all about the big order you placed over in Pottsville. Biggest TV them folks at the Sears and Roebuck ever sold."

Nods of agreement all around as the chief lost the moral high ground.

"Besides," chimed in Jeb again, ganging up on the chief, "don't tell me you ain't planning on sellin' no spirits at that brand new casino you been talkin' 'bout buildin'."

Buck couldn't believe his ears. Things were gettin' way out o' hand. "Just where the hell is all this stuff y'all dreamin' 'bout gonna' go? I'm thinkin' we're gonna run into some zoning issues."

Chief proudly offered in reply, "Casino conserve space with multipurpose parking lot. Miss Sarah agree to share parking with her new megachurch going up next door."

"Megachurch?!!" came a unified grown from the others who hadn't been privy to Sarah's godly aspirations. They couldn't help imagining endless Sunday morning traffic jams full of out-o'-

towners as they flocked from all over tarnation to lil' ol' Sweet Spot on some pilgrimage hoping to get a little closer to the Lord.

"Now hold on there," objected Buck. "I know she's got quite a thing for the Lord goin' on, but that just don't sound like our Sarah."

"That's what I say," agreed Mrs. Butts. "I bet it's that little business manager o' hers lookin' to make a killin' on sweet tea at the concession stand."

Scarlet and Charlie had only come along upon hearing all the commotion thinking maybe there was some news of Pedro and the Winchesters. But now they were beginning to feel a little uncomfortable amid all the bickering. It was the first time since arriving in town that they'd felt anything less than harmony among the folks of Sweet Spot. They sure were beginning to miss the good ol' days.

Buck couldn't have said it better, addressing his flock from on high. "Just listen to y'all peckin' at each other like a bunch o' fightin' cocks. Ya'll should be ashamed o' yourselves."

"Besides, I don't see Miss Sarah and Little Felicity down there to defend themselves against a bunch o' hearsay. Where are them two anyways?"

Simon, who'd remained quiet until then, inwardly blaming himself for all the strife his government check had seemed to bring to town, spoke up in reply.

"They couldn't make it. Some people were coming from over in Pottsville to talk to them. Sarah seemed to think maybe it was about some fancy school they had in mind for Felicity. Thought it might be a good thing seeing as Sarah was having a hard time keeping up with Felicity in the homeschooling department. She's convinced that little girl's going to be President one day and she doesn't want to be responsible for holding her back."

Nods all around confirmed a uniform respect for Felicity's mental prowess.

"Well, I don't know about no President..." began Buck, causing more than a few eyebrows to rise in objection to his lack of faith in their little prodigy. "I mean why she settin' her sights so low. Seems Emperor would be more befittin' the Felicity I know."

The ensuing laughter from the crowd abruptly stopped when Sarah Pritchard broke through the crowd out of breath and fell into Simon's arms crying inconsolably.

All eyes were on the couple. No one had ever seen Sarah express anything but joy.

"S... Sarah, wh... what is it?" Simon protectively wrapped her in his arms, visibly shaken himself by the change in the woman that had become his rock, his guiding light.

"It's Felicity," she squeaked between sobs.

The crowd was all ears. What had befallen their Felicity?

Simon felt a chill run down his spine. "What is it? Is she hurt?"

A murmur of concern broke out among the folks.

The words came from Sarah in a wail of mourning. "They've taken her!"

Simon looked about him, confused. "Who? Who's taken her? Why?"

Sarah rubbed her watery eyes and nose on Simon's shirt. "The people from Family and Children's Services. They were sent by the state to take her away after they saw her on the TV, on CNN's disaster coverage."

"What?" Simon didn't get it.

"They said they couldn't allow her to live on no bus without parents."

"Oh, Honey," began Simon. "How could they say that? You're better with her than any parents I've ever seen."

"I tried to tell 'em. So did Felicity, poor girl. But they weren't havin' it. They said they'd be liable if they left her in the care of some teenage drug addict. They had my records and everything." Everyone couldn't help but glance at her ankle bracelet.

Simon had heard enough. He felt something rising within him he hadn't known existed. The time for talking was over. The situation called for action. If the state of Mississippi wanted to take Felicity Barnes, they were going to have to go through Simon Goldfarb first.

He kissed the limp and broken Sarah, handing her over to Scarlet and Charlie, and ran off into the woods back towards town.

He'd try to catch them before they left Sweet Spot, but he'd run all the way to Pottsville on foot if he had to.

You see, Simon knew a little something about the workings of government himself. And if a person was ever in need of someone well-schooled in bureaucratic red tape, then Simon Goldfarb was their man.

Simon needed Sarah Pritchard and Felicity Barnes. But for the first time in his life, he felt needed too. And he wouldn't let his girls down. Simon Goldfarb wasn't coming back without that little girl.

Chapter 29

Everyone was giving Jennifer, Scarlet, and Charlie the evil eye. Let's just say it was a good thing no one had a rope.

Scarlet certainly wasn't feelin' the love herself, but she was more concerned for little Felicity than herself.

"I'm so sorry, Sarah. How did Felicity take it? Poor thing must be scared out o' her wits, all alone with a bunch o' strangers."

Sarah almost had to laugh through her tears at that one.

"Oh, not our Felicity. She ain't scared o' nothing, that girl. Almost have to feel sorry for them government people what took her. Why, the state o' Mississippi gonna have its hands full with that one. I can still hear her shoutin' at 'em from the back seat demanding her one phone call to her lawyer, how she was gonna have all their jobs, threatenin' to sue the state for reckless endangerment by placing her in that government vehicle with no kiddie seat."

Nods of approval from the rest of the crowd.

Well, that was all well and good, but Mrs. Butts wasn't ready to forgive and forget.

"How do you like that Miss Scarlet actin' all concerned now, when it was her what caused the problem in the first place." Turning to the others, "All you TV folks what got our Felicity took."

Her twin, Jimbo, piled on. "That's right. I seen all that CNN disaster coverage on the television at the Sears and Roebuck over in Pottsville, about our livin' conditions here. If not for y'all, our

Felicity would still be back home where she belonged sellin' her sweet tea."

A guilty Scarlet looked over at Charlie who looked up at Jennifer. They all felt just terrible about the situation.

Jennifer was devastated. She didn't know where to look. She should have been more sensitive to the ramifications of putting a small child on national TV. But she'd been seduced by the mission. Everyone knows nothing pulls at the heart strings like children in need. Mrs. Butts was right. What was she thinking?

But Sarah wasn't having it. "I never heard such a bunch o' horse shit in my life, excuse my French," she retorted, beginning to lecture the angry mob.

"The nerve o' all y'all, blamin' these poor reporter folk. They was just doin' their jobs. Y'all was the ones what brought 'em here in the first place. We all were," she added, knowing she was complicit in the whole charade.

"We only got ourselves to blame," she continued, tears welling up again. "We was wrong to do what we done. And now this is the Lord's retribution, our chickens come home to roost."

Even Buck began to regret his role as the mastermind in the whole affair. He'd never imagined such unintended consequences. Yet the genie'd already spilt the milk comin' out the toothpaste tube and there was no unringing that bell. Didn't see much point in makin' things worse.

That's why he suddenly grew concerned over the direction of the conversation. He knew he'd better take control of the situation before there was any regrettable slip of the lip.

"Now, now. Let's not lose our heads here. Ain't no use pointin' fingers at each other. I'll just run right over to Pottsville and get this whole mess straightened out."

But it was too late. Mikey Dunham had stepped forward from the crowd and stood alone, his shoulders shaking in crying spasms.

"It was all my fault," he confessed, his voice cracking.

Scarlet and Charlie went to console the distraught young man, knowing how close he was to Felicity. Scarlet offered words of comfort.

"Don't be silly, Mikey," Scarlet began. "It weren't nothin' you did."

Mikey brushed her hands from his shoulders, wiping the tears from his face. "Course it was. I was bad. And that's what happens when people are bad. They lose their best friends."

Scarlet tried to keep her own tears from welling up. "Oh Mikey. I can't imagine you would do anything bad. What is it you think you did?"

It was all clear as day to Mikey. "I lied. We all did. Miss Sarah's right."

Scarlet wouldn't believe him. "What? I don't understand. What did everyone lie about?"

"Don't answer that!" shouted Buck.

Jennifer looked at Buck. "What? Why not?"

Buck had to think fast. "Why not? Well... uh... the boy's obviously distraught. He don't know what he's sayin'. Let me run on over to Pottsville and—"

Jennifer smelled a rat. "Let him talk," she began, one eyebrow raised suspiciously at Buck. "Let Mikey tell us what he thinks he lied about. Maybe he'll feel better just getting it off his chest."

"But..." Buck glanced down at the townsfolk, looking for help.

Jennifer followed his gaze and did the same. "What? Does anyone down there know what Mikey lied about? What everyone lied about?"

But everyone was just looking down at their feet, guilty as sin.

Jennifer felt a chill down her spine. She turned back to Buck. "What? What's happened here?"

Buck Jones had never been at a loss for words in his life. But there he stood, with the girl of his dreams demanding answers, and he froze in panic. He couldn't look her in the eye.

Jennifer grabbed him by the chin. "What did you do?"

The silence was deafening as everyone looked at everyone else. Even Lizzie across the fishin' hole was all ears.

It was Mikey who saved Buck, not from his fate, but from having to be the one to break the code of silence.

"It was all a lie. About the twisters. We made it all up. Sweet Spot ain't never been hit. We just did it for the money."

The reporters were all at a loss.

Something told Jennifer she was supposed to be furious, incensed at being duped so. Yet, she just couldn't get her head around it. She wasn't ready to concede the impossible.

She'd seen the damage with her own eyes. If anyplace could ever have been declared a disaster area, Sweet Spot was it. Everything was either falling down or had already done so. No electricity or running water. People living in teepees and caves, living on roadkill for God's sake. These poor people had been thrown back into the dark ages.

Unless... No! Could people be forced... no, choose, to live this way? Could this be their natural state of affairs?

And if so, who could have the balls, the unmitigated chutzpah, to attempt such a scam? What manner of sick individual could come up with such a scheme? No one could be that deceitful. What kind of person could be so slimy as to defraud the government out of aid money, money that could have been allocated to real victims?

She looked up at the unshaven man with bed-head standing next to her in his boxers. Could the man be that devious? She didn't want to believe it. But one look in his eyes and she knew. She just knew.

And Jennifer Steele's world fell apart.

Unwelcome flashbacks to her childhood surfaced, ugly hurtful things, memories she'd thought long ago extinguished like the butt of a cigarette.

She'd thought that was all in the past, that she'd moved on. Just as soon as she was old enough to read a compass, she'd followed that arrow pointing due north all the way to New York. She'd written off all those men like Buck Jones and vowed never to return to the Southern backwoods so infested with them.

Yet somehow here she was again. She'd thought it was love. But apparently there was something about the concept that just kept eluding her.

Is this all that love was? Being used and made a fool of? All for money, for ill-gotten gain. Well if that were the case, then Jennifer Steele must have been head over heels.

Hers was a love story sure to end happily ever after. Right, with our two star-crossed lovers serving 25-to-life in federal prison as co-conspirators in an ill-fated scheme to defraud the United States government out of millions of dollars.

Well, things could have ended worse. After all, just look at Bonnie and Clyde.

Jennifer had no idea where she'd left her clothes. Didn't care. She'd mail the muddy dress shirt back to its owner as soon as she got back to New York. In the meantime, she started descending the rope ladder hanging from the duck blind.

Buck didn't know what to do but instinctively tried to defend himself. "We're not the ones came up with the idea, you know. We never claimed no damage. It was all you New York elite lookin' down from your ivory towers never seen how real folks live. Y'all came lookin' for victims and cast us all in your little play. We didn't think it was our place to set the story straight. Shoot, y'all a bunch o' big shots from CNN. Who was little ol' Sweet Spot to contradict The Most Trusted Name in News?"

Probably not the most effective means of winnin' the girl.

Jennifer had no intention of getting into a debate with the man. What was the point?

Buck stood there in the duck blind scratching his head as he watched her storm off down the trail back to town.

Scarlet and Charlie looked up at Buck as if he'd just told them Santa wasn't real and turned to follow Jennifer, taking the distraught Sarah and Mikey along with them.

The others picked up their bickering right where they'd left off.

"Now look what you done," accused Jeb, pointing at Mrs. Butts.

"Me?! I ain't the one suggested coming to the mayor as referee."

Jeb continued his attack. "You just had to be greedy, didn't you Gladiola? You coulda sold all the food you wanted. All I asked was that you leave the liquor store to me. But no, you wanted it all."

"Who you callin' greedy?" barked Jimbo, jumping in to defend his sister.

Chief tried to mediate. "Please, people, no let's fight. There plenty to go around for everyone. Better to smoke peace pipe and bury hatchet."

Jefferson just turned away in disgust and headed down the trail after the others, calling back over his shoulder. "Like to bury Chief's hatchet in y'all's heads. What y'all arguin' 'bout now? It's all gone. Ten million dollars, and y'all pissed it all away with your feuding. Shoot. Ten million dollars. Damn white folk."

The others were left staring at each other in silence. Finally Jeb and the chief left too, with Mrs. Butts and Jimbo not far behind.

Jimbo's voice could still be heard coming from the woods. "What did Jefferson mean, sayin' the money was gone? He sayin' they gonna make us give back the check?"

Gladiola wasn't in the mood for conversation. "Shut up, Jimbo."

Jimbo wouldn't drop it as their voices faded down the trail. "Like to see 'em try. Shoot, they gonna have to kill me first."

When no more voices could be heard from the trail, Buck found himself all alone. Standing on high in his duck blind, Buck began to understand how Moses must have felt when he descended from Mt. Sinai with the Ten Commandments only to find his people worshipping that golden calf. Things sure had gone to hell in a hand basket.

Just moments ago, he'd been on top of the world, had the money and the girl. Didn't get no better than that. And now it was all gone. Like in that pathetic old Wide World of Sports opening where that skier doin' the long jump careens off the side of the ramp and breaks every bone in his body bouncing limply off the ground. Buck had gone from the thrill of victory to the agony of defeat.

He just stood there in his boxers, unsure what to do, wallowing in self-pity. Buck was just thinking of that old saying how it's always darkest just before the dawn, when he turned his face skyward to curse the Lord and froze. Something wasn't right. It still seemed so dark. Would that sun never rise?

Then he noticed the clouds rolling in. They were black. And he wondered if he had that old saying right. Was it "just before the dawn" or "just before the storm?"

That's when it started to hail. Hail in August?

It only took a minute to set in, but then it hit him. He realized what was happening.

"You shittin' me?!"

There wasn't much time. Buck had better get to town. He jumped back into the duck blind only to grab his pants... his pants and that damn check.

Chapter 30

No one ever thought it would really happen. Not in Sweet Spot. So while all of the neighboring towns held periodic drills on what to do in the event of a tornado, everyone training to proceed in an orderly fashion to the nearest designated underground shelter, the Spotters were woefully unprepared. To describe them as running around like a bunch of chickens with their heads cut off would have been an insult to the chickens.

The New Yorkers didn't have a clue. At first, when the hail started on their way back to town, they thought maybe it was some crazed army of squirrels bombarding them with nuts from the trees overhead. But when they looked up and caught a glimpse of the clouds through the treetops, at least they knew it was a storm, but that was all, nothing more.

It was the locals set them straight. They might have been tornado virgins themselves, but they'd heard all those endless accounts from their neighbors, seen the usual television coverage over at the Sears and Roebuck, the nonstop blue-white flashes of lightning, the green-black clouds swirling like a giant toilet bowl.

Jeb and the chief headed directly for Jeb's cave, while the others all broke out in a frantic foot race following Sarah toward the church.

Their illustrious mayor wasn't far behind. Buck passed Jeb and the chief coaxing a skittish wild-eyed Conquistador into the cave and continued on toward the church.

What he found when he got there was nothing short of pandemonium.

The front doors were flung wide open, banging in the wind, as the church-goers argued out on the front porch. They were still pointing fingers over who was to blame. It seemed little Felicity wasn't to be the only victim of the town's little deception. No, as it turned out, they were all to feel the full fury of God's wrath. Sarah was right. What they done was wrong, plain and simple, and now they were paying the price.

Scarlet was crying, refusing to go in without knowing that Pedro was safe. Charlie was just as concerned about Eustace but managed with the help of Scarlet's new cousin, Jefferson, to wrestle the screaming girl inside.

Despite Mikey tugging at her sleeve, Sarah was similarly hesitant to take refuge and bar the front doors without first accounting for loved ones. Felicity and Simon were out there somewhere, God only knew where. She stood alone at the gate to the churchyard, bent against the wind, eyes closed, hands together in prayer.

Buck didn't hesitate, sending Mikey ahead and calmly scooping the girl up in his arms, carrying her with him into the shelter of the church, right behind Mrs. Butts and Jimbo herding their prized 800-pound sow, Miss Piggy, ahead of them.

Once inside, Buck took one last look at the sky thinking it might be his last, wrestled the doors shut, and started dragging pews to barricade the doors.

But when he'd finished and turned back to the inhabitants of the church, he froze. Someone was missing.

"Where's Jennifer?!" he asked to no one in particular.

Silence.

"Jennifer!" he called. She had to be there.

Everyone just looked at one another.

Buck was dumfounded. "But she headed down the path right in front of y'all. You must have passed her. Someone must have seen her."

"Oh my God!" from Scarlet. "She's still out there!"

"Shit!" exclaimed Buck, turning back toward the door, tossing the stacked-up pews left and right. "Damn that woman! When I find her, I'm gonna kill her!"

When he opened the doors again, they almost knocked him over. As he bolted out into the storm, he shouted instructions over his shoulder for everyone to barricade the door behind him.

First thing he thought to do was to retrace his steps along the path to the fishin' hole. But by the time he got back to Jeb's cave, reality dawned on him. She wasn't on the trail. She must have passed the church and just kept walking. Walking home. That fool girl was gonna walk herself right back to New York.

The chief was outside the mouth of the cave doing a weather dance to ward off the monster storm.

"Hey Chief," shouted Buck. "Better knock it off. I think you're makin' it worse."

The chief stopped and looked up at the sky. "You think so, Mayor?

"To be honest, Chief, at this point, I don't really think you have much say in it no more. Looks to me this horse has already left the barn."

The chief didn't get it. "But not supposed to happen. Not in Sweet Spot."

Jeb poked his head out of the cave, sipping a little something from a mason jar just to calm his nerves. "First time for everything, boys. Remember Jefferson sayin' America would only elect a black president when pigs fly? So what up and happens the very year the man takes office? Swine flu. Get it? Swine flu." The man almost spilled his drink laughin' at his own joke.

Buck didn't have time for political humor. "Speakin' of horses leavin' the barn, I need to borrow Conquistador. Got a damsel in distress needs fetchin'."

* * * *

Maybe Jennifer hadn't thought things out, going off half-cocked the way she did. She'd always suspected her temper would do her in one day. But never literally.

What was she thinking, heading out on foot? But that's just it, she wasn't thinking. All she knew was that she had to put some distance between herself and that bastard snake oil salesman.

Only, things hadn't turned out quite the way she'd intended. There'd been some... uh... complications. Complications beyond her control, beyond anyone's control.

Jennifer had never seen an actual tornado before. Yet now, once the adrenaline from her tantrum had finally run its course and she looked out across the flat Mississippi landscape, that's all there was, nothing but tornadoes as far as the eye could see.

They seemed to sprout like weeds in every direction. She was surrounded, and they were closing in fast. There was nowhere to run.

That's when Jennifer Steele knew she was going to die... barefoot and naked, except for that muddy ol' shirt. She should have known some redneck man would be the end of her. Seemed to run in her family.

She'd always thought it would be different for her. She'd always considered herself a fighter, never one to give up. But she was no fool. She knew when she was beat. Maybe this was just how her mother felt in the end. Hopeless. So Jennifer decided she'd just take a seat and watch the show, just sit herself down in the middle of the road and wait for it... the end, that is.

As she sat there looking out at Mother Nature, in all her fearsome beauty, she couldn't deny there were worse ways to go. She started wondering which of the deadly corkscrews jockeying for position out on the horizon would finally come for her. Then she saw it. The monster seemed to expand, wider and wider, until it was maybe a mile across. It seemed to be coming right down the road at her, like some grotesque, nightmarish form of public transportation.

It wasn't long before the thing filled the horizon, obscuring all the other twisters, competing for the lead, upstaging them, stealing the show. At some point, it was all Jennifer could see. It was so close that, squinting against the wind in her face, she could start to make out chunks of debris it had stolen from previous victims, objects sucked into the beast, caught up in its insatiable appetite for anything and everything in its path.

One particular shiny white object, probably some poor family's Kenmore refrigerator, seemed to be hurtling toward her from the leading edge of the storm. She wondered if it still had all those magnets on it, you know, the ones holding up those drawings the kids made for Mother's Day, that report card from two years ago documenting perfect attendance, or the sign from the gym specially made for the fridge that said "no trespassing." As the Kenmore grew larger on its approach, she began to wonder if that's how she'd go, crushed to death at the hands of some major appliance.

So she sat there, focused on that gleaming white fridge, as the sky began exploding in flashes of lightning and cracks of thunder all about her.

It was a full minute before she realized she'd been mistaken. That was no refrigerator. It was a white horse. It was Conquistador, and he was galloping his heart out to beat all hell right at her. She recalled the last time, in the cow pasture with the bull, when that horse had appeared out of nowhere to save her ass.

Only this time it wasn't some fine tanned Latin lover aboard the magnificent white steed.

It was a shirtless and barefoot Buck Jones, the pasty white flesh of his jiggling muffin-top love-handles gleaming with an amalgamation of rain and sweat. He pulled up in a cloud of dust, inches from where she sat in the road, only maintaining control of his bareback mount with a handful of mane as Conquistador reared skyward in another flash of lightning.

"Come on! Let's go!" he shouted, holding out his hand to her while looking back at the black curtain of death closing down upon them. Conquistador could barely hold his ground in the pummeling gusts of wind.

When he didn't feel her hand take his, Buck turned away from the larger-than-life spectacle approaching and looked down at Jennifer, still sitting in the road. She hadn't moved an inch. Maybe she was frozen in fear, afraid to get to her feet.

But when he saw her face before it turned away from him, Buck saw something much worse than fear, maybe worse than the storm that was coming to take them both to kingdom come. It was pure rage, the proverbial wrath of a woman scorned.

"What?!" he barked. "You're so mad at me, you'd prefer to sit there and die than take my hand?!"

Jennifer turned toward him just enough so he could hear over her shoulder.

"You're smarter than you look, cowboy!"

"But I'm saving your life. Let's go!" Buck looked back at the bloodthirsty beast closing in.

"I wouldn't care if you were the last life jacket on the Titanic. I'm not going anywhere with you! Not even to save my life. I'd rather die right here in the middle of the road."

As appealing as that was beginning to sound, Buck began to wonder if she might be better off taking her chances with the twister after all, because at that particular moment he was seriously considering killing her himself.

"Get up on this horse right now and I promise, just as soon as the storms pass, I'll get you home to New York or anywhere else you care to go for that matter. You have my word."

Jennifer couldn't help but throw him a cynical look, bringing into question the true value, if any, of the man's word.

"Really?! Really?!" he shouted, an impatient Conquistador rearing and spinning in circles.

Well that crazy bitch may have been ready to die, but Buck Jones wasn't. Not yet. And he wasn't leaving without her. So he prayed the buttons on the shirt she'd borrowed held fast as he bent down from the back of the horse, clutching Conquistador's mane with one hand and grabbing her by the back of the collar with the other. In one graceful swing, he pulled her kicking and screaming up over the horse and across his lap.

Apparently she carried more than just emotional baggage, because the girl wasn't the only thing Buck pulled just then, feeling simultaneous spasms stabbing at his lower back and groin. He wished he'd listened better all those times he was told to lift with his back, not with his legs... or was it the other way around?

Well, it wasn't anything a handful of Demerol and a pint of Jack couldn't cure. At the moment, though, he had some unfinished business to take care of. He didn't need to kick the horse to spur him onward, away from the killer storm. Conquistador knew what to do. He bolted from the road and took off across the plain in a beeline for the trees at the edge of Sweet Spot.

Before her lungs could come bouncing out of her mouth, Buck's reluctant passenger quickly managed to right herself to where she was sitting up, locked safely between his arms and legs.

Buck looked out over the horizon, now dotted with twisters, and realized Sweet Spot wasn't the only victim, noticing one particularly angry churning tornado pummeling earth off in the immediate vicinity of where Pottsville used to be. God help those poor souls.

But frankly Buck had too much on his own plate just then to dwell too much on the plight of his neighbors. Despite flying across the field on Conquistador, who would have given Secretariat a good run that day, everything seemed to be happening in slow motion. Buck prayed the horse could keep them out of the storm's grasp. Would they ever reach that tree line?

Should they be lucky enough to make it, Buck was trying to think of the most direct way home when he noticed a swath of cleared trees cutting deep into the woods, a clearing that only moments ago hadn't existed.

Buck took advantage of the newly-formed shortcut heading directly toward town and the church, but frankly wasn't too sure of what he'd find when he got there... if anything.

Chapter 31

Thankfully, the particular whirling demon from hell so kind as to clear the way to town for Buck and Jennifer wasn't prepared to take on the church, instead deciding at the last moment to veer off to the left when confronted by the big white cross standing sentry at the front gate.

Conquistador, however, had no such qualms, leaping the gate and pulling up within a nose length of the church doors. Buck jumped to the ground, throwing Jennifer over his shoulder, and smacking Conquistador smartly on the rump. The horse would follow its instincts and know where to go.

Buck began kicking at the church door, glancing back at the storm bearing down upon them. He didn't know if this one would follow the lead of the last and veer off as well. Buck had his doubts. Was it following him? Was it Buck it wanted? Had it become personal? Should he have taken one for the team and led it away from the church? He almost laughed at the nonsensical thought, realizing he was beginning to lose it.

Finally the doors flew open, barely controlled in the wind by Charlie, Jefferson, Jimbo, and Mikey. Buck dove inside, tossing Jennifer at the ladies huddled at the back of the church, and threw his weight behind the other men to shut the doors.

When they'd finished restacking the pews to block the entryway, everyone started peppering Buck with questions.

"No sign of Pedro?" asked a teary-eyed Scarlet.

"No," answered Buck. "But assuming those Winchester boys tracked him down, he couldn't be in better hands. They been preparin' their whole lives for Armageddon."

Charlie took what relief he could from Buck's declaration.

"What about Simon and the little girl?" asked Mrs. Butts. "Looks like they're probably better off over in Pottsville anyway."

All eyes went to Sarah who knew it didn't really matter what any of them had to say on the subject. It was out of their hands. Instead she remained on her knees at the church altar, head bowed, appealing to a higher authority.

Buck didn't have the heart to tell them what he'd observed on his way over, that other tornado off in the distance shredding poor Pottsville to pieces. He thought Sarah had the right idea though, praying to God, because from what he could see, it was going to take a miracle to save them folks over there.

But the people in Pottsville weren't the only ones gonna take it on the chin that day. Buck had seen what was headed their way, right for Sweet Spot. In fact, that damned twister must have found religion, cause it was headed straight for church and it wasn't even Sunday.

As bad as it was outside with the storm, Buck began to wonder if maybe it was worse indoors, unable to see what was coming, sheer terror gripping everyone's faces as flashes of lightning and cracks of thunder announced the storm's arrival. The building was beginning to creak and shudder under the buffeting gusts of wind.

Buck didn't kid himself into believing the lopsided church would offer much protection against a bonafide tornado. But there was nowhere else to hide. And given Sweet Spot's perfect record, no one had thought to add a storm cellar under the church.

Well, maybe they'd never been hit themselves, but they'd heard all the horror stories. So when they heard the proverbial roar of a train approaching, they knew full well what that meant. Their number was up. This was it.

Everyone braced themselves, grabbing one another and huddling together as if their combined weight could somehow keep them from being carried off. Buck longed to hold his Jennifer for what could very well be the final moments of their prematurely aborted romance, but she was surrounded by Charlie, Scarlet and Jefferson, while Mrs. Butts and Jimbo latched onto their Miss Piggy. Buck pulled Sarah and Mikey from the altar into the fold of trembling bodies, the girl's eyes still closed, mouth still moving silently in prayer.

While the well-worn floor shook beneath the conglomeration of torsos and limbs clinging to one another, they could hear the hideous groans of 100-year-old nails un-nailing themselves, freeing roofing and wall boards one after another to take flight for parts unknown.

Everyone could feel the air being sucked from the room as soon as the first sideboards began flying from the walls of the building. As others rapidly followed suit, it became apparent the Church was being shucked like an ear of corn, peeled from the outside in. The steeple was the next to go, plucked from the roof like a cork from a jug of cider, exposing the angry black heavens above.

By that point, they were all frozen in place... waiting... waiting for whatever was coming next. They had no idea what to expect, whether they were to be buried in one mass grave under the debris of the church, or sucked out through the roof en masse, transported directly to the gates of Saint Peter.

All eyes were screwed shut in anticipation... that is until they felt one of their own abruptly pulled from their communal grasp. They couldn't help but open their eyes in terror to see who among them was the first to be taken.

That's when they saw Miss Piggy making a run for it, squeezing through the naked studs of an exposed church wall, jumping to the ground, turning, and burrowing her way into the crawlspace beneath the church.

While the others were briefly relieved to see all were accounted for, despite Mrs. Butts's concern for what she considered a member of her family, Buck saw it as a sign, an opportunity. If Conquistador instinctively knew what to do in the event of a tornado, why wouldn't Miss Piggy? And they say pigs are a whole lot smarter than horses.

"Everyone! Let's go!" he shouted, starting to shove the tightly entwined knot of humanity after Miss Piggy, toward the opening in the wall.

"What?! Outside?!" they shouted. "We'll all die out there!"

Buck took one glance at what was left of the roof above them oscillating in the wind like a loosely-pinned bed sheet flapping on a clothes line.

"Well, we'll sure as hell die if we stay put in this death trap! Follow the pig! She's smarter than all of us!"

They didn't know if it was the right thing to do, but they had to admit anywhere seemed a better place to be. So they heeded their government official and shuffled as one to the wall until those closest began falling off the edge like suicidal lemmings, immediately darting one after another under the church, crawling through the dirt after the pig.

They could hear the church being dismantled board by board above them as they huddled like gophers in their subterranean burrow, spooning as if on some polygamous honeymoon, Mrs. Butts clutching Miss Piggy, followed by Jimbo, Charlie, Scarlet, Jefferson, Sarah, Mikey, Jennifer, and lastly Buck.

As he breathed in the scent of her hair and relished the touch of her body, Buck couldn't help but feel a sense of contentment, of inner peace, despite the war raging above them, because as he lie next to her, holding Jennifer in his arms, knowing that's just how they would be found, it seemed he would get his dying wish after all, to be buried by her side.

He'd hoped they'd have had a lifetime to grow old together before going to that final resting place, but it didn't look like matching rocking chairs on the front porch were in the cards that day, dust raining down through the floorboards as the church finally gave up the fight and collapsed on top of them. When the opening to the crawlspace, the only way out, was sealed by the fallen debris, so was their fate. Their shelter had suddenly become their tomb.

It was closing time and they'd missed last call as the Lord turned off the music and the lights, locking the door behind him on his way out.

Chapter 32

Pedro was buried six feet under...

...alive and well, having ridden out the storm as one of two guests of honor in the Winchesters' impenetrable underground bunker.

Built to withstand multiple nuclear attacks, the shelter was comfortably equipped and stocked to allow its inhabitants to hibernate through the longest of nuclear winters. Food, water, medical supplies. If only they'd had a couple of spare X-chromosomes lyin' around the storage locker, they'd have been prepared to reconstitute civilization and repopulate the barren post-apocalyptic planet in their image.

Bubba quietly chuckled to himself munching his Honey Bunches of Oats as he watched Sponge Bob on the portable satellite television. Judging by the TV's reception, the storm must have passed, a great relief to Pedro, eager for word from the outside world, news on how his friends had fared. He blamed himself for not being there for his Scarlet.

He was feeling much better since his ordeal in the woods. He couldn't say the same for Rocco.

But it almost hadn't turned out that way. Eustace told them they should have come in all stealth-like to secure the hostage before lowering the boom on the enemy, but his macho brothers overruled him and opted to go in guns ablaze with a maximum show of force.

That strategy turned out to be a mistake, resulting in a literal Mexican standoff, with Rocco threatening to kill the very Mexican they'd been commissioned to fetch.

But the boys always came prepared with a contingency plan. Whether it was better equipment, superior training, or simply overwhelming force, failure was simply not an option.

AR 15's locked and loaded, the Winchesters had three separate laser sights simultaneously trained on Rocco, who couldn't see the red dot flickering between his own eyes, nor the one entering his open mouth and lighting up the back of his throat. But he could plainly make out the one just below his Gucci belt hovering over his crotch. And that's right where the taser struck him.

Once the enemy was subdued and the hostage freed, a small difference of opinion arose.

"I'm the one what zapped him in the nuts, so I say I'm the one that gets to shoot him," claimed Earl.

"Yeah, well, was my hound what picked up the scent, so I say he's mine," countered Bubba.

Earl called for order. "Don't matter who did what. Miss Scarlet said we couldn't shoot him."

"Well, that's not entirely accurate," debated Earl. "She said we couldn't shoot Pedro. She didn't say nothin' bout this here varmint," he added, kicking the man writhing in pain on the ground.

Unfortunately the debate was cut short by the sudden onset of a patch of inclement weather, forcing the team to bug out back to headquarters. So they quickly untied the friendly from the tree, gently helping a bruised and battered Pedro into the cab of the truck, and tossing the incapacitated prisoner into the cargo bed.

The truck's onboard radar system clearly delineated the incoming weather system so they headed straight for the underground bunker, arriving unscathed, to ride out the storm.

The Winchesters made sure the few hours underground were well spent, using all manner of psych-ops to gather intelligence from the prisoner, torturing Rocco with an endless loop of Lynyrd Skynyrd and Hank Williams, Jr. hits. They didn't often have the opportunity for play dates, so the boys were beside themselves over the opportunity to practice their waterboarding skills on someone other than each other.

But all good things must come to an end as Pedro impatiently broke up the party, reminding the others they all had friends to go check on.

* * * *

Sweet Spot was a ghost town. They drove right by the church, or what was left of it, understanding full well they'd find no survivors there. Any poor souls unfortunate enough to have taken refuge in that pile of sticks were goners for sure.

So they drove on to Jeb's place next, hoping to find some signs of life. But it appeared they were out of luck. At least this time, though, they could account for the bodies. Jeb Clancey and Chief Firewater were found in each other's arms huddled at the back of the cave. The cause of death was unclear. No obvious signs of trauma. It appeared they'd passed uneventfully, still clutching their individual bottles of hooch.

The Winchesters would miss their friends.

"They look so peaceful-like," commented Eustace, wiping a tear from his cheek.

"Well, no use cryin' over 'em," said Earl. "They wouldn't want it that way. On the contrary, I believe a toast is in order. Drinks all around, that's what they'd want."

"I don't know," offered Bubba. "You really think ol' Jeb would want us messin' with his stash?"

"Well I don't know 'bout you boys, but I sure could use a stiff one after finding Jeb and the chief all laid out this way. 'Sides, it ain't like Jeb's gonna need it now."

Earl went to gently take the bottles from the deceased but was having a hard time prying the hands open, what with rigor mortis settin' in. "Shoot," began Earl with a little chuckle. "Coulda figured they'd put up a fight before givin' up the drink. Give me a hand Bubba."

But when they'd each gotten a solid two-handed grip on the bottles and began pulling in earnest, they experienced the shock of their lives as Jeb and the chief both awoke from their drunken stupors in time to defend what was theirs.

Eustace was overjoyed. Pedro nearly fainted.

Once the two dead men were roused to the point of semi-coherence, inquiries were made about the others, but they had nothing to offer, only that Buck had taken Conquistador.

Just saying the horse's name evoked a loud whinny from outside the cave. Pedro bolted outside, hoping for news from Buck. But as glad as he was to find Conquistador unscathed, he couldn't help feeling disheartened that there would be no word from Buck.

The horse, however, seemed agitated.

"It's OK. The storm's over," said Pedro, calmly stroking the animal's neck.

But the horse wasn't having it. He kept poking at Pedro with his nose and turning as if to run off.

Pedro didn't know what to do, but began to wonder...

"Is it the others? Miss Scarlet?"

This seemed to really set the horse off as Conquistador pawed the ground, reared up on his hind legs, and finally circled behind Pedro, forcefully shoving him back toward town.

Pedro was already mounted when he shouted back into the cave, "We're headed back to town. Keep searching."

The Winchesters had had their break. No longer parched, Earl put his fingers to his mouth, sending out a shrill dog whistle. Time to call in the reinforcements.

* * * *

Conquistador ran like the wind, carrying Pedro to where he'd last dropped his riders off, but when he got there, he grew confused. Something had changed. There used to be a big white building there.

Pedro sensed the horse's confusion and began to fear the worst, looking at the pile of rubble in front of him. "Please God, no, not in the church."

He started trying to toss the debris aside by hand, praying there were survivors, but soon realized it was futile, the lumber too heavy. So he jumped back on Conquistador and headed up the road looking for some rope. He rode past JW's Serious Bar-BQ which seemed completely intact. The Butts place also looked no worse than it usually did. It seemed ironic how the church was the only thing destroyed, as though that storm had only one thing on its mind, sent directly from hell, by the devil himself, to make some kind of statement.

Pedro finally found a good-sized clothesline at the Butts place and raced back to the church. He soon had Conquistador hauling debris from the pile of rubble with the aid of the rope, like a true workhorse.

As patches of floorboard began coming into view, Pedro began to wonder if maybe they hadn't sought refuge in the church after all. He experienced mixed feelings on the subject. Bad, in that he still didn't know where they were. Good, in that he hadn't unearthed any familiar bodies.

He was just about to give up the excavation project when Conquistador reared up once on his hind legs and then began pounding the floorboards with his front until one of the boards splintered. Maybe it was just a snake that riled the animal, but Pedro shoved the horse aside, dropping to his hands and knees, hoping to see through the splintered floor.

He had trouble making anything out in the thin shaft of light admitted through the crack in the floor, but finally, he thought he could make out a large pink object. Miss Piggy! Must have been some determined sow for something that size to squeeze under the church. Then he saw the pig's motivation. Apparently it was a mother's instinct that drove her underground during the storm to protect her young. Pedro had counted up to nine good-sized suckling piglets nuzzling at their momma's teats when the last one turned to Pedro and yelled, "Pedro, thank God! Get us the hell outa here!"

Pedro thought at first that he was hallucinating. "Meester Buck, is that you? You're alive?" When his eyes finally adjusted to the darkness, he saw nine faces, all human, not porcine, staring back up at him, all very much alive and never looking better, especially his beloved Scarlet.

The relieved voices were soon drowned out by the braying of the hounds, a hopped-up monster truck, and ultimately chainsaws, as the Winchesters got down to business. It was only a matter of minutes before the underground inhabitants were making way for an impatient Miss Piggy fighting to emerge first through the escape hatch cut through the floor. But once the giant sow was clear, the others came flying out like the afterbirth from a difficult delivery.

There was much rejoicing all around as Pedro squeezed the life out of Scarlet, Charlie kissed Eustace, Jefferson and Mikey were high-fiving and chest bumping, Gladiola and Jimbo were trying to get their arms around their life-saving pig. Yes, even Jennifer appeared caught up in the euphoria as she buried her face in Buck's chest, relishing in the comfort of his no holds barred bear hug...

...that is until she'd gathered her wits enough to kick him in the shins for invading her personal space, demanding to know when the next flight home was.

Scarlet was in no such hurry, drinking in the sight of her Pedro. She couldn't stop touching his pretty face. "What ever happened to y'all, Sweetie? How dare you stand me up at that party?" she joked.

Earl cut in by way of explanation. "Were that fella from ICE. Me and the boys found him ruffin' up your Pedro there, so we had to take things into our own hands."

"Oh?" asked Scarlet, looking about, concerned again for Pedro's safety. "Well, what happened to him?"

"Oh, you don't need to worry 'bout the likes o' that varmint," replied Bubba. "We got him back at headquarters. We're still runnin' a few tests?"

"Tests? So he's alive?" she asked, unable to hide her disappointment.

"I guess you could say that, in a manner o' speakin'," Bubba answered.

Earl couldn't resist. "But I bet he wishes he weren't."

Jefferson seemed distracted, looking off toward the horizon. "Well, at the end o' the day, looks like we all been pretty lucky after all."

The others turned to see what he was looking at.

"By the track o' that storm damage headin' out to the east," he continued, "I'd say Pottsville been hit pretty bad."

Everyone couldn't help looking, worried their neighbors over in Pottsville hadn't fared as well as they.

"Pottsville?" asked Mikey. "Isn't that where them people took Felicity?"

The revelers stopped in their tracks, more than one covering their open mouths in shock.

"What?" asked Pedro who'd been out of the loop since his abduction. "Why would anyone take the leetle girl? And where is Meester Simon?"

All eyes turned in sympathy to Sarah... but she was nowhere to be found.

She'd certainly emerged from the church crawlspace with all the others, but the celebration was all way too premature for her. She still had loved ones unaccounted for. And when Jefferson alerted everyone to Pottsville's plight, Sarah knew there was no time to waste. She still had some unfinished business to take care of.

The bus was destroyed, buried in debris from the adjacent church, the metal roof of the bus impaled by the church steeple.

Sarah might have taken it personally, being targeted so by the very thing that had saved her from a life of ruin. But she hadn't lost her faith, not yet. After all, it was only a church, merely a wooden fabrication of man, and as such, inherently imperfect. She would appeal to management, to the big cheese.

They found her sitting among the debris of the bus, hugging what few personal objects remained, praying. She clutched Sarah's tattered party dress to her face and Simon's battered briefcase in her lap. She was rocking back and forth babbling less-than-coherent scripture, and no number of her fellow survivors' comforting hands could stop her.

They were about to give up when Sarah suddenly stopped all on her own, opened her eyes, and smiled her beatific smile. She threw the dress and briefcase aside, jumping to her feet, and stared at the tree line to the woods.

Mikey was already there, his sixth sense tipping him off before even Sarah.

All eyes turned to see them pop from the woods, beaming at the sight of a bedraggled Simon, clothes shredded and glasses broken, a jubilant waving Felicity on his shoulders.

Even smothered in Sarah's embrace, no one could keep the child from answering every one of their questions about her exodus from Pottsville, how she'd been delivered in her own personal Rapture.

"You shoulda seen him, how he took control. Simon stormed into the office where they were holding me prisoner and demanded my freedom. They said they couldn't allow me to live with no unmarried teenage drug addict, and unless he was claiming to be my parent, who the heck was Simon to demand custody of me. Well, Simon wasn't havin' it. I thought he was gonna knock their heads off or somthin'. He may not look so strong, but when he gets riled up... Anyways, Simon goes to take me by the hand, and a struggle ensued likes to tear me in two. Well my jailers kept on about drugs and only bein' able to release me to an official guardian or parent, so what does Simon up and say? Well Simon says Sarah ain't no drug addict and how dare they speak about his wife in such a manner?"

All eyes widened at that one, especially Sarah Pritchard's.

"But wait. That wasn't all," Felicity continued. "Know what else he tells them nosey do-gooders. Mr. Simon Goldfarb tells 'em he's my daddy!" At that, a jubilant Felicity hugged Simon tightly around the head from where she still sat on his shoulders, sending what was left of his glasses flying.

The others all looked at each other, when finally Sarah spoke up. "Now Simon, there's been more than enough fibbin' goin' on around here without you fillin' the child's head with more. This whole town's payin' the price for the last one. I know you meant well, but the end don't justify the means. It's only bound to lead to no good. I won't stand for no more lies."

Finally Simon spoke. "It wasn't a lie. Or it won't be as soon as Mayor Jones here, as Justice of the Peace, marries us."

Justice of the Peace was in fact one of Buck's many titles, along with Notary Public and Coroner.

Sarah was speechless, the others looking for signs of consent.

Simon continued. "And just as soon as we're married, we can file papers to officially adopt Felicity."

"Yay!" shouted Felicity. She then looked right at Sarah, bouncing on Simon's shoulders, hands together in prayer. "Well? Please, please, can we keep him?"

Finally Sarah found the words, barely able to mutter them through a new set of tears, only this time, tears of joy.

"Yes, Felicity, we can keep him. And yes, Mr. Simon Goldfarb, I thought you'd never ask. It would make me the happiest girl in the world."

She finally walked over to Simon and held him as if she'd never let him go.

Once heartfelt congratulations were expressed all around, Jefferson asked Simon how they'd survived the storms.

"Well, the people at Children and Family Services still weren't prepared to let me take Felicity, but that storm came out of nowhere, hitting the building like a bomb. As soon as the windows shattered, they lost all interest in us and ran for their lives. Me, I scooped up little Felicity, walked out what used to be the front door, and headed home."

"You just walked right through all them twisters?" asked Jefferson, incredulous.

"Well, we didn't really have to walk through them. It was more like between. Those things were popping up all around us, but something told me to just keep walking. Felicity and me. It was as if someone was clearing the way for us, like the parting of the Red Sea. After that initial impact at the downtown office took my glasses and half my clothes, we never got hit by so much as a raindrop. It was a miracle."

All eyes looked at Sarah, the only one who showed no surprise at the unbelievable tale.

"And what about Pottsville?" asked Jefferson. "How did the rest of them fare?"

Everyone looked to Simon for a blow by blow description, but the report was excruciatingly short.

A glassy look came over Simon's eyes at his nearly inaudible reply.

"Pottsville? Pottsville's gone."

Chapter 33

So Sweet Spot finally experienced its first tornado, its much celebrated pristine meteorological reputation now gone with the wind. And yet, compared to Pottsville, as it turns out, Sweet Spot barely suffered a scratch. Even the mayor's mansion, the trailer home with the target painted on the roof, got off scot-free. Apparently it was just the church and Sarah's bus parked out back that bore the brunt.

Except for Sarah, the irony was enough to make folks question their faith. On the other hand, there was no loss of life, and everyone could be thankful in the knowledge that the Lord indeed works in mysterious ways.

There was one casualty, however. Whatever blossoming romance had existed between Jennifer Steele and Buck Jones had been firmly nipped in the bud.

Poorly timed comments from Jimbo and Gladiola Butts immediately following Simon and Felicity's rising from the ashes were just the icing on the cake.

"Well, Pottsville weren't the only town hit. Sweet Spot been hit too. Just look at our church," said Jimbo.

An excited Gladiola turned to Buck. "Hey, that's right, Buck. So does that mean we get to keep the money? They can't take it away from us now, can they?"

Jennifer looked over at Buck in full on evil-eye. "That's right, Mr. Mayor, now that Sweet Spot's really been hit, I guess you get to keep your precious money."

Buck pulled the cursed check from his pocket, wishing he'd never laid eyes on the thing.

Jennifer wasn't looking for a reply. "Right. I thought so."

She abruptly turned away, looking at Scarlet and Charlie. "Well, I guess the party's over. Our assignment here has concluded." Turning back toward the church, "Besides, our equipment is a total loss, and our accommodations are in sore need of repair." She then turned to Earl Winchester. "Speaking of repair, how are the repairs on our rental vehicle progressing?"

Earl looked to Buck for guidance before responding.

Buck remembered his promise to get her back home as soon as the storms had passed, yet still took a quick moment to see if there was some way to keep her. But when he checked his hand to see what cards he had left to play, he found no ace in the hole, and knew in his heart all was lost. In the immortal words of Kenny Rogers, "You've gotta know when to hold 'em, know when to fold 'em, know when to walk away…"

So when he forlornly looked over at Earl, it took every bit of strength he had left to slowly give him the obligatory wink and nod.

Earl knew the man's meaning and turned back to Jennifer. "Funny you should ask, Miss Steele. Why I believe the boys got your ride all fixed up just before the party last night. Looks like you're good to go… on the house."

* * * *

The trip to the airport went by in a flash, uneventfully, compared to the previous pilgrimage to Sweet Spot. Their load was considerably lighter, having lost everything in the church. Not a word was said on the ride back to the airport, each of the travelers immersed in their own private thoughts.

At the airport, Jennifer called CNN collect to comp them three tickets home, but an apologetic Charlie tugged at her arm mouthing, "Just two."

"What do you mean?" asked Jennifer, covering the phone.

Charlie hesitated, looking for the words. "I think I'm going to stay. You know, give it a chance with Eustace."

Jennifer was caught by surprise. "What are you saying? You're staying? Here? I mean, in Sweet Spot?"

Charlie nodded, feeling like some kind of traitor.

Jennifer took a moment to absorb the news, but saw he was serious, and returned to the phone, shaking her head in disbelief. "Make that two. Just two tickets."

"One," blurted Scarlet, switching to the other team.

"Not you too?" Jennifer asked, feeling blindsided.

"I'm sorry, Sweetie. I just can't go. I can't leave Pedro," answered a guilt-ridden Scarlet, unable to look her in the eye.

Jennifer was speechless. What was happening?

Scarlet took the momentary silence to jump in again. "You should stay too. Honey, that man loves you, and you know it. You see the way he looks at you."

She paused to see if Jennifer was softening, but saw no signs of surrender, and continued, "He was only doing what he thought was right... as mayor... for his town. He knows it was wrong now, and he's grown as a man... thanks to you."

Jennifer wasn't buying it.

Scarlet pressed on. "Word to the wise, you're lookin' for somethin' don't exist. You're lookin' for perfection, but he's just a man. Girl, you're more likely to find Sasquatch in Central Park than you are the perfect man. Between you and me, if perfection's what you're lookin' for, you're bound to end up a lonely old spinster."

Was that a chink in Jennifer's armor, as she visibly contemplated Scarlet's words to the wise? But the old steel curtain quickly dropped as she raised the phone back to her mouth.

"Make that one. One ticket. One way. And yes, that's my final answer."

* * * *

As she watched the uninhabited Mississippi countryside shrink to nothing through the window of her puddle-jumper connecting to Atlanta, Jennifer tried to digest what had just occurred.

Two highly-trained media professionals just gave up everything they'd worked so hard to achieve. Well, maybe Charlie was highly trained and hard working. Scarlet had big boobs and was annoying. Nevertheless, they'd both scratched and clawed their way up their respective ladders, against all odds, and made it, made it to an elite level of their fields that few obtain.

And now what? What would become of them? Would Scarlet learn to rope and ride? Was Charlie to become a roadkill master chef? The world was spinning out of control. And for what? Love? Ridiculous.

Their parting at the airport was... well... uncomfortable. Prior to Sweet Spot, Jennifer had only known them as coworkers, Charlie as an extremely competent camera man, and Scarlet as... well... a blonde bimbo. But through their common ordeal, they'd come to be more than that. The hugs were warm and heartfelt, the tears free-flowing. Jennifer would miss them.

At least they wouldn't be alone. Jennifer couldn't say as much for herself. She'd thought she'd been alone back in New York even when the others were there with her. Now what? Now she was really on her own.

But there wasn't anything she could do about that. The others found loves worth throwing everything away for. Eustace, artistic and reliable, able to overcome any situation. Pedro, sweet and romantic, treats a girl like a queen.

What did Jennifer get in Buck Jones? Redneck, born and bred, sneaky and low, like a snake. Nothing worth giving up a satisfying career for just to move to Hooterville. No, she was doing the right thing. A couple of days back in civilization and she'd forget all about that scheming mayor from Sweet Spot.

And Jennifer Steele was already well on her way toward her goal... after that second margarita during her layover in Atlanta, where they even had electricity and running water. What more did a girl need?

Well, maybe something to get rid of that migraine she felt coming on. Funny, she hadn't had one of those bad boys in a while.

* * * *

Speakin' o' bad boys, Buck felt quite a load off his mind, having handed that damn FEMA check over to Jefferson for safe keepin'. The damn thing was givin' him heartburn, bad joojoo. It was just for a little while, 'til he could work out exactly how to proceed, maybe give the feds a little time to renege and ask for the money back. Better to allow 'em a little grace period before spending the dough than havin' to come up with it after it was already spent.

Too bad about Pottsville. Buck had toured the devastation himself. Simon hadn't been exaggerating. And now it looked like those poor souls were gettin' stiffed by the powers that be up in DC. Could Jefferson have been right after all? Not a penny in aid money gonna' be comin' to Pottsville. Apparently, the feds had already filled their quota of obligatory pre-election news coverage, saving the day by handing out other people's money. But the media had since grown bored of natural disasters, pivoting back to its usual staples of abortion and terrorism. After all, the government couldn't be expected to bail out every podunk little town with a wind problem. No, there wasn't a penny to spare for no emergency food or housing for Pottsville. Now if they was lookin' for a green energy subsidy, or money to protect some endangered tick, well, all they had to do was ask. There was still plenty o' green stuff around for buyin' votes.

Of course, them folks over in Pottsville didn't have no monopoly on sufferin'. Buck Jones was feelin' mighty low himself these days. Whoever said it was "better to have loved and lost than never to have loved at all" obviously didn't know his ass from his elbow.

How did things go so wrong between him and the girl? And, more importantly, could it be fixed? Not likely. He'd seen the way she looked at him ever since she'd discovered the truth, you know, like somethin' crawled out from under a rock. No, that train already done left the station.

Buck knew he did the right thing, letting her go. It never would have worked out between them. Woulda been just a matter o' time 'til the girl had Buck puttin' on airs. First thing a woman like that tries to do is change a man, mold him into somethin' she read about in that Cosmopolitan magazine. 'For you know it, he'd o' been gettin' facials, pedicures, and lessons in elocution. What next? Holdin' her purse at the mall? That is, if they'd had a mall.

No, Buck Jones was much better off on his own, just him and Lizzie, and his good buddy Jack... Daniels, that is, out at the fishin' hole, livin' the good life, doin' what the good Lord intended a man to do. Fishin' and drinkin'. And no women lookin' to run the show.

Buck couldn't help rememberin' what a disaster it was the last time he'd been fishin', what a mistake it had been bringin' the girl along. Damn near cost him a perfectly good rod when she'd decided to play around with the gator.

Then there was the infamous berry pickin' episode, lettin' that bear chase them up a tree and drink all his wine 'cause she'd misplaced the firearm.

No, the girl was nothin' but trouble. Shoulda cut her loose a long time ago. No way around it. Just a matter o' time 'fore she got him killed.

But if that were so, then why did he already feel dead inside? Why couldn't he stop thinkin' about her. Her eyes, her hair... her ass. That first kiss right there at the fishin' hole, not to mention that night together in the duck blind. Man, them fireworks surely put the Winchesters' little show to shame.

Oh well. Case closed. Time to move on. Shake it off. But Buck would need a little help. And only one person could kill this kind o' pain. Paging Doctor Daniels. Doctor Jack Daniels.

As Buck took another swig from that little square bottle, he looked over across the fishin' hole at Lizzie. She was watchin' him. Buck first thought maybe it was just his imagination, the way she was lookin' at him like he was some kinda idiot. But when she abruptly turned her back on him, there was no escapin' it. That damn lizard was givin' him the cold-blooded shoulder. Just like a woman to take the girl's side.

Chapter 34

"Jennifer, is that you?"

"Scarlet? Where are you calling from?" Jennifer hadn't heard a thing from anyone back in Sweet Spot for a week or so, not surprising seeing how they had neither land lines nor cell service.

"Callin' from Pottsville. On a payphone. Imagine? Haven't seen one o' these babies in years. I feel like some kind o' time traveler fallen through a black hole."

"Pottsville? I thought the place was destroyed."

"No shit, Shirley. Flatter than a pancake. This darn payphone seems to be the only thing still standing, you know, like how they say only cockroaches will survive a nuclear blast."

There was a pause as Scarlet fed the antique relic some coins.

"So how are things in New York?"

"New York? Oh, great. You know. Can't beat New York," she bluffed, unwilling to admit how much she'd come to hate everything about it, the smog, the crowds, her job. She hadn't seen a star in the sky since her return. Just the thought of crawling into that rat tunnel they call a subway made her physically ill. And writing about the damn weather was never going to win her a Pulitzer.

"Oh, I don't know," replied Scarlet. "This country air really grows on you. Never felt so good in all my life. Hey, how the migraines behavin'?"

"Migraines? Oh, I haven't had one of those since I've been back," she lied, rubbing her forehead over her left eyebrow, which seemed to be the bullet's point of entry. "How's Pedro?"

"Oh, Pedro's his same gorgeous self, keepin' momma happy, if ya know what I mean. He says for me to tell ya Olá. That means hello. He's teachin' me Portuguese."

"Portuguese?"

"It's a long story. Anyway, on the subject of men, I thought I should just tell ya what's goin' on here with Buck."

"Buck? Buck Jones? Why would I want to hear about him?" Jennifer asked, feigning indifference.

"When are you gonna' forgive that poor man?"

"Poor man?"

"Oh, Honey, he's just pining away for you. You should see him. It's so sad. The man don't eat nor sleep. At first, he was just fishin' and drinkin'. Now he don't even fish no more."

Jennifer was unwavering. "Well that's a shame because he certainly can't afford to lose anymore brain cells."

"Well you can joke all you like, but I'm beginnin' to get worried. There's no tellin' what the man might do?"

"Really? Like what? Plead guilty and return the stolen money?"

"I'm serious. You're gonna be the end o' that man. Just seems a shame, the way you two was meant for each other and all."

"Meant for...?! What are you talking about? You been getting into Jeb's stash? Or maybe it's the heat. You better keep hydrated."

"Well, all right. You go ahead and keep fightin' it. I just hope there's still somethin' left o' that man when you come to your senses and begin to appreciate him."

Before Jennifer could object, the conversation was interrupted by an automated voice asking for more money for the phone.

"Listen girl, I'm outa coins. Now you think about what I said. I'll call ya back in a few days to see if you come to your senses. Adeus, Sweetie. That's Portuguese for goodbye."

"Come to my...?!" Click.

The call ended before Jennifer could express any further indignation at the idea of her ever forgiving Buck Jones.

Unbelievable. Why would anyone believe she and Buck Jones would wind up together? A country hick like him, with a city girl like her. Well, maybe she was fudging her resume just a bit. After all, she was born and raised in Tennessee. But she'd left that all behind her. And she didn't mean just her accent. More than anything, it was that bastard father of hers, and all those men just like him. Men like Buck Jones.

Well, that wasn't entirely fair. Maybe she was painting with too broad a brush. Buck Jones was a lot of things, but violent wasn't one of them. Just the opposite. The man had saved her ass on more than one occasion. Let's see. There was a little incident with an alligator, and another with a bear, not to mention her little sit down strike in the middle of a tornado.

No, the man would die for her. That was clear enough.

And, she had to admit, the mayor was more than adequate in the love-making department. Quite the over-achiever, in fact. A girl doesn't just forget a night like that.

But a girl doesn't forget being lied to, betrayed, and made a fool of either. No, Jennifer Steele would not be forgiving Buck Jones any time soon. Not ever.

Well... maybe if he gave that damn money back...

* * * *

Buck had forgotten all about the money. He'd nearly forgotten his own name by the time of the intervention.

It was all Sarah's idea, but everyone knew it was long past due. They couldn't just sit back and watch their mayor and friend drink himself to death. She told them all about the twelve steps and what a big part the Lord could play in Buck's redemption. However, while they all agreed on the importance of intervening, they didn't quite think the religious slant would be effective in Buck's case. So they decided to take a more scientific medical approach.

They decided to go with the chief, the closest thing they had to a medical doctor. Not that he had any actual medical training, but his grandfather had been a medicine man back in the old days and that had to count for something.

The first thing the chief did when they found Buck at the fishin' hole sprawled out amid a landfill's worth of discarded booze bottles was to take the half-empty bottle of Jack Daniels from the unconscious man's hand. The chief immediately chugged the remainder of the bottle's contents himself... just so Buck couldn't continue drinking himself into an early grave... you know... for his own protection.

The next thing he did was kick Buck in the ass to wake him up. When that didn't seem to bring the man around, the chief grabbed him by the scalp, something that might have ended differently in days gone by, and dunked the mayor's head in the fishin' hole, bringing a sputtering angry drunkard to the surface.

"What the...?! What'd ya' go and do that for?!"

"Mayor drink too much," stated the chief.

"Well, that's sure callin' the kettle black." Then taking in the crowd around him. "Say, what is this, some kind o' lynchin'?"

"We're here to help, Meester Buck," answered Pedro.

"That's right," added Jefferson, kicking the bottle away. "You're better than this."

Buck turned to Jeb. "And what about you? You and Chief better than this? Y'all givin' up the drink too?"

"Ain't the same thing," answered Jeb.

"That right," added the chief. "Chief and Jeb drink the firewater only to celebrate life, not to end it. The gods would not approve."

Buck looked at the chief. "So you're a religious man now, are ya?"

"Not like your religion, but yes. The gods of nature very strong. Look at storm we have when gods angry. You not want provoke them again."

"How did I provoke...?" But Buck knew the answer to his own question as he saw Sarah nodding her head in agreement.

"Who my gonna anger by drinkin' my way through a little rough patch?"

"One day or two, maybe. But not like this. Over week now. Bad medicine. Girl not coming back."

Ooh, the chief didn't pull no punches. Buck looked over at Scarlet who confirmed the chief's declaration by quickly looking away to avoid eye contact with him.

Buck lay his head back down on the ground wondering if perhaps there wasn't a quicker way to end the pain, but the chief seemed to read his mind.

"Chief have better way. Way of ancestors. They no find answers to problems in bottle."

"So where then? Tell me, Chief, where are these answers?" asked Buck, humoring him.

"Walk."

"Walk?"

"Long walk. Brave must go on journey to find answers. Sometimes journey is physical, sometimes spiritual. Different for each man. But clear to Chief that Buck need go for walk, go on journey in search of future... before Buck die in past."

The chief's words struck a chord in Buck. Maybe that was it. A trip. That's what Buck needed. Why hadn't he thought of it? He opened his eyes, looking up at all the concerned faces of his friends. It was his friends and neighbors that saved Buck Jones. He'd been so self-absorbed in his own little world that he'd forgotten how important good neighbors were. It was in those faces that he found the strength to carry on, to do what had to be done. The right thing, this time. And not just for himself, but for all concerned.

And yes, as the chief suggested, he would go on his personal journey, but first things first. There was still some unfinished business to take care of, a small matter of a big check.

Buck went to get up, but quickly changed his mind when the world started spinning.

"Hey Jefferson, you got any coffee brewin' over at your place?"

"Sure do, Buck."

"Good. I'm gonna need a couple of cups before puttin' on my mayor's cap. Ladies and Gentlemen, I'm callin' an official town meeting for one hour from now at JW's. We got some important business to tend to."

Everyone looked at each other, wondering what was up, but smiled in the knowledge that whatever it was, it was a good thing. They could see that old fire in his eyes, the rusty wheels of his still alcohol-soaked mind already beginning to turn. The mayor was back. Their Buck was back.

With the cobwebs rapidly clearing, Buck could barely keep up with his own thoughts. It was all becoming perfectly clear what had to be done. First, the meeting. It was painfully obvious what they had to do with that money. They were all just too afraid to be the first to say it. Not Buck. Not anymore. There comes a time when a leader must lead. It was time to do the right thing.

And then there was that journey. The chief was right. Buck would go on a journey... a journey far away. And Buck knew just where that journey would lead him.

Chapter 35

Buck knew better than to take the chief literally. It wasn't exactly a walk. But it was a journey.

The New York City skyline was not unfamiliar to Buck Jones, as the 747 made its final descent into LaGuardia airport. The island of Manhattan certainly was a sight to behold, with its mountainous skyscrapers, lines of traffic and crowds of people streaming like ants being flushed down a soiled toilet bowl, all headed toward Wall Street, the financial capital of the world.

That had been Buck Jones's world, long before Sweet Spot. When he left, he thought it had been for good. He'd promised himself he'd never return. Yet now, after more than ten years, he was back. Buck Jones was home.

He'd only kept the one vestige of his life back in The Big Apple, the last of his Armani suits, just for an emergency. Only an emergency could have brought him back. Well this was an emergency. He couldn't live without her.

He may have been born and raised on the upper east side of Manhattan straight through prep school, followed by Yale, then Wharton school of business, but the day he'd escaped the Northeast to Sweet Spot, Mississippi, there was no turning back. He'd planned to stay as far away as he could get from the only life he'd ever known.

Hong Kong may have been New York City's polar opposite, geographically speaking, but spiritually, it was Sweet spot, Mississippi. The air, the sky, the water. The pace, the people, the attitude. Everything.

He'd never missed his old life in the city and all its painful memories, not for a minute. The only thing that had ever mattered to him had been in New York. And when that thing had been suddenly taken from him, he'd left, never looking back. Yet, here he was, right back in the mouth of the beast, all for a woman, for Jennifer Steele.

He'd left the folks back in Sweet Spot without a hint of his destination. He didn't want word to get back to Jennifer too soon. He had some ground work to lay first. Besides, he honestly had no idea whether things would work out and didn't want to look the fool having to return in failure.

Of course, that wasn't his intention... to return. If everything worked out as he'd hoped, he'd be staying in New York for good. They had no idea he wasn't coming back. But that was the plan. Because New York was where Jennifer was. And if Jennifer Steele would have him, Buck Jones would follow her to the end of the earth, even New York City, the last place he wanted to wind up.

Sweet Spot would get along just fine without him. After voting on the disposition of the FEMA money, the town agreed that Jefferson Washington was more than capable of standing in as interim mayor for the duration of Buck's "walk." And if that "walk" was one-way, and Buck's absence became permanent, well so could Jefferson's tenure as the next mayor.

Besides, with the destruction of the church and the bus, Sarah, Simon, and Felicity were overjoyed to move out of their transitional accommodations at JW's Serious Bar-BQ and into Buck's trailer, the mayor's mansion, during his "temporary leave of absence." Little Felicity had never lived in a mansion before, and had assumed she'd be at least 18 before she could buy one of her own with the earnings from her sweet tea business.

* * * *

Buck was impressed at how quickly the doorman at his old place recognized him. Then again, they shared some history. Even the doorman hadn't gone unscathed that fateful night.

"Mr. Jones, is that you?"

"Yep, it's me, Frank. I'm back."

"Really? Never thought I'd see you again, not after what happened and all."

Buck took a moment's pause, not having heard the incident discussed anywhere but in his head in more than ten years. He felt a pain in his chest.

"Oh Jeez, I'm sorry, Mr. Jones. Didn't mean to open old wounds."

Buck didn't hold it against the man. "That's OK, Frank. Life goes on. You look like you've made a full recovery."

"I guess you could say that. I've always been pretty hardheaded," he joked. "Just sorry I couldn't have done more... you know... at the time."

Buck patted the man firmly on the shoulder. "I know, Frank. I know."

"Well, it sure is great to see you, Mr. Jones. Was worried about you. Hey, the place is just as you left it. Made sure to check on it and have it cleaned once a month."

"You're the best, Frank. Really appreciate it."

* * * *

Buck dumped his bag on the marble apartment floor, taking in the expansive view of midtown. Better that than look about the apartment itself. It was indeed spotless, just as Frank had claimed. Before he'd left, Buck had scrubbed it of anything that might bring back the pain, but it didn't matter, Buck could see them all the same. Missing photos, empty closets, the absence of items just as conspicuous as their presence would have been. He'd never wanted to think about it before, but now that he was back, he knew he couldn't handle it, he'd have to sell the place and look for new accommodations. Didn't think he'd find a place for no double-wide in midtown Manhattan.

Buck was beginning to feel a bit parched, beginning to miss his old friend Jack Daniels, when he decided it would be best to get some air and head on over to the bank.

Apparently leaving his investments on autopilot, conservatively diversified, was the best thing he could have done during the recent economic downturn, instead of trying to time the market anymore. It seemed he'd not only ridden out the bottom, but had continued to experience steady returns. The expenses of managing his eastside flat didn't even represent a rounding error. The people at the bank were fawning all over him with new schemes to leverage his millions.

Most of the old guard that would have remembered Buck as the whiz kid right out of business school who'd made a killing on Wall Street were gone. Buck Jones, the boy genius oracle who'd owned the close of the twentieth century, knew enough to stay all in through the infamous correction of '98, and continued on a tear even as the market tanked between 2000 and 2003, shorting everything including the kitchen sink, Buck's term of endearment for precious metals. He then, just as miraculously, suddenly cashed out around 2003 while the rest of them suffered a bumpy and relentless downward spiral into oblivion through the collapse of 2008, one economic bubble after another popping like a drowning victim's last signs of life at the water's surface.

Of course, Buck couldn't claim credit for his last decision, to pull out of the market entirely. Not that time, not in 2003. It wasn't the market that Buck was responding to that year. There were... unforeseen circumstances.

It was only after several aborted attempts and more than a few deep breaths that he could get himself to pay his respects to what lay securely stowed away in that old bank safe deposit box.

The box seemed oddly empty, compared to the weight of what it carried, the emotional weight, the oversized part of Buck's life represented by the scant contents within. It was just some old photos of a woman and a little girl, a wedding ring, and a love-worn stuffed rabbit. Just objects. Nothing to get upset about, not as if they were real flesh and blood. But to Buck, there was no difference at all. They might just as well have been living breathing people. He could still smell the woman's perfume and the child's sweet breath. He could still hear them both giggling in the midst of a tickle attack, his beloved wife and child. They had missed him, his visits to their new home at the bank. And Buck had missed them too.

At first he felt a burst of joy at seeing them again, flashes of sheer happiness. But then, as always, those initial pleasant memories were inevitably supplanted by the ugly finale. What kind of cold heartless city could allow such things to happen? Allow innocent women and children to be dragged kicking and screaming from their beds in the middle of the night by psychopaths ransacking the place only to feed their drug habits. Buck would have gladly given them more than they could have dreamed of. There was no call to tie up and execute his family just to keep them quiet lest they identify the burglars for taking some stupid diamond earrings and a Rolex.

But Buck couldn't buy their lives... because he wasn't there. At least the doorman, Frank, tried to stop them, even though his efforts were only rewarded with two weeks in a coma. But not Buck. Buck didn't do a thing... because he wasn't there.

He was at a late dinner meeting with clients... again. He was working... again. He wasn't there to protect them, not when they needed him. That was the last day Buck worked. He didn't need to. He couldn't.

He had to leave, get away from that concrete jungle, a place so mean and twisted that no one in their right mind would live there.

He remembered back to his summers as a child at his grandmother's place in the rural South. It was so foreign to him, like going to another world. But it was peaceful there. Fresh baked pies and dips in the swimmin' hole. Yes, that's where he would go, where he needed to go. Gram and her place were long gone, but there must have been plenty of places just like it all across the South. He remembered closing his eyes and poking his finger at a map of the southeastern United States. Voila. Sweet Spot, Mississippi. His new home.

So he locked his heart up in the little metal box and buried it in that vault at the bank.

And now he was back once again, all the bad memories mixing with the good. This visit to pay his respects ended just as they always did. Perhaps he'd forgotten the routine over the years. After all, it had been a while. But he should have seen it coming. He shouldn't have been surprised when he collapsed over the box, sobbing uncontrollably.

Chapter 36

"What do you mean, he's gone?!" shouted Jennifer into the telephone receiver. She hadn't meant to sound so concerned about that snake, Buck Jones. It just came out that way. But that almost overlooked comment thrown in at the end of Scarlet's latest update caught her off guard.

She'd thoroughly enjoyed all the chit chat about Charlie and Eustace's fledgling dreams of a catering business, Simon and Sarah's upcoming nuptials, and even Scarlet and Jefferson's Technicolored family tree. But when she heard about Buck leaving town... leaving no word about his whereabouts or when he might return, Jennifer grew worried. She didn't know why she would even care. But she did.

And when Scarlet continued to nag about how much he loved Jennifer, and how the only thing missing from his place was some old suit, Jennifer suddenly wondered, he couldn't possibly be on his way to New Y... No, never. Not that man. He'd starve. Fishing in the pond at Central Park was strictly prohibited. How would he support himself? After all, there were plans to do away with those horse-drawn carriages. No, that backward redneck couldn't survive a week in a town like New York. The whole idea was ridiculous. Jennifer had to stop letting her imagination get the better of her.

"I wouldn't worry about it," said Jennifer. "Probably just licking his wounds, holed up with some toothless big-city hooker over in Biloxi. I'm sure he'll be back in no time," she assured Scarlet, as much as herself.

Scarlet was persistent. "You sure you won't come back?"

If only Jennifer could tell her how much she wanted to, how much she hated her job, how she'd hardly managed to even get herself into the office anymore, what with her constant debilitating migraines. Pretty much the only thing she did there was wait for Scarlet's calls.

She was embarrassed to admit just how much she actually missed little old Sweet Spot. She'd even gone over to that ridiculous Manhattan country bar again hoping to rekindle the magic, just for old times' sake, but all those rhinestone cowboys only left her more depressed than ever. It would take a lot more than cowboy hats and boots to turn those dandies into real men.

She kept recalling her visit with Doc Miller at the Pottsville Post, how she began dreaming about running her own show, doing something important with her life. But it didn't have to be anywhere near Sweet Spot. She could join the Peace Corps, go on a mission to Central America... or even Africa.

To hell with love. Some people just weren't meant for it. Jennifer Steele didn't need any man. Too bad about Buck though. Was a time she thought maybe she'd stumbled upon the real thing.

"Back to Sweet Spot?" she replied in answer to Scarlet. "Well I must say things are looking up over there in Sweet Spot now that Buck Jones is gone."

"Don't be such an ice queen," Scarlet lectured. "I still think you two would make quite a pair."

"Really? You think I should associate with criminals? Or did Mayor Jones finally do the right thing and decide to give the money back to the government?"

Scarlet was eager to reply. "In fact, for your information, he did call a meeting, and everyone voted."

"And..."

"Well... as to giving the government its money back..."

Jennifer could tell by the way Scarlet was hesitating. "They voted 'No,' didn't they? I knew it."

"Well, not exactly."

"Not exactly?"

"Shoot, girl, you kidding me? Them yahoos voted 'Hell No!' It was unanimous. And I quote more than one citizen of Sweet Spot shoutin', 'Over my dead body! Them thievin' feds will have to pry that damn money from my cold dead fists!'"

The payphone interrupted to extort more money from Scarlet.

That figures, thought Jennifer. Buck Jones had set the tone. He could have stopped it. All he had to do was call FEMA and tell the truth. No, he was complicit in this. Maybe he was just covering his own ass for instigating the whole thing. Oh well. Whatever. It is what it is.

As Scarlet plunked more quarters into the payphone to resume her gossiping, Jennifer was thinking how one of those missions to foreign countries to help the poor was sounding better and better. She fired up her computer wondering just where one would enlist for one of those things anyway.

* * * *

It took Buck longer than planned to arrive at Jennifer's office. He'd started and stopped a dozen times, each time pulling up short, second guessing his sales pitch, weighing every word he'd planned to say, over and over, every nuance in his presentation. There was simply no denying it, he was scared, afraid she'd spurn his apology, tell him to get lost, laugh at his plea to take him back. He knew the odds were against him.

He'd had the Armani cleaned and pressed. Probably should have just bought a new one, but the custom tailoring would have delayed him even more. No, the dozen roses were a better idea. Or did it make him look desperate? Well, so what if it did? After all, that's exactly what he was... desperate. He didn't know what he'd do if she sent him away.

By the time the elevator doors at CNN opened, his palms were sweaty and his heart palpitating like some high school loser about to ask the head cheerleader to the prom.

He pried himself from the back of the elevator and approached the receptionist.

"I'm here to see Ms. Jennifer Steele, please."

"Nice roses," smirked the sassy young man at the desk. "Is she expecting you?"

"Uh… no. But…"

The young man with the eyeliner cut him off with a wave of his hand. "Don't worry. I got this. She may not be expecting you, but for a dozen roses, I'm sure we can make an exception. Name?" as he pressed the button for Jennifer's department.

"Um… just say it's an old friend." Buck was feeling lightheaded. He couldn't feel his legs.

"Ooh. Mysterious. I like it." While they waited for a reply from Jennifer, the receptionist hungrily drank in Buck's newly-pressed Armani like he was slurping his third appletini.

"Yes, I have an old friend here for Ms. Steele," he said into the headset. "What's that?"

"…"

"Where?"

"…"

"Really?"

"…"

"Oh, that's a shame. OK, I'll tell him." He hung up and looked at Buck, bad news written all over his face.

Buck knew it. She didn't want to see him. She was sending him away. Buck slowly turned to leave.

"She's not here," called out the receptionist, not wanting Buck to get the wrong impression.

Buck spun around on a dime. There was still hope. "Not here? Is that all? When will she be back?"

The receptionist didn't know how to break it to the poor guy. "Well… uh… that's just it. She won't."

"She won't see me?"

"No. She won't be back. She quit. Just yesterday."

Buck was confused. "Quit? Why? Never mind. Can you give me her address? Would that be OK?"

"Listen honey," he said, leaning in, "I'm not averse to bending the rules when it comes to matters of the heart. I'd gladly give you the address if it would help. But it won't."

"Why? Did she say she wouldn't see me?"

"Oh, no. Nothing like that. It's just... she won't be there. She's gone."

Buck was getting nervous. "Gone? Gone where?"

"Just gone. No forwarding address. Some kind of hippie granola deal about going on a mission to help the poor, something about wanting to make a difference."

Buck was trying not to panic. "Well, OK, a mission to help the poor. Where exactly are we talking about here? The Bronx? Newark?"

The receptionist would have chuckled if he hadn't seen the fear in Buck's face. "Look. I don't know how to break it to you, Honey, but they say it sounded more like some extremely depressing foreign country, you know, maybe Haiti, or Rwanda."

Buck turned without hesitation and started pounding the down button before his legs could give out from under him. His mind was racing for answers. Where could she be? What should he do? Was it truly all over? Would he never see her again?

Buck didn't hear the words of sympathy coming from the apologetic receptionist. He didn't hear a thing, preoccupied as he was with scrambling for a plan, some solution to the recent turn of events.

The receptionist knew when to throw in the towel. There was nothing to be done for the lovesick cutie behind the closing elevator doors. On the other hand, things weren't a total loss.

"Hey, thanks for the roses! I better get these babies in some water."

* * * *

Out on the street, Buck felt disoriented in the blinding sunlight. It made his head hurt, but not so much as his chest. It wasn't a heart attack, though, not exactly. It was a broken heart. She was gone. He was too late. He'd blown it big time.

He didn't know how he made it back to the apartment. He didn't remember Frank's words of concern, his offer to call an ambulance.

He didn't leave the apartment for a week, other than once, on a half-hearted whim to find a size 44 homeless man to give the Armani to. Buck had no use for it anymore. But Buck and the homeless man lying in his own urine appeared to have a lot more in common than just their suit size. They both had that lost, hopeless look about them, not to mention being unshaven and reeking from a general inattention to personal hygiene. Buck never did give him the suit, because, like the poor soul in the street, it didn't take long for Buck to forget why he was even there in the first place.

He spent the week all alone in the apartment, without even his old friend Jack Daniels to keep him company. No, he didn't need any painkiller this time. Because he couldn't feel a thing. Nothing at all. A little pain would have been a welcome distraction.

It was only the daily intrusions by Frank pounding at Buck's door, checking up on the patient, sniffing the air for any signs of decomp, that drove Buck away. He just wanted to be left alone. He would leave. Go away. Anywhere.

So he pulled that old map out again, the same one that had randomly led him to Sweet Spot ten years back. Only this time, he knew Sweet Spot was off limits. He couldn't go back there. Not like this. Not without the girl.

No, Sweet Spot was definitely out. So was the entire southeastern United States for that matter. It would only remind him of her. So he opened up the map to show the entire world.

Where could he go to escape the memory of her? And not just her, as he thought of that little metal box, all the women in his life.

He found himself staring at the map. How hard could it be? He had the whole world to choose from. And it didn't matter where he ended up. But his eyes kept wandering to all those poor troubled spots of the world, the Haitis, the Rwandas, wondering if she could be there, helping the unfortunate, bringing what relief she could to their suffering. What if that's where Buck ended up? What if, by some strange coincidence, Buck randomly ended up in the same spot as she, the same neglected corner of the globe.

Buck sat up in bed, suddenly fixated on the question. Why not? So what if she wasn't in New York? Or Sweet Spot, for that matter. What difference did it make where she was... as long as he was there with her?

How hard could it be to find her? He jumped out of bed still holding the map. She was an American citizen. She'd recently bought a plane ticket... with a credit card. She would have needed a travel visa. Surely she could be tracked. Maybe not by the Winchesters with a pack of hound dogs, but there were other ways. He could hire a detective to track her down. Buck was not without means.

He couldn't remember when he'd last eaten, but as he reached for the phone to dig up a private investigator, he noticed he'd never been so hungry in his life. And what was that awful smell? Somebody needed a shower.

Chapter 37

As it turned out, that detective would have put them Winchester hounds to shame. After all, the girl hadn't felt the need to cover her tracks. Buck hadn't even made it to the shower before he got the call. Next thing he knew, he was trying to curb his hunger pains by scarfing down some complimentary peanuts aboard a jet bound to some godforsaken place as yet untouched by civilization.

He kept peeking out the window at the desolate landscape below wondering if she were OK, how she was surviving down there without him? But he already knew the answer. She didn't need him, not any man. It was Buck that couldn't live without her, precisely because of her independence. He never wanted a helpless needy little thing. He was attracted by her strength, her indomitable will. She was a force of nature, as strong as any old tornado. And Buck had been caught up in her whirlwinds like a mere fallen leaf, unable to escape. Since then, without her, he'd lost his footing, his direction. And God help him.

The humidity hit him like a wet blanket as soon as he deplaned at his final destination, waves of heat dancing off the runway like tribal spirits.

Fortunately, the indigenous population had mastered a dialect of English comprehensible to Buck, enough to understand he would have to use some ingenuity finding transportation out to the lesser populated regions.

Buck finally arrived at the outskirts of the little village, hopping off the back of a truck overloaded with chickens onto the dusty dirt road. He gave the kindly driver of the truck a wave of thanks and slapped at his Armani to remove the bulk of the clinging feathers. He hadn't even taken the time to change when the detective called, immediately racing to the airport. But that same smell that had evoked more than a few angry looks from fellow passengers on the plane could easily have been sold as fine cologne compared to the strong odor of chickens now permanently embedded in the Armani's expensive gabardine wool.

Initially, the natives didn't know what to make of the man in the strange attire. After all, they'd had no previous experience with such modes of dress as Armani. Nevertheless, Buck was welcomed with open arms by the friendly villagers, like a fellow tribesman, and immediately pointed in the direction of the pale-faced female outsider come to help their neighbors immediately to the east.

The larger neighboring tribe was much worse off than this one. They were the ones she'd come to help. The other village looked like a war zone, with dire shortages of food, clean water, and shelter. Given the precarious conditions there, Jennifer was forced to reside where she was, outside the perimeter of the carnage, making daily pilgrimages to the east to aid in the import and distribution of emergency provisions. Her current accommodations, primitive as they were, were much more palatable than what little was available to the east.

So Buck hightailed it down a narrow footpath leading to where they said the volunteer could be found fishing. Despite her gracious hosts' offer to care for all her needs, the girl said that was unnecessary, that she would carry her own weight, contributing her share to the sustenance of the tribe.

That sounded just like his Jennifer, thought Buck as he made his way down the trail. He only hoped she'd taken adequate precautions, venturing out all on her own into treacherous backcountry.

He knew it was she as soon as he emerged from the trees into the clearing at the edge of the water. Her back was to him, busy in her role as hunter gatherer, but the unmistakable combination of all those things that made her Jennifer Steele, the same things that always made his heart jump and took his breath away, could not escape him.

He found himself staring at her, mesmerized, feeling a general sense of peace and well-being such as he hadn't experienced since the day she'd left Sweet Spot and his shredded heart bleeding on the ground. He'd never let her go again. He would do whatever it took, apologize, promise her the world, grovel as no man had ever done before.

He just wanted to run up to her, throw his arms around her, and never let her go.

On the other hand, he felt mixed emotions when he saw that she had indeed brought precautions, the great white huntress's elephant rifle propped up against the tree right next to her, easily within reach. After all, Buck may have realized he couldn't live without her, but he wasn't so sure the feeling was mutual. And that gun, perfectly capable of dropping a full grown lion, could just as easily take down a little ol' two-legged varmint like Buck. He was debating whether to announce his presence or try the silent approach.

No sooner had the thought entered his mind than Jennifer, in one well-oiled motion, dropped her fishing rod, lunged for the rifle, and spun about, simultaneously bringing the butt to her shoulder and training her sights on whatever unfortunate jungle beast dared stalk her from behind.

"Don't shoot!" he shrieked, raising his hands in surrender and throwing himself on the mercy of the court. "I'm sorry. I didn't mean to deceive you. It's just that our real tornado was a no-show. So when you showed up instead, assuming we'd already been hit, it was too good to be true. I thought it was fate. I got carried away in the moment." The man was babbling.

"Buck?! What the hell are you doing sneaking up on me like that?! I could have killed you!"

Although she'd withdrawn her finger from the trigger, and her exclamation implied that killing him was not her initial intent, Buck kept his hands raised where she could see them, not quite sure he was off the hook yet.

"I saw your little bazooka there and didn't want to frighten you. I didn't make a sound. How did you even hear me?"

"Hear you? Are you kidding me? I could smell you for the past 20 minutes. I just couldn't imagine what sort of beast could give off a stench like that."

Buck looked down at what was left of his poor Armani still shedding its feathers.

Jennifer resumed her interrogation, eying him suspiciously, wondering what kind of cheap Biloxi hooker might be impressed by a man in expensive designer clothes.

"So what's with the suit anyway? Where've you been?"

"Where've I been? I've been searching the world over trying to find you."

"So what took you so long?" she insisted.

"Well, this was certainly the last place I would have looked."

Jennifer thought back to her last phone conversation with Scarlet, the one where she'd learned the town had voted to keep the money, and how furious that had made her. She knew Buck could have changed the outcome of that vote. He could have influenced the people of Sweet Spot to do the right thing. But hearing Scarlet's account, Jennifer thought Buck had let her down... again.

Yet when Scarlet finished dropping more coins in the payphone, Jennifer heard the rest of the story. Of course they weren't going to give that money back to the federal government, the same government that would stiff the poor people of Pottsville in their time of need simply for political reasons. Why, them Spotters would have just assumed taken one of the Winchesters' flame throwers to that money before giving it back.

But they didn't do that either. Calmer heads prevailed. Buck's head, to be exact. And it was all his idea, with Sarah Pritchard cheering him on.

Pottsville. It was Pottsville needed that money. Needed it bad. And the helping hand of the government was nowhere to be found, except maybe in someone else's pocket. No one was surprised by that. Failure of the federal government was to be expected.

But what was also to be expected was for neighbors to be neighborly. Call it Southern hospitality, being good Christians, or just a matter of common decency. Sweet Spot had a check for ten million dollars and it just so happened Pottsville needed that much and more.

It was Buck made sure everyone knew the gravity of Pottsville's situation, and explained to them Sweet Spot's obligation, as members of the local community, as friends and neighbors. He then made the motion himself with, an enthusiastic second and Hallelujah from Sarah, and called the vote. It was unanimous. They'd give the money to Pottsville, every last penny.

Jennifer'd nearly dropped the phone when she'd heard the news. She couldn't believe it. Buck's idea? Was that the same Buck she'd thought she had all figured out? The lying, cheating, stealing one? Had she underestimated him? Perhaps there was more to this man than she'd thought.

As soon as she'd stopped crying over Buck's unabashed act of kindness, Jennifer booked her plane back to Sweet Spot to find him, to find this sweet, kind-hearted soul, to apologize for misjudging him, to ask him for forgiveness for doubting him, to drag him up to that damn duck blind, pick up right where they'd left off, and show him just how much she'd missed him.

Only, when she got to Sweet Spot, she realized she was too late. He was gone. And no one knew where he'd gone, or even if he was coming back... ever. She thought she'd lost him, and with him, her only chance at love.

So as a distraction, to ease the pain, she'd thrown herself into charitable endeavors, dedicated her life to helping others less fortunate, wherever that might take her. She'd traveled to the end of the earth and found her neglected corner of the globe, to make herself useful, to forget him.

Yet now, here he was, at that same end of the earth, standing right in front of her, wanting her every bit as much as she wanted him. Staring at him down the barrel of her gun, she only wanted to run to him, wrap her arms around him, and never let him go.

But then again, there was that smell, that suit. She tried not to imagine what had been going on all this time with that skanky hooker over in Biloxi. She hadn't lowered the rifle just yet. She didn't know whether to kiss him or shoot him.

On the other hand, she had only herself to blame for leaving him. She wouldn't leave him again.

As soon as she put the gun down, he came running toward her. She opened her arms to him and steadied herself for the embrace of her life, ready to be literally swept off her feet, body and soul.

Only, that's not exactly what happened, not at all. He ran toward her, all right, but he didn't stop there. He kept going, right past her, diving for the fishing rod being dragged out into deeper water by that evening's main course.

It was one thing for Buck to try to solve complex riddles of love and relationships, where he was completely lost, unsure even where to begin. But when it came to fishing, he was in his element. It was all instinct. He saw the rod she'd left unattended about to be lost, and his legs sprang into action. He was waist deep by the time he got control of the thing and started reeling in her catch.

And it was a whopper, enough to feed the whole village. Buck and his smelly, now drenched, Armani were making slow progress back toward shore as he struggled to land that night's dinner. The 20-pound largemouth bass could be seen leaping from the water more than once, breaching like a whale, as it put up the fight of its life.

Buck nearly had the beast landed when a sudden yank on the line pulled him off his feet, sending him sprawling face first back into the water. That unexpected amount of force may have been generated by something with a big mouth all right, but it wasn't no bigmouth bass. Seemed more like maybe a full grown male hippopotamus.

Buck could barely keep his head above the water, but wasn't about to give in.

"Let go of it!" shouted Jennifer, racing into the water to save her man. "Give it up!"

Buck didn't know the meaning of the word, at least not when it came to fish... or now women, for that matter, feeling a rush as his Jennifer joined him in the fight.

"Never!" he replied. "Ain't no fish gonna get the best of Buck Jones!"

Jennifer didn't know what she'd gotten herself into with this man, morphing into Captain Ahab at the sound of a spinning reel. He would go down with that cursed white whale before he gave up the fight.

But with Jennifer's help, Buck managed to regain his feet, and begin slowly backing toward the shore again, Jennifer towing him from behind by the belt of his pants. They'd just managed to reach the muddy bank when whatever held their line so taut gave up the tug of war and suddenly released the fish, which then came hurtling toward Buck and Jennifer as they both looked up just in time to see 20 pounds of flying fish flying their way. They both suffered direct hits to the face as the bigmouth slapped them across the mouths, sending all three of them flopping onto the muddy bank like bullfrogs.

It was The Return of the Monsters From the Black Lagoon, as the two mud-covered anglers sat up laughing just in time to see exactly what sort of beast had suddenly released their line, deciding they could keep that fish they'd risked life and limb for.

And lo and behold, it was none other than their old friend Lizzie who floated to the surface of Sweet Spot's fishin' hole and looked back at them with a wink, welcoming them home, before slithering away through the muddy water.

You see, when all was said and done, the very godforsaken place as yet untouched by civilization where Buck's detective tracked Jennifer to turned out to be none other than that sorry-ass neglected corner of the globe known as Sweet Spot, Mississippi. While Buck had gone to New York looking for her, she'd gone to Sweet Spot looking for him. And until he came home, her plan was to help out any way she could with the local relief effort for the poor victims in Pottsville.

Now happily reunited, Buck and Jennifer, still clutching their slimy flopping prize catch between them, turned to one another, looked into each other's eyes, and finally enjoyed that big wet kiss they'd both longed for so long, the first of many to come since that night in the duck blind. They were both glad to be back home in Sweet Spot, together...

...as was the entire population of Sweet Spot, erupting in cheers and catcalls from the edge of the woods, where they'd just watched the entire show go down, for it was only an hour earlier that Felicity Barnes, soon to be Goldfarb, had sent Mikey Dunham running to town to alert the folks as soon as she'd seen the man in the strange clothes jump down from that chicken truck. She hadn't recognized the mayor at first, all gussied up in his travelin' suit, thinkin' it was just another potential customer.

But once she'd made a positive ID, she knew just what to do. She'd practically dragged the weary traveler down the path to town to reintroduce the long lost prince to his princess, his lady in waiting, who'd returned a week or so earlier looking for him.

By the time Buck had embarked down the trail to the fishin' hole to find her, the word that he'd returned and gone to find Jennifer had spread like the clap— pre-penicillin— until all of Sweet Spot was infected with the good news. They wouldn't have missed this reunion for the world, and the jubilant crowd of folks heading down the trail after Buck grew steadily until the whole town was there to witness the long-awaited head to head no holds barred rematch between the mayor and the feisty reporter. They expected there to be no shortage of fireworks, good and bad, and no one wanted to miss the show.

So when they came upon her holding him in her rifle sites, they thought it best to observe from the safety of tree-cover. This was going to be good. And nobody left disappointed. Oh, the epic bigmouth battle was exciting and all, but that was just the icing on the cake, tasty as it was.

For it was the kiss they'd all come to see... between their homecoming king and queen. And it was quite the kiss at that, inspiring men to remove their hats, and women to cry. It just hadn't been the same without those two knuckleheads. But now they were back, and Sweet Spot was finally whole again.

Chapter 38

Shit! Jennifer Steele had completely lost track of time, absorbed as she was in her special edition of the Pottsville Post commemorating the one-year anniversary of the deadly twisters that had leveled the town, a set of storms so bold as to even take a sucker punch at the never before hit neighboring town of Sweet Spot.

Jennifer was running late for a very important engagement as her thoughts drifted back over the past year. She couldn't help but marvel at how far things had progressed since then, since Sweet Spot's first, and hopefully last, tornado.

It had taken a full year, but the Pottsville Press was finally back up and running, and its first issue since the previous year's disaster boasted an article about the day's planned ribbon-cutting ceremony over in Sweet Spot unveiling their brand new church.

It had been quite an undertaking for the tiny town. The ten million may have all gone to those suffering over in Pottsville, but Sweet Spot, nevertheless, was not without means.

That's because during the mayor's brief sabbatical in New York in the aftermath of the storms, he'd left the town in good hands. As interim mayor, Jefferson Washington was in charge of the FEMA check. And Jefferson knew better than to let that much money sit idle under his mattress, so he immediately placed half in an interest-bearing account. He took the majority of the remaining half and started trading in foreign currencies. But the coup de grace was his leveraged investment in pork bellies, something the man definitely knew a little something about.

All told, in just a couple of days, before handing the ten mil over to Pottsville, the interim mayor had made quite a killing, netting more than enough to rebuild Sweet Spot's little white church.

Jefferson had planned to use some of the money to buy Sarah a new bus, but Buck wouldn't have it. That was no way for a growing family of three to live. And as Buck was not without means himself, he was more than happy to supply some seed money for the little family. Besides, the sooner Sarah and Simon's brand spanking new trailer home could be parked alongside the church, the sooner Buck could reclaim the mayor's mansion for himself and his girl.

Buck also did a little something for the new parents' adopted daughter, Felicity. He quietly set aside enough to fund four years of college for the little entrepreneur, but somehow Buck suspected she wouldn't be needing it. After all, not everyone on the Fortune 500 had ever bothered with a college education.

Buck remained cagey whenever Jennifer insisted on knowing through what illicit scheme he'd stolen all the money he was throwing around. But Buck wasn't quite ready to talk about his former life in New York yet. He was still afraid to jinx the deal with Jennifer by revealing that there'd been another woman in Buck's life, and always would be... two of them, in fact.

For all Jennifer knew, Buck and his Armani'd spent his lost week after the storms with some cheap hooker in Biloxi. But that was only after Jennifer'd thrown him to the curb. He'd have no cause to visit Biloxi any time in the future, and Jennifer knew she'd have to be a little more trusting of her man when he assured her everything was now on the up and up.

Of course, Jennifer's silence on Buck's unexplained largess may have been bought with a little gift of her own from Buck. No, Buck's first gift to Jennifer didn't exactly fit in a tiny jewelry box. You see, Jennifer's new dream career would need a building to house it in. As the new proprietor, editor-in-chief, reporter, and delivery girl of the reinvented Pottsville Post, her first order of business was to rebuild the little office over on Main Street to house the old printing press she'd inherited from Doc Miller.

Ol' Bessie, Doc's beloved printing press somehow managed to weather the storms without a scratch. Unfortunately the same couldn't be said for the rest of the building, or Doc, for that matter. So Ol' Bessie'd been sitting idle since the day they'd found William J. Miller, PhD's still body sheltered under the giant machine like a baby bird under its momma's wing. As always, Bessie'd done her job. His body had survived the storm completely untouched. Must have been his heart gave out in all the commotion.

At first they thought he was asleep again, only this time it was for good. They found him clutching his revolver in one hand, and his last literary publication in the other, a quickly scribbled Last Will and Testament, leaving whatever part of his newspaper business survived him to "that spunky little girl from his alma mater back in New York."

So Jennifer became the proud owner of an antique printing press buried in a pile of splinters that used to be the Pottsville Post, and she couldn't be happier. But it just didn't seem right to use the town's limited FEMA funds to rebuild a dead man's building, so Jennifer's new mysterious benefactor, Buck, vowed to take care of that himself.

Of course that was only Buck's first gift. The other he picked up on a brief clandestine mission to New York to put his old place up for sale and empty out an old safe deposit box. That trip to New York served both to bring Buck's old family home with him, and to start his new one with the diamond ring he'd picked up on Fifth Avenue.

Turns out that special edition of the Pottsville Post was special in more ways than one for Jennifer Steele, because the little announcement about the ribbon cutting over in Sweet Spot wasn't the only event taking place that day at the little white church. You see, the Post also happened to include, on the society page no less, the wedding announcement of its new proprietor and editor-in-chief to one Honorable Buck Jones, Mayor of Sweet Spot.

In fact, that was the very engagement Jennifer was running late for that day. What with getting dressed for the wedding, she'd been delayed in getting the last of her papers delivered. So it was quite the treat for her customers shouting well wishes to their paper delivery girl jumping out of the limousine in her white wedding dress to hand deliver their papers.

Rocco Buttafuoco was enjoying the free advertising for his limo service, driving the bride around in his black Lincoln Town Car delivering newspapers.

That's right, Rocco had decided to stay in the area too, at least for now. No, not locked away in chains at the Winchester compound. You see, Rocco Buttafuoco was a changed man. It's truly amazing what can be accomplished with a little waterboarding and a twelve volt car battery. Ever since his rehabilitation at the Winchesters' patented catch and release program, Rocco had become a model citizen.

Only time would tell if the change was a permanent one. But for now, he'd decided to stick around, Rocco and his Lincoln Town Car, serving to fill a void by providing airport limousine service for the steady stream of contractors and consultants coming and going as Pottsville was rebuilt from the ground up. But that was only part of it, as Rocco's connections in the concrete business paid substantial dividends as well.

* * * *

The guests at the church were beginning to wonder if the girl'd finally come to her senses and jilted their small town mayor for a life in the big city over in Pottsville.

So a nervous Buck Jones was profoundly relieved to see his beautiful bride finally come running up to his trailer out of breath, cursing about a splinter she'd picked up racing barefoot down the trail from the road.

Her maid of honor, Scarlet Witherspoon, immediately sprang into action, painting on the bride's makeup. Scarlet would have run away to Rio de Janeiro with Pedro if she'd had to. But since Rocco, with the help of the Winchesters, had taken care of Pedro's little public relations problem with the boss back in Palm Beach, the renowned Nacho Garcia had decided to stay in the States permanently. Scarlet loved jet-setting about the world for polo season so she could keep those pesky female groupies off her man. But her favorite thing was always coming back home to Sweet Spot, to the small horse farm she and Pedro'd started at the outskirts of town where Pedro molded Tennessee thoroughbreds into highly-sought-after polo ponies.

Speaking of polo ponies, the next day's Pottsville Press would boast a front page photo of a gleaming white Conquistador making quite the entrance as he arrived at the church, bearing the bride and groom.

And a review on the society page would describe how Mikey Dunham's inspired piano playing brought tears to the crowd, while former CNN cameraman, Charlie Green, memorialized the whole spectacle on video, from little Felicity's show-stealing flower girl, to Chief Firewater's performance of the ceremony decked out in full headdress.

Other than Jefferson's famous pulled pork, the entire reception was catered by Eustace Winchester, who'd finally given in to Charlie's prodding to open a small bistro in the up-and-coming Pottsville, utilizing all local natural ingredients, of course. Felicity provided the sweet tea... at cost, and Jeb provided the rocket fuel. The joyous festivities ultimately culminated in a characteristic full on Winchester aerial assault that lit up the night sky into the wee hours.

This time, however, the bride and groom opted to miss the Winchesters' display entirely, instead slipping out early for a little moonlight stroll down to the fishin' hole. Once there, the couple bid their old matchmaker Lizzie a hasty goodnight and quietly retired to their honeymoon suite. Buck insisted on carrying his lovely new bride across the threshold to the duck blind where, finally alone, the two newlyweds could begin creating some fireworks of their own.

* * * *

Of course, over time, those newlyweds would have a few more secrets to learn about one another than just how their parts fit together, like how Buck's city girl was actually born and raised country, and how Jennifer's redneck man was, in reality, a thoroughbred city slicker.

In fact, you could say it was that Yankee drive of Buck's in the first place that led him to try to better little ol' Sweet Spot against its will. But while Buck enjoyed makin' money, it was only the thrill of the chase that drove him. Actually havin' it seemed to bring more pain than pleasure. So he gave all that ill-gotten FEMA dough away, kind of like catch and release, and with it, all the trappings of money that had the whole town at each other's throats. You could even say that government check was carried off by the very tornadoes that followed, carried off to Pottsville where it belonged, leaving Sweet Spot just as it was before all the commotion began.

So in the end, Sweet Spot finally had its cherry popped, its innocence lost, along with its long-held previously untarnished reputation for never having been hit by a tornado. And yet, that damn twister never destroyed Sweet Spot after all. Not even close. On the contrary, it saved it, restored it, and rising from the ashes, not unlike Sarah Goldfarb, Sweet Spot, Mississippi was born again.

ALSO BY DAVID ABIS

THOUGH I WALK THROUGH THE VALLEY

Her daddy was just a small town preacher. But that was before. He ain't nothin' now... except dead. What truly happened between 19-year-old Jaime Jo Tremper, Tommy Harris, and her daddy would be the subject of conjecture for years to come. Yet secrets always trump gossip in a small town, and only those involved, and their maker, can ever really know the truth. Jaime Jo and Tommy have a history together, and the scars to bear for it, both mental and physical. No one ever expected to hear from Tommy again after being packed off to war. Yet two years later, resilient as a cockroach, the Special Forces psychopath comes home to the mountains of North Carolina to claim his girl. The overwhelmed local sheriff does his best to separate the two, but love can be a powerful thing, not everything is as it seems, and only Jaime Jo and Tommy know the truth. As a desperate young woman places her fate in the hands of her Lord, a vengeful Vietnam vet takes matters into his own, coming home to save his girl and finally end the nightmare that began the day Tommy Harris met Jaime Jo Tremper.

PURE CANE

Coming of age on a sugarcane plantation during the 1986 Philippine revolution, young Lisa Salonga, pampered niece of the wealthy Delgado family, lives only for hacienda socials amid the sweet scent of the cane harvest, that is until her idyllic childhood ends when she falls hard for a mere cane worker from the other side of the tracks who turns her carefree world upside down. Even though her relationship with Johnny appears doomed from the start by a class-conscious society, Lisa remains determined to unravel his mysterious past in America and the unspoken taboo surrounding his family ties to the plantation. Their fledgling romance only grows as Lisa and Johnny play pivotal roles in the church-led people's revolution overthrowing the corrupt Marcos regime, but soon, amid a growing communist insurgency, the lovers are caught in the crossfire and Lisa begins to wonder which side her Johnny is really on. It's only when a deadly typhoon threatens to destroy them all that she discovers just who her Johnny really is and what he represents for the future, both the plantation's and hers.

VILLAGE IDIOTS

Just a naive young medical student from Manhattan's Upper East Side, Benjamin Walker's cloistered world is thoroughly rocked by his very first patient on the psych ward. Angel McGovern, exotic dancer by trade, is a nymphomaniac genius with two and a half PhD's. An overwhelmed Ben is kidnapped by Angel and taken on a wild and crazy road trip to the tropics, accompanied by two other zany escaped inmates from the asylum. Makesh Guptah is a rocket scientist who believes aliens plan to destroy the Earth. Juan Martinez is a slow-witted giant who wouldn't hurt a fly, but is headed for the electric chair if found mentally competent. Will Juan beat the rap? Will Makesh save the planet? Will Angel ever scratch that itch? Will Ben make it home alive? VILLAGE IDIOTS, a sexy farce with heart, is kinky, crazy, and ultimately out of this world.

* * * *

If you enjoyed
CALAMITY IN SWEET SPOT,
please like it on Facebook at
Sweet Spot Publishing